ONE GOOD THING

JENNIFER MILLIKIN

JNM, LLC

ISBN: 978-1-7326587-6-9
www.jennifermillikinwrites.com
Cover by Okay Creations
Editing by My Brother's Editor

For my readers.

1

ADDISON

HOT SWEAT ROLLS DOWN MY RIBCAGE. IT ACCUMULATES IN MY bra, soaking through my tight-fitting black leggings.

My plans for today did not include jogging down a busy street wearing clothing better suited for a chic restaurant with over-priced cocktails. Neither did they include being woken up by my assistant's phone call. *"I can't get into the store,"* she'd told me tearfully. *"There's a lock on the door handles."*

When I saw her name flashing across my phone, I'd had a fleeting thought she needed help with something at the store; a question about a recipe, or the combination for the cash box that she keeps forgetting. Panic surged through my veins as I listened to Ashton, and I rushed from my apartment wearing the first clothes I grabbed.

Forgetting the hot, humid Chicago weather is only the icing on my cake of troubles.

My lungs fill with air and I keep going. Finding a parking spot closer to my bakery would've been smart, but I'm out of sorts.

Scratch that. *Out of sorts* is for a harried young mother trying to quiet her toddler while breastfeeding her infant.

I'm much worse off.

Who does this beating heart belong to?

These thoughts… are they mine?

They can't be. They. Cannot. Be. Mine.

Because if these thoughts are true, then my life really is a broken, bloody mess.

And the culprits are the last people in the world I would've thought could do this kind of thing to me.

Warren's parents. *My fiancé's parents.*

I choke back a sob.

Ex-fiancé. I think, anyhow. It's not a determination that is easily made, considering the circumstance.

I spot Ashton ahead, picking at her thumbnail. I slow, then come to a stop in front of her. Gently I touch her forearm and manage a huffed greeting. My *hello* feels out of place given the situation, but what is a person supposed to say?

"What are you going to do?" Ashton asks, choosing to forgo a greeting altogether. Her eyes are wide, frightened, and she uses a flattened palm to shield them from the sun. She's looking to me for direction, a leader to follow, and I don't have a clue what my next step should be.

I stare up at the sign in the window of my bakery. *For Lease*, it declares, with the name and number of the leasing company below the script.

A wide variety of bad names float through my mind. I picture my soon-to-be (would've been?) mother-in-law and throw every crude name at her scrunched up, judgy, permanent makeup face. I'd yell at her husband too, but he is only guilty of having rubber for a backbone. The *For Lease* sign is the work of his underhanded, vindictive wife.

My gaze moves from the sign to the door, and I think of how I rushed to get here. What was I in a hurry to see? The lockbox on the padded copper door handles, denying entry even to me? Or the giant white sign in the window, announcing my failure in big blue letters to everyone who passes?

If only I could tell Warren about his parents, how cruel his mother has become. Her about-face would shock him as much as it did me.

"This must be a mistake," I assure Ashton. It's a lie. I know the sign and the locked doors are not a mistake, but she looks like a fawn in search of its mother, and I feel the need to protect her. "Take the day off. I'll get this sorted out." I pat her back, a gesture meant to soothe and also propel her into action. I have a call to make.

Ashton offers me a weak, worried smile and starts off down the busy street. Chicago isn't the city that never sleeps, but it's the busiest place I've ever lived. The bakery is tucked away on a side road, but it's hardly quiet. The foot traffic on this street rivals the number of cars zooming past.

Ignoring the curious looks of passersby, I take my phone from my purse and call Vivienne. As it rings and rings, I picture all those names I threw at her in my head. I'd really like to throw them at her in person and watch her forehead try to move as she takes umbrage with them.

"Addison." My name has apparently replaced *hello*, and it's being spoken not by Vivienne, but by her daughter, Shannon. Warren's sister.

"Shannon, I need to talk with your mom." Obviously. That's why I called her phone.

"My mom asked me to tell you there's no need to have a discussion. If you're going to turn tail and run away from Warren then she has no choice but to pull her funding."

Funding. As if this is a passion project instead of my livelihood.

My teeth clamp together as I work to control my anger. "It's a trip to Oregon to clear my head." Shannon knows how much I love Oregon, how deeply I miss my grandma. I'd told her on more than one occasion. She must know I'm not running away, just attempting to heal.

"Call it whatever you need to call it to make yourself feel better about deserting Warren." Her voice is cold, and it only solidifies what I've known for awhile now. We'll never be sisters-in-law, and we're no longer friends either.

I squeeze my eyes shut. I have nowhere to put my frustration, nowhere to send the injustice I'm experiencing. "This is my bakery, Shannon, and—"

She snorts loudly, disbelievingly, in such a cruel way it stops me short. "It was never yours, Addison."

No matter what she says, no matter who paid the mortgage, that bakery was mine. I worked for every dollar it earned, I made each baked good that touched someone's lips.

"I don't foresee us needing to talk again. Have a nice life."

There is no click, no obvious sign she has hung up. Only silence.

I tuck the phone back into my purse and stare up at the sign above the door. *Addison's.*

This place was mine. *Mine.*

And I've learned how to lose what's mine.

In the past ten months, I've lost an entire life.

At least I made it to my car before the tears began pouring like rain.

Normally I hate traffic, but this morning it's almost soothing, the stop and go, as dictated by something mechanical and not a vengeful puppeteer pulling the strings.

I choke on a sob and touch the brake, gliding to a stop at a red light. My hand dips into my purse, finding my phone. I need to read someone else's bad news. I've been sitting in my own for so long.

It takes three seconds to navigate to a gossip site. Two seconds to see the top story: Self-Help Guru Needs To Help Herself. I skim the body of the article. Essentially, her football boyfriend slept with the stripper from his bachelor party. I scroll down to the comments section. Most of them have a pitying tone. Some berate her for not seeing this coming, because apparently her boyfriend's career makes him a guaranteed philanderer. And from a few vitriol spews.

DrummerGirl423: I mean, really, who cares? She probably doesn't even have a heart, and if she does, then this famewhore got what was coming to her. She can go cry into 1000 thread count sheets about her NFL fiancé, then tomorrow accept an even bigger diamond and go on social media to spout more stupidity and tell us all that 'mistakes are part of the process'.

A short breath pushes from me. *Geez.* And I thought Vivienne and Shannon were cruel.

DrummerGirl423 probably didn't give this woman a second thought after she hit publish. She stepped away from the screen and microwaved her dinner, or wiped a child's runny nose, or who knows what else.

Outrage spreads across my chest.

I'm going to respond. I'm going to tell every one of these mean people just how nasty their comments are and how their words affect others. I'm going to stand up for myself. I mean, for this woman.

A flash of anger streaks through me, and I stomp my foot.

Right onto the gas pedal.

And into the car in front of me.

Metal kisses metal, an unmistakable sound.

"Nooooo," I groan, my forehead falling down onto my steering wheel. A second later I lift my head and watch the driver of the car I've just plowed into step out of her car. She looks like she's twelve, but obviously she's at least sixteen.

I hit the hazard button and climb from my seat, meeting her at our enmeshed bumpers.

"I'm so sorry," I say, at the same time taking in her creamy, unlined skin.

She looks scared. Another fawn looking for its mother.

I take a deep breath and try to calm her with an apologetic smile. "We're going to exchange insurance information. Tell your parents you were rear-ended and it's not your fault. My insurance will pay for your new bumper." Her car is one of those little starter cars, the kind with more plastic than metal.

She nods and agrees, going back to her car. I duck into mine and reach for my glovebox. I'm not even sure my insurance card is in here. It's one of those things you don't think you'll ever need, so you shove it to the back of some dark place and forget about it.

Turns out I have it. And my registration too. Apparently I'm more than prepared to get in an accident or interact with law enforcement. Speaking of, I'd like to wrap this up before any red and blue lights arrive and start directing traffic away from us. People are figuring out to go around us without any help from the boys in blue. I meet her on the passenger side of her car. We snap photos of each other's insurance cards.

And that's it. It took all of eight minutes for my life to get just a little bit worse. I'm not even going to wonder how much worse my day could get from here, because at this point it might actually come true.

You should extend your stay. That's what my grandma said this afternoon when I called to tell her about the bakery. I told her I'd think about it, but really, what is there to think about?

Relationship? That's gone.

Career? Vanished.

Reason to stay in Chicago? Also elusive.

I want the outdoors. I want air that smells like earth, not exhaust and a mix of cuisines. I want soft dirt that slips through my fingers, leaves and twigs crunching under my boots. I want my grandma. And I'm sure she could use some help running her bed and breakfast.

Planning a visit home to Lonesome, Oregon is what put Vivienne on the warpath. If she didn't want me going to Oregon, she could've just said it. As it is, her behavior has had the opposite effect. My visit just morphed into a trip without a return date.

There are things to do now. Matters to handle. My apartment, or I guess mine and Warren's apartment, will go up for rent, fully furnished. In this market and in this neighborhood, it'll be snapped up.

I called Ashton and told her what I couldn't bear to tell

her this morning. She said she'd assumed such, and I offered my name as a reference when she starts looking for a job.

I gathered personal items and put them in boxes, and then realized I needed help getting the boxes to the storage unit I rented. The problem was easily fixed by knocking on the door of the apartment across from mine and recruiting the two teenage boys who live there with their mom.

It's shocking how easy it is to rearrange a life. It's happening faster than I can keep up. This day has been punishing, bloated with change, and I haven't had a chance to really breathe. I'm not sure how I'll feel when the dust settles.

The boys from across the hall show up and help me load my car with the new dent. They're sixteen and eighteen, miniature men, filling out but not quite there yet. Warren was the same way; I've seen pictures.

We make six trips in total. There isn't much in my apartment anymore. Vivienne came and cleared out Warren's things two weeks ago when I told her I planned a visit to my grandma. Too bad I didn't realize she was planning to clear out my career along with his favorite shirts and running shoes. She doesn't have everything though. Before she arrived, I hid some of his things, mostly his concert shirts, ones she couldn't possibly know about because they were concerts he and I went to together.

After the final trip to the unit, I pay each kid (man child?) a hundred dollars. Money well spent.

I make my way back to the apartment for my final night for who knows how long. I pass an upscale restaurant, the kind of place that is more bar than restaurant. It's crawling with the after-work, happy hour crowd. Men in collared shirts with the sleeves rolled up, their blazers hung over the backs of chairs, and women in pencil skirts and blouses. They must be hot wearing that in the summer.

After a lingering glance in the window, I move on. I'd like to have a glass of wine, dull the sting of the day just a little, but I don't have time. Instead, I pick up a bottle from the little store on the corner, and drink more than I should while I scrub countertops and floors, checking every drawer and forgotten corner for artifacts of my life with Warren.

When I finally collapse into bed, mentally and emotionally exhausted, I can't fall asleep. I look up, seeking out the design in the textured ceiling that resembles a strawberry. I only know it's there because of all the time I spent on my back in this bed, Warren moving on top of me. It wasn't always that way, but I'd be lying if I said I'd never mentally sifted through the contents of my refrigerator while Warren was hard at work.

That was back when life was normal.

Then the stable surface I'd been standing on transformed to vapor, and I fell down, down, down.

2

BRADY

"We're sure going to miss you, buddy."

Gabriel winds an arm around my shoulders and sips from his vodka and soda. Gabriel's the biggest asshole at my firm, and I don't believe for one second that what he just said is true. This is his third drink, and it's doing the talking for him.

"Where is it you're going again?" His question is directed at me, but his eyes are on a woman seated at the bar, her long legs extending from under a short skirt.

"Oregon." I sip from my own drink and wait for him to respond with some comment about what could possibly be in any place that's not a major metropolitan city like Chicago.

His gaze stays on the woman, and after a few seconds he mumbles, "Ohio, that's great."

"Sure is," I agree. I'm not interested in correcting him.

Gabriel takes his arm off me and shrugs his shoulders twice, like he's prepping for a big moment. "There's a fish to catch." He rips his gaze away and looks at me, wiggling his eyebrows. "Excuse me."

I watch him walk to the woman. He says something to her, she looks up and smiles, and he sits down next to her. I should tell her that he just referred to her as a fish, but I know that I won't. Feeling a twinge of guilt, I down the watery remains of my drink and set it on the round table beside me.

Looking around at the crowded bar, I stifle a sigh and think about when I can get the hell out of here without coming off as rude. It was nice of my colleagues to put together a going away happy hour, but I'm ready to head home.

This place is packed with men and women dressed in professional attire. No blue-collar beer drinkers in sight. Is that what I'm going to see in Oregon? I'm picturing lumberjacks with meaty arms lifting steins of frothy beer, but that's probably due to my exposure to television and obvious lack of knowledge thanks to growing up in the Arizona desert.

Maybe I should do some shopping before I leave, though. Just in case. I could pick up some flannels?

I sigh quietly.

I'm not sure why I'm going anymore.

That's not true. I know *why* I'm going. I just don't know why I chose Lonesome, Oregon as my destination. I mean, yeah, the name drew me in. I was feeling shitty on a Saturday night, and instead of answering the phone when Lennon called, I watched it ring. Then, when the phone said I had a missed call, I felt like saying *no kidding. I just watched me miss it.*

I reached the bottom of a bottle of red wine at just about the same time I found Lonesome, Oregon. According to the website, it's a retreat for those in search of solitude. Twelve free-standing cabins, each featuring a set of rocking chairs on the front porch and personal barbecue, promise a peaceful and relaxing departure from the overload of everyday life. The main house, where the owner lives, serves breakfast each morning. After typing *escape* into the internet search bar, Sweet Escape Bed and Breakfast popped up. I didn't waste even two seconds thinking about it. I selected my stay date, whipped my credit card from my pocket, and typed in the numbers.

Wham, bam, thank you ma'am.

That spur of the moment decision brought me here, to this crowded bar drinking goodbye drinks with my soon-to-be former colleagues.

I flick my wrist, attempting a surreptitious glance at my watch. We've already been here an hour. I have another half hour left in me, then I'll split. Ninety minutes is enough time to devote to people who were, at best, surface level friends.

Honestly, calling them friends is an overstatement. I probably know more about them than they do about me. A majority of the people here have families. I know their wives and husbands' name, and kids too, thanks to the note app in my phone. Referring to that app before walking into a meeting has awarded me several surprised and appreciative *he remembered my kid's name* looks.

Conversely, these people know little about me. They know nothing of how I grew up, only that I came to Chicago from Arizona. Their questions about Arizona ranged from intelligent to idiotic. *What crops are grown in the desert? Have you ever been stung by a scorpion? Are there rattlesnakes, just, like walking around all over the place?* The last one was from an intern. He didn't last long, and I don't know how he even made it into the firm at all. I told him there are indeed rattlesnakes *walking* around everywhere, then congratulated myself on ensuring an embarrassment to humankind like him would never go to Arizona. *You're welcome, great people of state forty-eight.*

"Brady?"

I'm stirred from my memories by Lindsey Tovani, a new-ish lawyer. She's been at the firm fewer than six months. I haven't worked with her much, but my impression of her is that she's very bright.

"Lindsey, hi."

"Looks like you're low." She inclines her head toward my drink. Her dark hair falls over her shoulder, and she tucks it back behind her ear.

Lindsey is attractive. Her hair is a warm brown, kind of like chocolate, and her eyes are dark too.

Similar to someone else I know. The same person who, for better or worse, plays a role in my escape to Lonesome, Oregon.

Lifting my drink, I shake it and watch the ice cubes tumble around. "I'll use the cubes for hydration."

She laughs, lifting her nearly-empty white wine glass to her lips and finishing it. "I'll get us another round."

My ingrained manners take over, but Lindsey is quick. She's already spun around toward the bar, so I move quickly, grabbing her hand. Or, I thought I was grabbing her hand. In my haste, I grabbed her hip.

Lindsey spins back around, her face upset. When she sees it's me, she relaxes.

She steps closer, leaning into my ear and shouting to be heard. "I was ready to throat punch a handsy asshole. Thank goodness it was only you." She pulls back, a little smirk on her lips, and turns back to the bar.

Either I'm hearing things thanks to the din of this place, or Lindsay had a flirtatious lilt to her voice. And she doesn't care that I've grabbed her hip. Apparently I don't qualify as a handsy asshole.

Lindsey has already ordered new drinks for us, but I'm taller, so when the bartender holds out a hand for payment, I get it in his hands before Lindsey can finish sliding hers across the wooden bar top.

"Hey," she yells, frowning at me.

I hold up my hands defensively. "I'm all for female equality, but there are some things I can't let go. And a lady buying me a drink is one of them."

She huffs, but I can tell it's playful.

We return to our table and make small talk. My brain feels foggier from the drink. One by one, my colleagues wish me well and go home. Two hours later, it's just me and Lindsey. So much for that half hour.

She places her hand on my arm and doesn't move it.

I respond by wrapping an arm around her waist.

She turns in and nuzzles my neck.

I lower my face, she lifts hers, and we kiss.

There aren't fireworks, but I don't think I believe in those anymore.

We leave together, and I know how this will go. This isn't the first time I've played this game since I came back to Chicago after spending some time down in Arizona eight months ago.

I'll close my eyes and pretend the girl in my arms is *her*.

The pain of opening them and seeing it's not Lennon will be worth it, because for the tiniest, most glorious slice of time, *it is her*.

She's still my Lennon.

She's the person who has owned my heart for longer than high schoolers have been alive.

And in that brief slice of time, she's not my best friend's girl.

She's mine.

One step closer. I'm really doing it. It would be hard to turn around now. I'm through security and by the gate where my flight will soon be called for boarding.

Instead of settling into a chair near the gate, I head for a place with a large, block-lettered sign that reads *Johnnie's Pub.* It's close enough that I should be able to hear my flight when it's called.

I grab a seat, hook my backpack over the back of the swiveling chair, and make eye contact with the bartender. He hands over a menu and I quickly place my order, and less than thirty seconds later he's setting an ice-cold beer down in front of me. I nod my thanks and take a sip.

People-watching is the best in airports, so I lean back and look around the place.

A man in a sleek, expensive suit sits three seats away from me. He's probably about my age but bald, with AirPods in his ears that communicate to everyone he's not interested in small talk.

Across the way, seated in a booth, is a man and a woman with two very rambunctious kids. As I watch, the little girl sticks her tongue out at the little boy, and he bares his teeth and gets in her face. The mom leans over, inserting one flattened palm between them before they can get physical.

I turn my head, and that's when I see her. Long, honey-blonde hair frames her beautiful face. She's on the other side of the square-shaped bar, and I can only really see her if I lean to my left, which looks embarrassingly obvious.

A worried '*v*' sits in between her eyebrows as she looks down at her hands, watching herself shred a napkin into tiny pieces.

What is it that has her so upset she's shredding napkins? Or who?

An odd feeling rips across my chest. It feels a bit like fire, an angry possession I have no right to feel.

I'm gallant on a normal day, but this gorgeous woman whose name I don't even know has me wanting to throw armor over my V-neck and joggers and slay dragons.

Shit, she's looking at me.

My first instinct is to avert my gaze, but it's too late and looking away now would be awkward. She's clearly caught me looking, and judging by the turned down position of her lips, she doesn't appreciate my blatant staring.

My traitorous lips do the opposite of hers. They turn up automatically. Into a full grin. As if I needed this to get worse, I'm giving her my mega-watt, you-know-you-trust-me smile I use on juries. Correction: I *used* to use on juries.

She makes a face, something between surprise and disgust, and picks her phone up from the bar top. Now her gaze is trained on the phone, her fingers swiping, and her point is made as clear as the businessman with the AirPods. *Don't talk to me.*

I sit up straight in my chair, making it so I can't see her. My food arrives and I get out my phone, scrolling through the news headlines while I eat. A smart man would've learned his lesson and kept his eyes trained on his phone.

Normally, I'm a very smart man.

But not today.

I lean left just enough to peek at her. I've done this five times. Okay, ten. I can't help it. She's stunning, but there's something else. Something inside her calls to me. She's a siren, and I'm the hapless sailor.

Overhead, a bored, crackling voice breaks through my thoughts as it announces that my flight will start boarding now. Pulling my credit card from my wallet, I toss it on the bar and push away my plate.

When the bartender grabs my card and turns back to run it, I take another peek at the woman and feel letdown when I find her seat empty.

The letdown feeling only lasts for two seconds, because suddenly there's a jabbing sensation on the backside of my shoulder.

I whip around and find myself face-to-face with the woman I haven't been able to stop staring at.

Happiness darts through my insides. *I didn't terrify her!*

"Hello." Reflexively I begin to extend my hand, but I don't get even halfway there because the angry look on her face stops me.

"You are the worst," she seethes.

"Uh... excuse me?" My head moves back an inch, as though her words have dealt literal blows. I glance around to see who's listening to this exchange. The businessman is standing beside his seat, wallet out and handing his card to the bartender. He's looking my way, a smirk playing on the corner of his lips. He's probably thinking what rotten luck I possess to have found a crazy one.

"Oh, let me just sit across the bar and try to hit on a woman I have no business hitting on." Her sarcasm is almost as shocking as the hurt I see flashing in her eyes.

"I apologize for offending you, but—"

She interrupts me. "Don't apologize to me. Apologize to your wife!"

"What?" I say loudly. My head shakes as I try to understand what the hell is going on with this woman. "Look, I don't know what you're talking about—"

I stop speaking when she rolls her eyes and her arms fly into the air like what I'm saying is just so unbelievable.

She points at me, and says, "Next time, you should remember to remove your wedding ring before you hit on women who *aren't your wife.*"

Oh. Shit.

I glance at my left hand. More specifically, at the fourth finger on my left hand. The finger that wears a simple, time-worn gold band.

"It's not what you think," I protest, shaking my head.

"If I had your wife's number, I would call her right now and tell her about you. She deserves to know."

Then, as I watch with a dumbfounded expression on my face, the only other woman whose soul called out to mine stomps off, hair swinging, and strides right into the line for her flight.

The same line I need to get in.

Lonesome, Oregon, here I come.

3

ADDISON

What an asshole.

I haven't been able to get his face out of my mind. The entire flight -which of course he was on- I stared at the back of his head. My fingers itched to reach over the rows separating us and grab a handful of his thick, shiny brown hair. I'd give it a good yank and listen to him squeal. Then maybe he'd stand up, enraged, and I'd throw my first ever punch.

Yes.

Then maybe I'd knee him in the crotch, right in the second brain he's obviously using to control his behavior.

Then—

I really need to calm down.

The unfairness of life took away my chance to reach the altar, and here's some guy who was lucky enough to say *I do*, but apparently had his fingers crossed behind his back during that part of his vows. My rage was misguided, but I couldn't help it. I knew it the second I slipped from my barstool after catching him looking at me for the tenth time. The anger had been building in my chest as I ate my chicken sandwich, getting hotter and hotter. Something inside me snapped, and instead of ignoring the married guy who was looking for who the hell knows what, I stomped over and told him off.

Loudly. And with passion.

At first I'd felt flattered that the hot guy across the bar was checking me out. I'd noticed him as soon as he sat down and ordered a beer. Long before he looked my way. It wasn't until we made eye contact that I saw the gold band shining on a very important finger.

Non-starter, of course. But not for him, apparently.

And then he had the gall to look shocked, like he'd forgotten he was wearing a ring.

Prick.

It's over now. Maybe my outrage at his behavior has scared him straight. Maybe his days of flirting with women other than his wife are behind him.

But probably not.

I kept my gaze averted while we deplaned, and now I'm studiously looking at my white converse while we wait at the baggage claim. I have no idea if he's here, but I don't want to look around and find out.

The bell above our carousel rings and the belt begins to move. Out pops black bag after black bag. My bag is maroon. I chose the color so it would be easy to spot.

It's not more than a few minutes before I see it. The bag makes its way toward me and I lean over to grab it, but it's heavier than I'm used to. Straining my arms, I pull and get one corner off the belt and onto the side of the carousel.

But that's the thing with conveyor belts. They keep moving.

"Excuse me," I mutter, stepping in front of the couple beside me and trying to heave my bag up and over the side.

It doesn't want to move.

"Sorry," I apologize to two more people as I step in front of them.

I'm still struggling to lift the suitcase when a hand reaches out, closing over mine, and pulls the giant overstuffed suitcase off the belt, dropping it onto the ground.

My gaze lifts and my mouth opens to thank the person who helped me, but the words die on my lips.

Flight guy.

"Don't start," he says, holding up his hands and taking a step back. His eyes meet mine briefly before he spins and walks away, a backpack hanging from one shoulder and a suitcase wheeling along behind him.

"Asshole," I mutter under my breath. Just because he did something nice doesn't make him a nice person.

My phone buzzes from inside my purse.

I pull it out and see a message from my grandma.

I'm parked on the curb. The attendant is giving me the stink-eye. Will you be out soon?

Grabbing the handle of my bag, I lug it behind me out to the curb where I find my grandma in her old green Jeep. She climbs from the car when she sees me, and as soon as I'm close enough, I let go of my bag and fling myself into her open arms.

She smells like cinnamon, and her bosom is big and pillowy and the comfort I feel takes me back to childhood, to skinned knees and tears being shed over youthful injustices.

My tears now? Adult injustice.

"Grandma," I whisper, but she shushes me, and the sound of the air rushing between her teeth lessens some of the pain in my heart.

"I know, Addy. You don't have to say any more."

I pull back, sniffling, and look at my grandma. She's

seventy-five, but still acts like she's fifty. There's a spring in her step, and her memory is probably better than mine. I hope to hell I got whatever genes have given her this gift of longevity. It's easy to think nothing could bring her down, not her husband's abandonment of her and a baby (my mom), or illness. She's impenetrable, except when it comes to me. I'm her soft spot.

"Ladies, you really need to move on. Other people need this space." The disapproving voice of the attendant breaks through our reunion.

We both turn to look at the frowning, middle-aged man standing with his arms crossed over his middle.

"Come on," Grandma says, dropping her arms and walking around me to my suitcase. She gives it a push and watches it roll only a few inches.

"Did you bring everything you owned?" She winks at me.

The man walks away, probably to bug someone else for breathing too heavily.

I grab the handle and tug it over to the Jeep. Together we lift it into the back, but I'm careful to take as much of the weight as I can. Grandma may be healthy, but she's still seventy-five.

We climb in, and as I'm buckling my seatbelt, I say, "I packed everything because I'm staying forever." Probably not, but right now it sounds good.

Grandma pats my knee, then puts the car into drive. "If only that were true," she says, searching for something over my head. Her eyes light up in recognition, and she raises a stiff middle finger high in the air. I don't even look to see who she's flipping off, because I'm certain I already know.

She gives me a mischievous wink as she lowers her

hand, then she looks over her left shoulder and pulls out into airport traffic.

"Home sweet home," Grandma announces when we park. She stretches her arms out toward the large house before us.

It used to resemble a giant Lincoln Log cabin, but three years ago my grandma renovated the entire place. She got rid of the log-style and brought in large wooden planks instead. The stone columns give the place a sophisticated look. The large front door has a copper metallic finish, and the two lights on either side of it look like large lanterns. It's more modern, while still maintaining that outdoor camp vibe.

The place screams comfort and luxury, and immediately makes me picture a glass of red wine and thick, comfy socks pushed down over buttery-soft leggings.

Too bad it's the start of summer. I'm in the mood for snow and freezing temperatures.

I heave the suitcase from the trunk of the Jeep, roll it over the sidewalk, and hoist it up over each stair.

We get inside, and I stare around in shock.

"When did you redecorate?" My head swivels left to right, taking in the new rugs, the cognac-colored leather couches, the large painting of a wild stallion over the stone fireplace.

"A few months ago," she answers, hanging her purse on a hook behind the door. "I told you I was hiring someone."

"I know, but..." I keep looking around at the little touches, like the stack of coffee table books. *The Illustrated Oregon Trail. Coast to Coast. Getting Lost to Find Yourself.*

"It's warm and inviting." It's everything I need. It's exactly why I came.

Growing up, this is where I spent my summers. Mom and Dad brought me here as soon as school let out in June, and they came back at the end of August. They traversed the globe while I explored the woods and canoed on Lonesome Lake. They called weekly to report their explorations, and I happily told them about the tide pools I'd found and the bonfire Grandma and I had built on the beach.

It sounds bad to leave your kid for the summer, but I was so happy at Sweet Escape with Grandma, I hardly missed my parents.

Now my parents are settled in Florida, and we don't talk all that much. They know what happened to Warren, but not much more. I saw them last Christmas, and there was nothing new to share. I didn't tell them about the bakery. I'm sure I will at some point, but who wants to constantly be the bearer of less-than-stellar news?

"I'll let you get settled in, okay, hon? A new guest is arriving in an hour, and I still have a few things to do." Grandma walks out of the living room and around the corner. From there she will either go into the kitchen or the master bedroom. My bedroom, plus two more, are upstairs. One is used as an office, one is a guest room, although I don't think it gets any use. My grandma is too busy taking care of all her B&B guests in the cabins to host a guest in her home.

It takes all my arm strength, but eventually I get the suitcase up the stairs and to my room. When I'm done unpacking, I lie down on my bed.

I don't know why, but I scroll through videos on my phone until I find the one I'm looking for. With a deep breath to steady my rolling stomach, I press play and watch Warren's face come to life.

He smiles, reaching forward to try and bat my phone away, but I step out of his reach and he misses. He's wearing the shirt I gave him from the football game we went to when my Alma Mater crushed his. It was such a good, fun day, filled with beer-flavored kisses and nachos.

"Addy love, turn that thing off." My heart twists at the sound of his voice.

Warren leaps for me, taking me by surprise, and the phone drops, capturing nothing but the carpet and my giggling pleas as he tickles me.

I pause the video and toss the phone on my bed. My chest feels carved out, my entire body hollow.

A childish shriek draws my attention outside. Scooting down my bed and closer to the window, I peer out, my nose pressed to the glass.

Below, coming up the big lawn, is a family of four. The younger boy chases the older girl with something held in an open palm.

I shudder. It's probably a bug.

They continue walking, and I watch them until they disappear from sight. From this window, I can see a lot of the property. The main house, where I am now, is on a small hill. This gives anyone on the second floor a view of most of the guest cabins. Beyond them is Lonesome Lake. Even farther than that, is the coast.

Maybe tomorrow I'll borrow my grandma's car and take a drive to the beach. Maybe I'll go for a walk around the property. Or, maybe I'll stay in my pajamas all day and do nothing.

Backing away from the window, I lie down on the bed and close my eyes.

4

ADDISON

"THIS SEEMS LIKE A GOOD CREW," I REMARK AS I HELP MY grandma carry in the serving dishes from breakfast.

Every morning Grandma gets up at five a.m. and works on assembling the complimentary breakfast for the guests. I slept in yesterday, but today I woke up and helped her.

She sets her armload down on the counter beside the sink. "These guests have been fun. Two weeks ago I had a crew who were hell bent on complaining. I could have given them a gold bar and they'd have complained it was too heavy."

"That's too bad." I frown, running the hot water and adding a squirt of soap to the scrubber. I don't like to think of my grandma running this place alone and having to deal with asshole guests.

"The good ones make up for it." Grandma reaches around me for the containers she uses to store uneaten pastries. She pauses, peers out the window above the sink, then resumes her task of depositing croissants in the container.

She's snapping on the lid when she looks up again, her

hands suspended. "The guy in cabin seven didn't come up for breakfast yesterday or today. And unless I missed it, he hasn't gone anywhere since he arrived two days ago."

I glance out the window in the direction of the cabin. "Do you think we should take him something?"

Grandma shakes her head, finishing the final snap and placing the leftovers off to the side. "This is supposed to be a place for solitude. Says so on the website." She winks at me. "He doesn't need an old lady harassing him about food."

I finish washing the breakfast dishes while Grandma goes to prepare a cabin for guests arriving later today.

My eyes fall on the container of pastries while I'm drying my hands. Again, I look out the window in the direction of cabin seven. It's not visible from here, but I can easily picture it. From the front, it looks just like all the other cabins, aside from the metal number seven attached to the door. Right now, it's the current inhabitant that makes it unique.

Why is he holed up? What is he hiding?

Or *who* is he hiding from?

What if he's a criminal?

I roll my eyes at my assumption of the worst. He's not a criminal and he's not hiding from anybody. Probably. But if I bring him breakfast, I can suss out the situation.

Besides, Grandma said he didn't need an *old lady* bringing him breakfast. And since I do not qualify as an old lady...

Before I can think about it any further, I assemble a plate and wrap it in plastic. Two croissants, one plain and one chocolate, and a side of fruit. Who wouldn't be happy when handed a plate like that?

I stop to refill my coffee and fill a thermos with coffee for the guy in cabin seven. I hope he likes it black because my arms are too full to carry creamer.

Cabin seven is a little farther than most of the cabins. The crispness of the morning is already burning away, and before long, it will be warm enough to wear a bathing suit and head to the lake. Maybe that's what I'll do today, after I help Grandma prepare for the new guests. It'll be cold, but that's okay.

Cabin seven comes into view. Like all the other cabins, it's made of wood planks and mimics the main house. But I know what's special about it. Unlike the other cabins, this one has a little screened-in porch off the back.

I walk up the three steps and onto the front porch, stepping onto the mat with the words *Go Away* scrawled on it. It's meant to be a joke. All the cabins have a mat with some kind of snarky saying. My favorite one is from cabin four: *I'd answer the door but I don't want to.*

I knock, and a minute later, knock again.

After my third knock, I take a step back and look left to right. I want to peek in the windows on either side of the door, but I know better. Privacy, and all that.

I'm on the bottom step when I remember the screened-in porch. I should probably leave, but, well, isn't the guy hungry? And, if he's a bad guy, I'd rather it be me who finds out about it instead of my grandma.

I come around the side of the cabin and round the back, walking right up to the black screen. The position of the sun has left the porch in total shade, making it difficult for me to see in. Looking closer, I spot a figure in a chair. He's leaning back, with his feet propped up on a chair opposite. Squinting, I make out a half dozen bottles on the ground around him.

My lips twist. Maybe he's not a bad guy. Maybe he's running from something painful, just like me.

I feel bad for waking him up, but after the night it looks like he had, he needs sustenance.

Raising my hand, I knock quietly on the wooden door. When he doesn't move, I knock again, louder this time, and clear my throat.

The man startles, pulling his legs off the chair and staggering to his feet. He turns my way, but I can't see anything else. He's just a mass of body, and he's coming this way.

He pushes open the door, but his head hangs down like it's too heavy to lift. His messy brown hair flops over his forehead. He's wearing low-slung jeans and he's shirtless. He has abs for days, the kind that ripple. If I reached out, my fingers would *bump bump bump* over them. Good thing my hands are full. And that I have a brain. And a broken heart.

"Hi," I say, taking care to keep my voice low. "I work for Sweet Escape and noticed you didn't join us for breakfast this morning. Or yesterday morning," my voice falters and I feel flustered. *Way to kick the guy when he's obviously down.* "I thought you might want to eat."

Taking a deep breath, the guy lifts his head and looks me in the eye.

No.

The universe is playing a cruel trick on me.

I feel instant guilt for admiring his abs, so to make myself feel better I look at his hand, at his ring finger, and find the ring missing. "Where's your wedding ring?"

He says nothing. Instead he reaches out, unwraps the plastic, and grabs the chocolate croissant. He stuffs nearly half of it in his mouth, chews, and says, "I'm not married."

"You were wearing a ring. And just because it's gone now doesn't mean anything."

"I'm not married," he repeats, eating the rest of the pastry and reaching for the second one. He walks back to the table and sits down. He looks at me while he chews, and I find it annoying. Liars don't make eye contact like that unless they're really good at lying. It's even more annoying that he's so gorgeous it almost hurts to look at him. He should grow a big green wart on the end of his nose.

He opens his mouth to say something, but I turn around and hurry back to the path at the front of the house. His coffee is still in my hand, but that's too bad.

As I keep going down the path and into the trees, a nagging little voice reminds me who I really want to yell at. The person who should be on the receiving end of my venom is not that guy back there. He's a proxy for Warren, for his mother, and for life in general.

LAUNDRY CALMS ME. I KNOW IT'S WEIRD, BUT WHEN I'M overwhelmed, I start washing.

I switch the laundry from the washing machine to the dryer, then add a new load to the washer. Setting the timer on my watch for forty minutes, I leave the laundry room and grab my running shoes from the mudroom. A quick run should help me clear the cobwebs in my head. I feel tired, uneasy, and just plain weird.

I'm positive it was my run-in with the guy in cabin seven that left me feeling this way. I'm mad at the wrong person, and I can't talk to the people who deserve my anger.

"Hello?" a voice from the back of the house calls.

"Coming," I respond, using my sweetened guest voice.

I tie the last lace on my sneaker and jog out from the mudroom, skidding to a stop when I see who it is.

"Is there something I can do for you?" I grit out. Despite my disagreement with his loose interpretation of marriage vows, he's still a guest. A *paying* guest.

Cabin Seven rocks back on his heels, surveying me from under dark, thick lashes. I could look in my grandma's guest book and learn his real name, but I like calling him by his cabin number.

He tucks his hands into the pockets of his shorts and grins. "Did that hurt?" he asks.

I sigh. "You mean when I fell from Heaven?"

Cabin Seven chuckles and removes a hand from his pocket, rubbing his fingers across his chin. "No. Asking me if there was anything I needed. Being forced to help me when you've decided you hate me."

A flush warms my face, and I push away the smile that almost surfaced. "Oh. Uh, yes. It was excruciating."

He nods. His hand tucks back into his pocket. "I came to see if there's any coffee left. My head's pounding. I need my daily dose of caffeine."

I walk toward the kitchen and nod for him to follow.

"Are you sure that's the only reason your head is pounding?" I ask over my shoulder as we walk. He's a few feet behind me.

He laughs again. "There might be more than one."

I move around the kitchen, preparing coffee for him. He takes a seat at the island and waits. He doesn't say anything, and I'm grateful. I don't know how to talk to him. Up until now, I've only yelled at him.

I should probably wait for the coffee to be done, be a good hostess and all that, but I'm itching to get away from him. The way he stays calm while I'm upset unnerves me.

"Cups are here." I point to a cabinet. "There's creamer in the fridge."

Cabin Seven watches me with shrewd eyes, and it feels like he can see all the way down into my soul.

"Would you like to join me for a cup?" His voice is warm, his tone hopeful.

"You need to stop—"

"I'm not married. How many more times should I say it before you believe it?"

My hands go to my hips. I take a deep, slow breath and shake my head. "It doesn't matter if I do or do not believe you. It's not my business. You're here as a guest, so let's forget how we met and move forward. Please reach out if there is anything more you need to make your stay more enjoyable."

He opens his mouth to respond, but it's too late. I've already pivoted, and my quick feet are taking me away from the kitchen and the man I can't figure out.

The man I have no business figuring out.

5

BRADY

I SMELL A BIT LIKE BEER. I'VE ALREADY SHOWERED TODAY, AND I haven't had anything to drink yet. I think it might be seeping from my pores.

Sad but true.

Following an afternoon of doing nothing, I've decided to venture out of my cabin and go for a walk on one of the trails around the property. Aside from getting coffee from the main house this morning, I haven't been out since I arrived a few days ago.

It turns out licking wounds is boring. And lonely. And I'm not really sure it helps anything. I don't feel any better here than I did in Chicago. Hearts ache no matter where you take them.

My shoes kick up some brush on the outside of the path, and the tall, thick trees filter sunlight so that my arms appear dappled. There's no denying it's gorgeous here, or that it's as peaceful as the website promised.

Although the website failed to mention the heart-stoppingly gorgeous, angry woman who would be here. I haven't figured it out yet, but she's connected to the owner somehow.

How was it possible that the airport girl was headed to the exact same place as me? I think I might have bad luck.

First, Lennon chooses my best friend Finn over me.

Then, the first woman to pique my interest turns out to be stubborn and irate.

Supposedly bad luck comes in threes, so what the hell is going to happen next?

I look down at the piece of paper in my hand. When I checked in here, the owner, Louisa, gave me a photocopied map and pointed out a lake on the property. She said it's public, but a section of shoreline is for her guests only. *You'll see the signs*, she pronounced, in that cocksure, irreverent style of hers. She waved her hand in a way that relayed how, through just that single interaction, she believed me to be intelligent enough to manage her property on my own.

The map is hand drawn, I'm guessing by Louisa. It's incredibly accurate. Every twist and turn in the path is reflected on the paper.

After ten minutes of walking, I spot the lake in the distance. It reminds me of the lake behind Finn's cabin in Arizona. It feels like a lifetime ago I was there with him and Lennon. In reality, only eight months have passed since that fateful day, the one that caused Lennon to finally choose between us.

Different trees, same rippling dark blue water. Light glints off the ripples, like a thousand diamonds sparkling off the top.

A tiny sliver of calm slips through me as I make my way closer. Water has always had this effect on me. Maybe it's from growing up in the parched desert. Maybe the incessant heat desiccated more than just the cacti and clay soil.

As I walk I hear nothing but my footfalls on the ground. The silence is exactly what I came for. I may have spent my first couple nights here getting drunk and accomplishing nothing, and I'm not saying it's the end of doing that, but *this* is really why I chose Lonesome, Oregon.

I'm not sulking. I'm not hiding. I'm not running away from Lennon and Finn with my tail between my legs. I'm *searching*. For what, I don't know.

But it's going to be something good. Something that sets my soul on fire. Something that startles my heart, that makes me incredulous at the fact I ever lived without it.

Maybe I won't find that here. Maybe it's wherever I'm going next. Until this moment I hadn't thought about *next*. There had been no second bounce of the ball when I made the decision to come here.

Where should I go after my stay here is over? Somewhere tropical? Or maybe continue north. Seattle... Vancouver... Alaska...

For the first time in a long time, I feel the tiniest shred of something that isn't like what I've been inundated by the past eight months. I wouldn't call the feeling happiness, but it's a stop on the way there.

With my gaze fixed firmly in front of me, I try to think of nothing at all. Not Lennon, not my old job, not that gorgeous blonde with whom I keep having unfortunate run-ins. I'm failing at the last one. It's hard not to think of someone so fiery and passionate. Even when that fire and passion is taking the form of anger, and that anger is directed my way.

Whoever that woman is, she's made it clear she's not interested in me. This morning in the kitchen she did what she needed to do as an employee and split as soon as her responsibility was filled. She doesn't even want to know the story of how the wedding ring came to be on my hand. I prefer not to tell her, but I will if only to exonerate myself. I don't like being accused of philandering.

I'll probably never get the chance though, and I'll just have to come to terms with that.

According to the map, I'm almost to the lake. The sky that had been sunny when I set off has been steadily turning a burnt orange as I've walked.

I clear the last of the trees and step out onto the rocky sand. Tipping my chin to the sky, I fill my lungs with clean, earthy air, slowly releasing it and lowering my gaze to the water.

Movement to the left grabs my attention. Less than twenty yards away, a woman's head and shoulders emerge from the lake.

And though I can't see her features, I'm positive it's the beautiful girl I can't get out of my mind.

This is bad. So, so bad. She's going to think I was spying on her. I'd back up slowly, but any movement on my part will only draw attention. Not that it matters. There's no way she won't see me here.

My muscles clench in anticipation of the inevitable verbal dressing-down from her once she spots me.

Her arms wrap around her shoulders and she rubs them as if trying to warm herself. I'm not an expert on lake water temperature in the northwest, but my guess is that it's not exactly warm. With a nervous glance behind herself, she walks completely out of the water.

Wearing the tiniest bikini I've ever seen.

I know I'm supposed to look away. It's what a gentleman would do, and I consider myself to be a gentleman above most other things in my life.

I rip my gaze from her just as she steps gingerly across

the rocks. I'm trying to be as quiet as I can, shutting my eyes and hoping somehow we'll make it through this without her spotting me.

Suddenly she yelps and my eyes fly open. Without meaning to, without any volition of my own, my hand flies out toward the pained sound.

The movement catches her eye, and she whips her gaze toward me. Our eyes widen, mine in apology and hers in horror.

She wraps her arms around her chest, which confuses me. Why is she wearing a bathing suit like that if she's embarrassed by it? She wobbles, all her weight on one foot.

I extend my hands like I'm already begging forgiveness. "Are you okay?" I ask, remembering the pained yelp from only a few moments ago.

She doesn't answer, and I watch her try to take a step and wince.

"Can I help you?" I'm pretty sure I know her answer, but I'd hate myself if I didn't offer.

She looks at me with a mix of irritation and something that's hard to name. I don't know how to describe it, but it looks like a fervent wish for me to be gone.

"I was on a walk." I hold up the map, and see in her eyes that she recognizes it. "I wasn't spying on you. I'm not a creep."

It's getting darker now, the sky turning into a faint purple-blue, and from this distance I can barely make out the thin line made by her pursed lips.

After a moment of consideration, she lets out a deep growl of frustration. "I think I stepped on something sharp."

Keeping my hands out, as if I'm pacifying a wounded animal, I ask, "Can I come over there and help you?"

She looks down at herself and says in a distressed voice, "I'm practically naked."

Her state of undress makes her feel weak. I get it.

With tremendous strength, I keep my eyes from traveling down her body that is equally as beautiful as her face. "I'm aware," I grit out, my eyes locked on hers.

In all my encounters with this woman, I've never seen her as vulnerable. Brazen, yes. Harsh, yes. Vulnerable? No.

But right now, the fragile look in her eyes is tugging at my heart. Part of her wants to run from me, the other knows she needs my help, and both halves dance across her face.

Finally, she nods her head just slightly.

"You want my help?" I ask. I need clarification of the head nod, and I want to rub her need for my help in her face, just a little. This woman, whose name I still somehow do not know, hasn't exactly been warm and welcoming to me. A little nose-rubbing won't hurt.

"Yes," she growls, an irritated look on her face. "You know what? Never mind. I'll do it myself."

She lifts her injured foot and teeters as she attempts to balance. Usually when people balance their arms come out to their sides to help them, but she's still using her arms to cover herself. She tries to angle herself away, but now instead of seeing her front, I see her backside.

And what a fine back half it is. She's not wearing a thong, but it's one of those that might as well be called one. Thanks to the ever-darkening sky, it's not on full display, but from what I can see, it's the kind of backside any red-blooded male in his right mind would have a hard time looking away from.

She throws a dirty look at me over her shoulder. "I hope you're enjoying the view."

Her momentary glance throws her off balance, and she

instinctively lowers her injured foot to catch herself. Instead of yelping in pain, she whimpers and lowers her chin to her chest, defeated.

"Now can I help you?" I call out.

She nods in the saddest, smallest way. "Yes."

I take care to make my stride slow and even, not wanting to weird her out by being overeager.

Truth be told, I *am* eager to be nearer to her. Despite her prickly exterior, the glimpses of vulnerability I've seen in the past few minutes make me curious.

Her eyes are trained on me as I approach, but when I get within a foot of her, her gaze falls down to the rocky shore.

"Don't be embarrassed," I say softly.

"Um, okay." Sarcasm encompasses those two words. "I'm wearing a bikini meant for spring break in Europe, not a lake in Oregon. It was all I had, and it's from years ago. I didn't think to bring anything with me from Chicago."

She's embarrassed and on the defensive. Understandable.

Crouching down, I do my best not to stare at the perfect curve of her backside and reach for her slender ankle. She falters, using my shoulder to balance. Which means she's no longer covering her chest. It takes all my willpower not to glance up.

Why, oh why, is this woman reducing me to a hormone-addled teenager? Been there, done that. Teenage Lennon gave me years of embarrassing or otherwise ill-timed tightening in the front of my shorts, and damn it if it's not starting up at this inopportune time.

Stifling a sigh, I force my attention back to the task at hand. Shoved deep into the flesh in the center of her foot is a thick, nasty looking thorn.

I'm just about to pull it out when I get an idea. Careful to keep my eyes on her foot, I open my mouth.

"You're a captive audience, so I'm going to use the next eight seconds to tell you about that ring."

She starts to protest but I bulldoze through her words. "That ring belonged to my grandpa. My mom gave it to me before I left Phoenix to go back to Chicago. I found it in my dresser just as I was leaving my apartment for the airport."

"And you wore it?"

I open my mouth to respond, but then think better of it. I don't want to get into why I put that ring on and kept it on. Now that I've said my piece, it's time to move on from the subject.

Making certain her foot is supported in my left hand, I wrap two fingers from my right hand around the thorn. "I'm going to pull this out on the count of three," I warn her. Her fingers dig into my shoulder in anticipation.

"Just do it already," she pleads.

Swiftly I count to three and yank the thorn free.

She yelps softly, then chuckles. "That wasn't as bad as I thought it would be."

Without speaking, I stand, striding to the spot where her clothes are piled. Scooping them into my arms, I walk them back over to her.

I look away into the darkened trees as I hand them to her. "My name is Brady Sterling, by the way."

"I know. I looked in the guest book my grandma keeps." She says it simply, in a very matter-of-fact way.

So she is connected to the owner, like I thought. It's a family-run operation.

I keep my gaze averted as she dresses. After a minute, she says, "My name is Addison West."

I look back at her and see her hand extended. We shake, and when she looks into my eyes, I notice her guard is back up, but it's not as strong as it was before. It's still visible in her eyes, but it's no longer plain on her face.

"I'm sorry it has taken me so long to introduce myself. Three run-ins is a long time to wait."

Addison tucks her hair behind her ears. "Yeah, well, it's not like I gave you any real chance to tell me your name." She starts for the trail, and I follow, falling in step alongside her. "In my head, I've been calling you Cabin Seven."

I tuck my hands in my pockets and laugh. "I've never been called that before."

Addison sneaks a glance at me. "What have you been called?"

I think for a moment, but ultimately I'm unable to come up with anything. I shrug. "Mostly bad names, I guess. No real nickname."

Addison laughs, and I feel disappointed she's not looking at me right now, because I'd really like to see her smile.

"How do you know we're going the right way?" I ask. She's navigating the path as though it's the middle of the day and not almost night.

"Years of experience."

"You grew up here?"

"I spent summers here. With my grandma."

"Seems like a nice place to spend time."

"You're from Phoenix?"

"Technically. I grew up in a suburb called Agua Mesa."

"What are you doing here?"

I'm not sure how to respond. Normally, Lennon and Finn are the only people I'd talk to about my issues, but not this time. Not when they're the ones causing the problem.

Addison chuckles. "So, you lose the ability to speak when I ask you why you were wearing a wedding ring that didn't belong to you, and you can't tell me why you're here? Sounds like lady trouble."

"Something like that."

"I think it's exactly like that."

Now I'm the one chuckling. "Maybe." It's not an easy story to tell, and the words themselves don't paint the situation accurately.

Addison doesn't respond, and after a minute she points ahead, to a spot where light from Sweet Escape filters through the trees. "Here we are."

Every step closer brings Addison into better view. Her wet hair falls down around her shoulders, and from what I can tell, she's not wearing any makeup.

The path ends, dropping us off onto the lawn of the main house. Addison stops and looks up at me.

"That path will take you to your cabin," she says, pointing.

"I remember from earlier. The coffee," I remind her.

She nods. "Right."

We stand there awkwardly.

Addison slips her hands into her back pockets. "Okay, well, I'm going inside now." She turns and walks a few feet, then looks back at me. "You can stop envisioning my nearly naked backside."

Her words make the image spring to life in my mind. "What about your nearly naked front side?"

Her eyes squint and she gives me a mean look, but I think it's playful.

She turns back around, and I start for my cabin. It isn't until I'm stepping under the hot spray of the shower that I realize I didn't ask Addison why she came to Oregon.

Something tells me she's not just here to recreate the summers of her childhood.

6

ADDISON

I HAVE NO IDEA HOW MY GRANDMA DRIVES THIS JEEP. THE steering wheel requires all my arm-strength to turn, and I'm certain I could beat this beast in a five second race starting from zero.

Despite my complaints, I needed her car this morning. My oldest friend lives twenty minutes away, and I'm visiting her.

I need a dose of reality. I need to slip into the old me, into the person I was before I settled in Chicago. I need the wild girl who ran around barefoot and slept in the same clothes she wore that day.

And I need the person who makes me feel like that girl again.

The Jeep cranks to a stop in front of a low-slung house. I peer out at the silver metallic house number affixed to the front of the garage, making sure I'm in the right place. I haven't seen Charlie since her wedding three years ago. I'd gone alone, and a week later I met Warren in the produce section of Whole Foods. We were both looking for the ripest Cara Cara oranges.

I push back the memory just as the front door opens and Charlie steps out. She waves excitedly and I return the wave, a grin pulling up both corners of my mouth, my sadness at the thought of Warren vanished. I grab my purse and hurry from the car, using a considerable amount of my strength to slam the door shut.

"Charlie!" I call out as I round the back end of the Jeep. She's coming down the porch steps with her arms out.

I stop where I am, my mouth dropping open. "You're pregnant!"

Charlie puts her hands on her hips and turns to the side so I can see her profile.

"Really pregnant," I add, staring at her huge belly. Guilt blooms inside me. I haven't been an attentive friend since I went back to Chicago. Warren took over my life, first with the headiness of being in love, then with the daily struggle of his absence. I'd called Charlie during that time, listening to her gush about the joys of married life and adding my own anecdotes about my newfound love. And, right after the accident, it was Charlie I called. But in the past eight months, I'd pulled away. For me, there was nothing happy to talk about, and I didn't want to bring my dark storm cloud to our conversation. Charlie's phone calls went unanswered and unreturned.

But now, in the bright Oregon morning sun, my Chicago storm clouds have faded into a memory. Charlie beams, her hands lifting into the air. "Surprise! This little guy will be here in a few months." Her hands come down to her stomach, rubbing it lovingly. "My belly button popped this morning."

"I don't know what that means," I say cheerfully, closing the distance between us and wrapping her in a hug. It's an off-center hug, to make room for her middle.

I feel Charlie's laugh in the space where our chests meet. She steps back but keeps a hand on my forearm. "It means my innie is now an outie."

Her hand moves off my arm only to reach down and grip my own. "Come inside."

She leads the way as if we're kids again, her brown hair falling down her back like it did when we were twelve. I bet she still has a little mole on her right shoulder.

I follow her up the steps and through the front door. The house is small but decorated beautifully. The walls are painted cream, and the couches are teal suede. A white brick mantel over a fireplace holds a large framed wedding portrait.

Running my fingertips along the soft couch, I tell her, "I love how you chose a bright color."

"Thank you. The color makes me happy." Charlie leaves the living room and motions for me to follow. I'm a few seconds behind her, and when I turn the corner she walked around a moment ago, I step right into the kitchen.

It's hot pink.

I try not to gape, but it's nearly impossible to keep my lips closed.

Charlie looks at me and laughs. "I know, it's awful. I did it on a whim. Merch swears he's going to re-paint before the baby comes."

I examine the array of notes and magnets on the fridge, including a sonogram picture with Charlie's full name in the corner. *Charlotte Merchant.* "Do you ever call your husband by his first name?"

"Not even in the bedroom," Charlie answers, grabbing an oven mitt from a drawer and shoving her hand into it.

"Oh geez," I groan playfully.

Charlie pulls open the oven and grabs something from

inside, then sets it on the stovetop. She turns back around and gestures to her stomach with her hands. "Well, how do you think this happened?"

"Good point." I peer over her shoulder at whatever she placed on the stove. "What's that?"

"Quiche. I was hoping you'd come hungry."

"I'm always hungry."

She eyes me. "From the looks of you, I wouldn't say I believe you."

I make a face. "My weight is just fine."

"You're tiny."

She's right, and I know it. After Warren, I lost weight and it still hasn't fully returned. My appetite is starting to come back now though, and that delicious looking quiche hiding behind Charlie looks like a good place to begin.

I smile at her. "I guess I'll just have to have two helpings to rectify that situation."

Charlie's eyes soften around the edges. "Do you want to talk about Warren?"

My fingers find the frayed hem of my jean shorts, and I tug at a string. "No," I say in a low voice.

"It's not your fault, you know?"

And there, with that one sentence, Charlie has reached in and tugged at the heart of the matter. In black and white terms, what happened is nobody's fault. But nothing is black and white, so where in all those shades of gray does the blame lie on me?

"Fundamentally, I know that. But sometimes it seems like the blame should lie somewhere." My eyes fill and I use the backs of my hands to push away the moisture.

"Sometimes sad things happen, Addison. And there doesn't have to be clear-cut blame to place on somebody."

I nod my agreement, but my mind continues on to a place it knows well.

If that guy hadn't decided to ride his bike, then...

If Warren had wanted dessert instead of declining, then...

If I'd slept in our bed that night, then...

The *if's* are endless. The blame may not be clear-cut, but instead it's broken into pieces, little shards resting on all our shoulders.

Charlie removes two plates from a cabinet, her belly bumping against the counter. She keeps going as if she didn't notice, which makes me think it probably happens all the time.

With a smile, she turns to me, and asks, "Remember that time I called Cooper's mom and tipped her off about the weed he kept stashed in the toe of a boot in his closet?"

I bark a laugh, palming my forehead and looking up at the ceiling. "That was the best revenge."

"Cooper deserved it. What kind of guy lies about sleeping with someone?"

I think back to the pimply faced, sixteen-year-old I went on two movie dates with, then learned he'd told his friends I had sex with him in the back of the theater. "Cooper, apparently."

Charlie grabs a knife and cuts two slices from the quiche. "He went to college out of state and I haven't seen him since. And he never did find out it was me who told his mom." Her chuckle is playful and evil. She pats her belly and looks down. "You'll never do anything like that, will you?"

I help Charlie carry the plates and forks to the table. We sit and eat, our conversation a constant stream of chatter. She tells me about Merch, and I fill her in on what it was like to run a bakery. I don't tell her about Warren's family swiping the bakery out from under me. I don't want to bring down the cheery mood of our reunion.

We finish the food, and she shows me the nursery. It still needs wall hangings and the crib lies unassembled in a box, but it's getting there.

Before I leave, Charlie invites me to happy hour next week with some of her girlfriends, and I accept.

"They're all moms. A couple of them are rowdy, but they'll have two glasses of wine and then go home early because there's a good probability a kid will be up during the night."

"Sounds like a safe bunch."

Charlie tells me she'll text me when she knows the time and place, and we hug goodbye.

The road to Sweet Escape is just as bumpy as it was earlier, but I don't notice it as much. Charlie has brought a little sunshine into my life.

"MOM, HEY." I HOLD UP MY PHONE, MY ELBOWS PROPPED ON the kitchen island, and my mom's face comes into view. Her blonde hair is in a ponytail, and her bangs are in need of a trim.

"Hey, baby." Her eyes rove around my head, taking in my surroundings. "Where are you?"

"Grandma's."

"Oh." The corners of her mouth dip. "Why?"

"I wanted to visit."

She nods slowly. "Everything okay?"

"Not really, but I don't want to get into it."

Her lips twist as she surveys me. "How's your heart these days?"

"Mom, I just said I don't want to talk about it." My tone is gentle. I talk to my mom so infrequently, upsetting her isn't something I want to do.

She lifts her hands. "Okay, okay."

There's a sound behind me, soft like careful footfalls. I sit up and whip around, peering into the darkened living room. I know it's not my grandma. She wouldn't be sneaking around her own house.

"Hello?" I call out. It's probably a guest. "It's okay. Do you need something?"

I hear the footfalls again, this time not as soft, and they're coming closer.

He walks into the light, and I see that I've assumed correctly. It's a guest. Just not a guest I want to see, especially after the embarrassing incident at the lake.

"Mom, I have to go. A guest needs something."

"It's awfully late," she complains. She's always disliked that my grandma runs a bed and breakfast.

"Bye, Mom. Love you." I press the end button and look back to Brady. "How long have you been standing there?" I hear my tone, and it sounds accusatory. I'm still wary of him, despite the fact I believe him about the wedding band. My senses are heightened around him, and it makes me uneasy.

Brady takes two more long strides toward me, coming to stand a few feet away. He's dressed in jeans and a hooded sweatshirt. "I've been here long enough to know you came to Oregon for the same reason I did."

I frown. "You were eavesdropping."

He shakes his head. "Technically, no. I tried to back away quietly."

I stare at him for a moment, determining how I feel. I want to be angry he overheard, but I know that's stupid.

Mentally I put on my proprietor cap and ask, "Why did you come to the main house? Do you need something?"

His fingers press against his temple. "I have a headache. I was wondering if you have any pain reliever?"

"Sure." I hop off the stool and go to a cabinet. He has two choices from the stock my grandma keeps, and I hold up the bottles to show him. He points to one and I hand it over.

"So," he says, unscrewing the cap and tipping the plastic bottle into his hand. "You have a broken heart too?"

I lean back against the counter and eye him. "I knew I was right. Girl trouble."

He tucks the pills into his pocket and places the bottle on the counter beside me.

"I'll tell you mine if you tell me yours."

I'm already emotionally exhausted, and I don't want to go into it tonight. It's not an easy story to tell. Pushing off the counter, I tell him, "Another time."

His chin dips quickly, a curt nod. "You still don't trust me, do you? Even though I told you about the ring." Brady's eyebrows knit, and I can see how upset he is by the idea that someone doesn't trust he's telling the truth.

I grab a glass and fill it with water, letting the seconds pass before I respond. This question of belief, of whether I think he's telling the truth, makes me uncomfortable. It's like having some kind of weird inside joke, but it's not a joke. It's just something that binds us, when nothing should. We're two broken souls, spending a short time traveling parallel roads. He'll go on his way in a couple weeks, and I'll...well, I don't know what I'll do.

"I believe you," I assure him. It seems imperative to him that I believe him, and besides, I actually do.

"Honesty is important to me," he says, his arms crossing in front of himself.

His arm muscles flex because of his stance, and it doesn't escape me that he's attractive, so ridiculously attractive, even more so than usual thanks to the ardent expression on his face. I swallow down all those thoughts, and with the goal of ending our conversation, say, "I'm sure one day you'll find a girl who will appreciate that quality."

His gaze falls to his arms, and I feel like an idiot. I didn't mean to make him think of *her*. The girl who sent him looking for solace in wooded Oregon. I was just being a bit flippant, not careful of my words.

"Right. Well, anyway." He starts to walk out of the kitchen. "Thanks for the medicine."

I feel bad. "See you at breakfast?"

He answers with a wave as he goes, which isn't an answer at all.

I listen for the back door to close, then count to fifteen and follow his path, locking the door behind him.

7

BRADY

I NEED TO BLOW OFF SOME STEAM, AND EXERCISE HAS ALWAYS been the best way for me to do that. As far as I can tell, there aren't any gyms within walking distance, so I'm completing a circuit in my cabin. Push-ups, planks, jumping jacks, mountain climbers, and burpees.

I'm in the middle of my third set when my phone rings, cutting off the music I'd been listening to. I grab it and look at the screen.

Lennon Facetime.

I stare at the phone for a second, deciding if I should let it go. Guilt and a sense of duty win out. I reach for my shirt and pull it over my head. There was a time when I wouldn't have covered up before answering, hoping my shirtless self would send Lennon's libido soaring and she'd realize her attraction to me was far greater than it was to Finn.

That ship has sailed.

"Hi," I say, Lennon's face appearing on the screen. My heart twists at the sight of her. Her lips, her eyes, her collarbone. She's gorgeous, and painfully familiar.

"Hey, you." She grins. "Where are you hiding yourself?"

"What do you mean?" I hadn't told her or Finn I was headed anywhere, so I don't know why she thinks otherwise. The truth isn't something I feel like telling her. If I do, she's going to feel guilty. The guilt she feels already clouds everything we do, a dark tinge on every conversation.

"Don't you lie to me, Brady Sterling." Lennon points a finger at me, her voice stern. "I can tell you're thinking about lying."

I chuckle softly, lifting my hands in the air. "You got me."

"So?" Lennon urges. "Where are you?"

"Why don't you think I'm in Chicago?" I'm positive my mother hasn't spoken to Lennon, and even if she had, she wouldn't have told her my plans.

"I can see where you're sitting Brady, and it looks nothing like your ultra-modern apartment. And I ran into your mom when I had to go to Agua Mesa to sign some papers. She showed me a picture you sent her. I didn't make a big deal about it, but it's obviously not Chicago."

Right... I had too much to drink on the first night here and sent my mom a picture of the front of my cabin. "I'm doing some exploring in the northwest. I'm staying at a bed and breakfast in Oregon."

"Babe?" Finn calls out from somewhere in the background.

Ouch. My poor heart.

Lennon turns her head and looks off to the side. "Yeah?" she calls out.

"Do you know where the—oh, hey Brady. What's going on?" Finn drops onto the couch beside Lennon. He grins the same mischievous smile he always wears.

"Hey, man."

"Brady's in Oregon," Lennon tells Finn, but she's looking at me. She leans away from him a fraction. She's being careful of my feelings, trying to make certain I'm not subjected to the image of them touching. I appreciate her consideration, but unfortunately I have an imagination, and on dark nights it has run wild. Seeing their shoulders pressed together now would be the least of what my mind has conjured.

"Cool. Lennon was afraid you'd run off to an ashram or something. What are you doing there?"

"Exploring parts unknown and taking some R&R."

"Sounds fun." Finn nods and looks at Lennon, his eyebrows raised. She shakes her head ever so slightly, and he holds her gaze. I watch them have a conversation with their eyes, and it hits me that I can't read her like I used to. I don't know her thoughts the way Finn does. Not anymore.

The searing pain of her choice rips across my chest, the flames licking their way across my flesh. If I could, I'd rip my heart from my body, just so I can stop from ever feeling this way again.

"You guys good?" I ask. I don't know what else to say, and I need to recover from watching them. I need them to see that I'm fine with them being together, even when I'm not.

"Yep," Lennon pipes up, her voice chipper. She smiles at me. "How is it there?"

"Good, so far. Have you ever been here?" The question is directed at either of them.

Finn gives me a look, like I should know better than to ask that question of him. He grew up dirt-poor, and I grew up alongside him, although I wasn't exactly poor. Still, I know he didn't travel anywhere when we were growing up. In my defense, he could've traveled when we went our separate ways for college.

"Anyway," I say, taking a deep breath. "This place is a

stop along the way to somewhere else. I just don't know where yet. I'm wandering."

"Not all who wander are lost," they say in unison, as if they're reading the front of a T-shirt at an outdoor supply store. Most people would laugh and share a look after saying the same thing at the same time, delighting in their ability to be on the same page. But not Lennon and Finn. They don't need to do that, because finding themselves on the same page isn't remarkable anymore. It's typical. It reinforces the painful truth. Maybe Lennon really did make the right choice.

I see it on Lennon's face instantly. The guilt.

She covers it up, smiling out of one side of her mouth. I may not have won in the fight for her heart, but she's still my best friend, and I *think* I have an idea what she's thinking.

"You're a good guy, Brady."

I tip my head up, acknowledging her compliment.

We chat for a few more minutes, and I invent an excuse to hang up.

"Bye, you two."

"Bye," they respond, and Lennon waves. The concerned look is back on her face.

I hit the end button before I have to spend another microsecond looking at her worried expression. I don't want to be reminded of why she's wearing that look.

My stomach growls, but I ignore it and finish my set. When I'm done, I shower and dress, then head out of my cabin and up to the main house.

I'll have to plan to make it to breakfast a little earlier tomorrow. What's left is not so great. Two carrot muffins and scrambled eggs that were probably delicious when they were fresh.

"Good morning, Mr. Sterling." Louisa greets me with a smile when I walk in. I've yet to see her anything but friendly. Never rushed. Never put out by a request. "Let me get you some fresh coffee."

"Please call me Brady," I tell her, following her into the kitchen. The last time I was in here it was dark in the whole house, except for the overhead lights in the kitchen. I had the perfect view of Addison, seated at the island with her back to me. The shadows darkened her blonde hair, and I heard her mother ask about the current state of Addison's heart.

Her mom's question, and Addison's dismissive response, told me I'm not alone in my search for solace.

Louisa moves about, replacing the old grounds from the coffeemaker with a fresh filter and new coffee.

"Sorry for the slim pickings out there," she says, inclining her head toward the mostly empty platters on the buffet table in the dining room. "We have a new family who came in yesterday. Three teenage boys." Her head shakes while she talks. "Those parents must need an extra income to feed them."

"Rice," I tell her, watching the coffee drip into the glass carafe. "A lot of rice-based casseroles. They fill stomachs for not much money."

Louisa snaps her fingers. "Good idea. Is that something your mom did?"

"Oh. Uh, no. My best friend's uncle made a lot of rice." I can't remember being at Finn's place as a teenager and ever eating anything besides rice. It was usually mixed with something else. Sometimes chicken, and always a bag of frozen corn, peas, and carrots. My house though? Different story.

We weren't lavish spenders, at least not in my opinion, although I guess that's relative. We were very comfortable, and I wanted for nothing. Especially compared to Finn. And Lennon, to a degree. She was more fortunate than Finn, though. It gave him the chip he wore on his shoulder into adulthood. Oddly, what knocked the chip off his shoulder was that cabin he built up in northern Arizona. I think it had something to do with controlling a set of circumstances. We haven't talked about it, but I think it's the first time Finn has felt like he's at home.

"Well, then, I guess your friend's uncle knew how to get by on a little." Louisa hands me a cup of coffee and offers me cream and sugar. I politely decline and blow across the top of my steaming coffee.

"Is Addison around?" I'm aiming for a casual tone, but I'm positive the curiosity in my voice betrays me.

Louisa smirks. "I saw her earlier but—"

The doorbell rings and Louisa's sentence is cut off.

"Just a moment, Mr. Sterling." She brings a cupped hand to her lips. "Brady," she amends apologetically, as she hurries from the kitchen and through the living room to the front door.

I'm not trying to eavesdrop, just like I didn't mean to overhear Addison on her phone call last night, but I can't help but hear the conversation between Louisa and whoever is at the door.

A woman's voice drips with honey as she speaks. "...Your property is a prime location and..."

"Thank you," Louisa responds, her tone warily appreciative.

I take a seat at the table and pick my way through a

carrot muffin. I can't hear what the woman says next, but I hear Louisa say, "This property is not for sale."

The woman must not have a working set of ears, because she pushes her agenda despite Louisa's response. She says something else, and Louisa gasps.

I'm up from my chair in an instant, striding across the living room and joining Louisa at the door.

"What's going on, Louisa?" I ask, taking in her stricken face.

She opens her mouth, but she can't seem to get anything out. Her hand lifts to her chin and her pointer finger presses against the center of her lower lip, as if she just can't fathom whatever this person has said.

I look to the woman standing on the welcome mat. She's middle-aged, and she wears a navy skirt and ivory blouse. Her glasses are not a flattering shape for her face.

She peers at me, and I get the feeling she views my sudden presence as a nuisance. "I'm certain it's no business of yours." The sugary sweetness in her voice has evaporated.

I extend a hand across the threshold. "Hello, Ms.?" I fix my expression into one of polite interest.

"Campbell," she answers, her eyes narrowing in suspicion. She places her palm in mine and we shake.

I feel Louisa's hand gently squeeze my shoulder, giving me permission to help. Smiling my smooth courtroom smile at the woman, I inform her of the position I've just appointed myself. "Ms. Campbell, it's business of mine because I'm Ms. Craft's attorney. My name is Brady Sterling." I don't look to Louisa to see how she interprets my pretend role. My eyes remain trained on the woman.

"How lucky you were here when I dropped by." Her narrowed gaze hasn't lessened by even a fraction.

"Wasn't it?" I agree, my smile still in place. "Please fill me in on why it is you've come to visit Ms. Craft today."

The woman crosses her arms and glances to Louisa. "I have a client who'd like to buy the land this business is operating on. He's willing to pay more than this place is worth."

I nod. "I'm sure you heard Ms. Craft tell you it's not for sale?"

She raises an eyebrow. "I'm not hard of hearing, Mr. Sterling."

My own eyebrows pull together in a disbelieving way. "Why is it you're asking twice?"

"I'm giving Ms. Craft the opportunity to rethink her initial response. Money talks. People often require a second, third, or even fourth chance to reevaluate their initial decision."

"Chance? Is that code for coercion?"

The woman makes a clucking sound with her tongue. "Be careful throwing around such powerful words."

I ignore her issued caution. "Who is your client?" I ask. I'm really starting to dislike this lady, whether she's just doing her job or not. She has come here to make an offer, yes, but she's really here to force the issue if she's rejected by Louisa. What if Louisa weren't as keen as she is? What if she was confused by legalese and said yes to an offer she didn't agree with just to make her head stop spinning? I'm infuriated by the idea of an older person being taken advantage of just because their mental acuity may not be sharp.

"Brandywine Developers," she answers. I don't know who they are, but they must be a big name client, or she wouldn't have that hint of pride in her voice.

I look to Louisa. She doesn't look so stricken anymore. Some of the color has come back to her cheeks. Which reminds me that I still haven't figured out the reason for the gasp from Louisa that sent me to the front door in the first place.

"What was it you said that appeared to upset Ms. Craft?"

The woman adjusts her shoulders, a pleased look creeping across her features. "Local government is prepared to step in on behalf of Brandywine should Ms. Craft deny purchase and—"

I snort. I can't help it. The sound stops the lady short of finishing her sentence. "Don't begin talk of eminent domain." I wave my hand around. "You, and anybody with functioning eyesight, can plainly see the recent work done to update this property. Blight is not an issue, nor is it a problem for any surrounding properties. Eminent domain has no place here. And neither do you."

Gently, I guide Louisa back from the open door.

"Goodbye, Ms. Campbell. I sincerely hope we don't see you again in this capacity."

I close the door. Louisa turns to me, her hands cupped around her mouth and her eyes wide with astonishment.

"You were incredible!" She throws her arms around me, taking me by surprise. She steps back after a moment but keeps her grip on my upper arms. "Are you really a lawyer?"

"I am. But I'm not licensed to practice in this state, so I can't actually represent you."

Louisa wags a finger at me. "You are good," she says, then peers around me. "Wasn't he good?" she says to someone who is not me.

I turn around and see Addison standing on the bottom step of the stairs. She wears a long yellow skirt and a silky-looking white top.

"How long have you been standing there?" I ask. It's her question from last night, and I wonder if she'll recognize that.

She smirks, and I'm pretty certain she does. "Long enough to know you can talk circles around someone."

This could be a compliment, but coming from her, I just don't know.

I'm too hungry to take on verbally sparring with Addison right now. Turning back to Louisa, I ask her if Uber or some other car service will come out here. From what I can tell, we're a little over twenty minutes from the town. "I'd like to see Lonesome," I explain, not wanting to disclose that actually I'm starving. She'd probably insist on making me food, and I don't want to add to her workload.

"You don't have to worry about that," she answers, side-stepping me and going to stand in front of Addison. "Before you came in for breakfast, I asked Addy to go to the grocery store for me. She wouldn't mind being your tour guide, would you, Addy?"

Addison gives her grandma a long look, then drags her gaze over to me. "Sure," she finally answers.

She doesn't sound unhappy, or even put out. Wary. That's how she sounds.

"Great," I say, already heading toward the door that leads out of the house and to the cabins beyond. "I'm going to grab my wallet and I'll meet you out front."

I don't hear if she responds, because I'm already through the back door.

8

ADDISON

"Can we please get breakfast before we do anything else?" Brady asks the second the doors of the Jeep are closed.

I give him a look and he starts to explain. "I was late to breakfast."

I give him another look, remembering the coffee I made him a few days ago when he was hungover.

"I'm not making it a habit. And I wasn't hungover," he adds, smiling. "I was working out this morning and then a friend called. By the time I got to breakfast there wasn't much left."

I decide not to tell him I spent a few seconds watching him pick carrots from his carrot muffin before he flew to my grandma's defense. Instead, I ask, "What were you doing for a workout? Hopefully not going for a run in the woods. Don't want you to get lost." I smile to let him know I'm teasing.

"Very funny." He adjusts his seatbelt and sits back. "I was doing a circuit of various exercises."

I nod, trying not to picture those abs rippling with each

repetition. "Where do you want to eat?" I ask, to change the subject.

He shrugs, glancing over at me. "Aren't you supposed to be the tour guide?"

Oh, right.

"I know of a good place," I tell him, taking another turn and using all my arm strength to wrench the wheel.

"No power steering?" he asks.

I shake my head. "I don't know how my grandma drives this thing. Although, I don't think she drives often."

Brady nods thoughtfully. "Doesn't seem like a good car for someone her age."

I snort. "Try telling her that."

He lets out a derisive laugh. "Uh, no thanks."

We're quiet for the next few minutes until I pull into the restaurant parking lot and majorly curb it. The Jeep jumps and sputters, and I laugh.

Brady, however, grimaces and grips the handle on the doorframe.

"Sorry about that," I say, my cheeks warming.

"It's okay," Brady assures me, but his voice is off. "I'm still a little jumpy. I was in a bad car accident not too long ago."

"Crap. I'm sorry."

"Seriously, don't apologize. It'll just take time for me to chill out."

"Were you hurt?" I ask, twisting around and grabbing my purse from the back seat.

"Broken leg," Brady responds, getting out of the car. I'm digging in my bag for my Chapstick when I hear my car door open.

"Oh!" My hand flies to my chest in surprise.

Brady steps back to allow space for me to get out. "I'm sorry. Did I frighten you?"

"You took me by surprise."

"I was trying to be polite."

I nod, adjusting to the idea of someone getting my door.

"Are you going to open the door of the restaurant too?" I'm teasing him again.

Brady presses his lips together and nods. "Probably. It's how I'm hard-wired."

And then he does exactly what he said he would do. He opens the door and I step in, scanning the room for an open booth. I spot one and we get settled in. A server brings us menus and backs away with our drink order.

"I bet you put your hand on the small of a girl's back when you're opening the door for her, don't you? You guide her in?" My heart twists. Warren always did that.

"I'm not giving away all my moves," Brady says, laughing and winking.

My stomach drops, and for a second I stare, trying to determine if he was flirting.

Brady looks down at his menu and says, "Whatever happened, it was bad, wasn't it?"

Tears immediately spring to my eyes. "Yes," I whisper.

Brady looks at me, his gaze full of remorse. "I'm sorry, Addison."

I sniff. "We've managed to say I'm sorry a lot this morning and we've only been together for about twenty minutes. How about we make a deal?" I extend a hand across the table. "No more I'm sorrys."

He looks relieved when he places his hand in mine. "That sounds great."

The server approaches to drop off our coffee, and we place our orders. Brady orders enough for two people.

"Those carrot muffins didn't do it for you?" I ask. Immediately I realize my blunder.

A smug look creeps onto Brady's face. "You were there for way longer than I was behind you last night."

"I would've said something, but you shot out of your seat and raced across the room." I take a sip of my coffee. "Thank you, by the way. For coming to my grandma's rescue."

Brady drinks from his own cup, nodding as he swallows. "If they're determined, what I said this morning will only hold them off for so long. They might try to strong-arm your grandma. Hopefully they have the brains to know they have nothing but bloated threats. If not, she'll need a lawyer." He sees my raised eyebrows and adds, "And it can't be me. I'm not licensed to practice outside of Illinois."

"What do you practice in Illinois?"

"Family law."

He seemed right at home in his role this morning. I wonder if he's always that passionate when he's doing his job. He was articulate and clear, and his voice reverberated with his belief that what he was fighting for was the just choice. I'd believe him in a second.

"What do you do in Illinois?" He sits back in his seat and extends an arm, draping it across the top of the booth's cushion. It causes the sleeve of his shirt to creep up his upper arm, revealing even more of a large and impressive bicep. He said he was doing circuits in his room this morning, and now I'm wondering what they consisted of.

I tear my gaze from his arm and say, "I was a baker. I owned a bakery."

His head tips to the side. "Past tense?"

The fingers on my right hand drum against the worn wooden table. "You don't miss much, do you?"

He shrugs with only one shoulder. "Being perceptive was a job requirement."

"Past tense?" I ask, raising my eyebrows.

He grins, taking a sip of coffee. “Past tense, for now. I took a leave of absence.”

“Can I ask why?” My words come out slowly, my tone gentle. I know this is a sensitive subject.

“I had my heart broken. I needed some time to get over it.” He looks around for a moment, his gaze falling back to me before he speaks again. “And it seems I needed a change of scenery to make that happen.”

I nod but don’t speak. Memories of my own heartbreak creep in, but I push them away when Brady keeps going.

“As you already know, I grew up in Arizona. I had…” He pauses, shaking his head. “*Have.* Not *had*.” He smiles at me, and though I already know what he’s going to say, I’m shocked to find we’ve created an inside joke so quickly. “Not past tense. I have two best friends who still live there. Lennon and Finn. We’ve been best friends since we were really young. And then we grew up, and things, well” —he raps his knuckles on the table twice— “they got more complicated. By about tenfold. Long story short, Lennon chose Finn.” He smiles, but it’s the saddest, most melancholy smile I’ve ever seen. “I didn’t get the girl.”

My hand leaves my coffee and covers my heart. I don’t know much about Brady, not really, and for a majority of the few days I’ve known him I haven’t liked him. But last night he showed me how important honesty is to him, and this morning he rushed to my grandma’s defense, obviously disgusted by the idea of her being bullied. It’s hitting me, right now in this very second, that I might actually *like* Brady. And the idea of him not winning the object of his affection makes me feel dismayed. And maybe something else, something warm in the pit of my stomach, something I don’t have a word for.

“So they are still your friends?” I ask, at the same time

the server drops off our breakfast. There are so many plates I almost ask her to join us, but then I remember Brady picking at the carrot muffin earlier and let the joke pass.

"Yes," he answers, inhaling two bites of food before he speaks again. "Not being friends with them is impossible. They're... my everything. I can't imagine life without them."

I nod, scooping up a forkful of my food. The love and loyalty he shows his friends, even when hurt by them, is inspiring. We're quiet while we eat, until I think of something else to ask him.

"Was it really dramatic? It sounds like it would be." I wince as I hear myself. Talk about insensitive. I open my mouth to apologize, but remember I'm not supposed to, so I get creative and think of a way around it. "Please accept my remorse at my question."

Brady gives me a knowing look and shakes his head. "Roundabout apologies will be considered a violation of the agreement."

I cross my arms and pretend to huff. "Ugh, what a lawyer."

Brady chuckles. "Yes."

He sees my confusion and says, "That's the answer to your question about it being dramatic. But there probably wasn't any other way. Not after so long."

"You really loved her?" There it is again, that warm feeling in my belly. Still, I can't name it.

He nods, glancing down at the table. "I loved her for most of my life."

My heart. It hurts for him. And then I realize that I like how I hurt for him. Finally, I'm feeling pain for someone other than myself.

Brady looks up at me. "But apparently Lennon knew something I didn't. She chose Finn, and I have no choice but to trust she made the right decision. If she'd thought I was the right man for her, she would've chosen me. And she didn't."

Without thinking, I reach across the table and run my fingertips over the top of Brady's hand. "You're the right man for somebody."

Brady's gaze stays locked on mine, then he glances down to where our skin touches.

I rip my hand away, embarrassed. "I'm—"

"Don't say it," Brady warns, a playful look in his eyes.

His playfulness relieves some of the embarrassment I'm feeling, but I'm still largely mortified. Looking at my plate, I stab a bite, but before I can lift my fork, Brady reaches for my free hand and touches it.

"It doesn't bother me that you touched me. I was just surprised by how warm your touch was."

Suddenly my mouth feels dry. How long has it been since I've been touched? A hug from my grandma here and there the past few days, but before that? It's been a while. A long while.

It feels good. Too good. And, in a confusing way, it also hurts.

Slowly, I slide my hand out from under his, but now the absence of his touch is almost as excruciating.

To avoid hurting his feelings, I reach for the napkin in my lap and use it to dab at the corner of my mouth.

The server comes back to our table, coffee carafe in hand. She offers it to me first, but I shake my head, "No thank you."

"Yes, please," Brady says, pushing his cup closer to her.

I watch the dark liquid fill the cup, a few drops splashing onto the table. She sets our check down and tells us not to rush.

"So," Brady says, lifting his freshly filled coffee to his lips. He looks at me over the rim of the white cup, his eyebrows raised. "I showed you mine. You show me yours now."

Right. I knew this was coming.

"Addison!"

I turn to the familiar voice saying my name. Across the small room, Charlie and Merch stand beside a booth. I wave, and Charlie makes her way over, weaving through the tables that separate us. This is no small task, considering she has to navigate the tight quarters with a protruding belly. Merch follows his wife.

When Charlie reaches our table, she plops down beside me and lets out a heavy breath. "I swear to the man upstairs, I am bigger this morning than I was last night."

I look down at her stomach and see that it can barely fit in the booth. I open my mouth to introduce Charlie to Brady, but she beats me to it.

"Hi," she says, sticking her arm out over the table. "I'm Charlie. I'm an old friend of Addison's. This is my husband, Merch. Technically his name is Conrad, but I don't think anybody has ever called him that." Her gaze flickers over to him as she talks.

"Nice to meet you," Brady responds, shaking Charlie's offered hand. He slips from the booth and stands to shake hands with Merch.

"My last name is Merchant," Merch explains to Brady. "I played football in high school and the team started calling me Merch. The name stuck."

Brady chuckles. "I played baseball, but Sterling isn't the kind of last name that sounds good shortened."

Merch and Brady start discussing high school sports. It takes some effort, but Charlie turns her body to me. "Where did he come from?" she asks quietly.

"Chicago. He's staying at Sweet Escape." I glance at Brady. He's nodding at something Merch is saying. "Actually, he was on my flight out here."

"Serendipitous."

I sip my water. "It wasn't a cute first meeting or anything like that. I thought he was married, and I yelled at him when I caught him checking me out."

Charlie's eyebrows furrow. "Why did you think he was married?"

"Because he was wearing a ring."

Her eyes grow huge. "Please tell me there's a story here that involves him not actually being married."

I smile. "There is. It was his grandpa's ring that his mom gave to him."

"Why was he wearing it?"

I eye Brady again, biting my lower lip as I study him. "I think I may have just learned some of the reason." Looking back at Charlie, I say quietly, "He has a broken heart."

"Kind of like you," she says, only her reply isn't quiet.

I look away so I don't have to respond. My glance falls to the bulletin board above the cash register. A large flyer with block lettering announces the 65th annual Lonesome Day.

"Aw, I remember Lonesome Day," I say fondly with a lopsided grin, thinking back to my childhood summers. Mostly I remember flavored ice, caramel popcorn balls, and fireworks.

"You guys should go. It's a few weeks away. And this year is going to be amazing because—" Charlie's words screech to a halt and her eyes grow wide. She turns away from me and looks to Merch, grabbing for his forearm.

At first I think maybe her water broke, and I can tell by Merch's concerned gaze that's what he thinks also. Relief flows through me when a large smile takes over her face.

"Merch, remember what my mom said this morning? About Lucy's bakery?"

"Yeah," Merch says, the word drawn out to convey his confusion.

"Addison has to do it. She just has to." Charlie claps her hands with excitement.

"Addison has to do what?" I ask, trepidation filling me.

"You know Lucy's bakery?"

I nod.

"Lucy is retiring. Everybody and their mother wants the space, but she's refusing to rent it to anybody that's not going to use it as a bakery. And apparently she already has, like, five people who've agreed to use it for that."

"So?"

"So, she's holding a bake-off to determine who gets the place."

"Okay?"

"Oh my gosh, do I have to spell it out for you using mini-muffins?" Charlie shakes her head in exasperation. "You should enter the bake-off! The winner will be announced at Lonesome Day."

That would only work if I'm staying in Lonesome. And right now, I don't know that I am. I didn't come here with a purpose. I came to lick my wounds. Beyond that, I don't have a plan.

"I'm flattered you have such confidence in my baking ability, but I don't think it's a good idea."

Charlie makes an annoyed sound with her lips. "Just think about it. What else are you doing with your time?"

"Helping my grandma."

"Oh. Right. Okay, well, besides that?"

Does lying on my bed feeling sorry for myself count? If so, that takes up a lot of my time.

"Speaking of my grandma," I say pointedly. "I'm supposed to be running errands for her. We stopped for breakfast because someone was forced to eat carrot muffins this morning." I glance at Brady, and he smiles that same smug grin from earlier.

Charlie takes the hint and slides from the booth.

Merch and Charlie both hug me goodbye, then shake hands with Brady. They make their way back to their booth, and Brady and I walk outside. We don't make it more than three feet before the door opens behind us and someone yells, "Hey!"

We whip around. Our server is standing there, her hand on her hip, a piece of paper dangling from her outstretched fist.

"Oh, shit," Brady groans, but there's a little laughter in the sound, and he reaches into his back pocket. "We weren't skipping out on you. I promise." He pulls three twenties from his wallet, and even without looking at the check, I know that's probably more than twice the amount of the total. He presses the cash into her waiting palm, and she smiles at him.

"Usually it's the teenagers I have to watch closely," she says, joking now that she knows we didn't mean to pull a dine-and-dash.

Brady laughs and she retreats through the open door.

He slips his wallet into the pocket of his jeans and looks at me. His eyes are wide, his expression one of humorous disbelief.

I can't help it. I laugh like I haven't laughed in a long time.

Like his hand on mine earlier, the laughter feels good.

And also so, so bad.

9

BRADY

I'M BARE-NAKED, AND ADDISON IS FULLY DRESSED. Figuratively speaking, anyway.

We've managed to get through her list of errands without her telling me a thing about why she left Chicago for Lonesome.

I can tell it's been weighing on her. Our trips to the grocery and hardware stores weren't as comfortable as our time at the restaurant. She stiffened when I opened her door at the last stop and placed my hand on the small of her back. It wasn't a conscious choice. My fingers drifted toward her like there wasn't any other place they were supposed to be. I hadn't even realized it was happening until I felt her go rigid. We weren't supposed to be apologizing anymore today, so I let my eyes convey my apology. She looked away after our gazes brief meeting, but I know she got my message.

After we left the restaurant, I'd hoped we'd broken through a few of our barriers. The dine-and-dash incident had Addison howling with laughter, a deep, rich sound that until then I hadn't imagined could come from her. Her whole face had lit up, and she looked like the opposite of the person who yelled at me in the Chicago airport.

Now she's back to being the Addison I've come to expect: guarded and aloof. But there's something else now. A sadness. Her eyes look heavy, as if her soul is burdened.

I know it's whatever she hasn't told me. And when she tells me, she'll feel naked too.

We pull into the detached garage at Sweet Escape. It's tidy and organized, cabinets lining one side with pegboards running the length of the wall above the cabinets. Screw-drivers and other small tools hang in order of size from the pegboards. Lawn maintenance tools hang from hooks on the opposite wall. Obviously Louisa takes pride in her home and her business. And her car, which is old but in good shape. Although I don't know how she even drives the thing. Without power steering, it must be damn near impossible for her to turn. The muscles in Addison's forearm flexed every time she turned, and I can't imagine the effort it takes Louisa.

I get out of the Jeep and reach into the back, grabbing a handful of grocery bags. "Next time, will you let me drive?" I'd offered when we left the restaurant, but Addison had already descended into her current mood, and I'd known better than to push it.

"Sure," she says, coming up beside me and grabbing a fistful of bags.

She pauses, her arms extended into the back, and stares up at me. There's a heaviness to her gaze, carrying the weight of something still unknown to me. "I know I'm supposed to show you mine," she says slowly, a grin pulling up the corners of her mouth. Even though it's probably the choice of words making her smile, it's the friendliest she has looked since we were on the sidewalk in front of the restaurant. "How about this evening? There's somewhere I'd like to go."

"I'm up for it," I tell her, trying not to show my surprise at her invitation. The bags I'm holding make a crinkling sound.

"Good." She attempts another smile, but it's not natural. Her eyes still look burdened. "Meet me back here at seven."

I nod, then follow her into the house. Louisa isn't around, so I deposit the grocery bags on the counter and take the two bags that belong to me. Each cabin has a microwave and fridge, which suits me fine. I'm not a cook, but I can microwave with the best of them.

I hover near the island, unsure of what to say. Addison is in the pantry, up on her tiptoes to set something on a high shelf. She tries twice, failing both times.

I come up behind her, wordlessly taking the box and setting it on the shelf.

She glances at me as she sinks back down to flat feet. We lock eyes, and in that instant I watch her make a decision.

She leans in, her lips coming to rest on my cheek for the most fleeting of seconds. If it weren't for the heat searing my skin, I might not believe it happened at all.

Without a word she steps away, retreating to the counter and pulling more items from the grocery bags.

I do the same, silently leaving the house and walking across the sloping yard back to my cabin.

It was just a kiss on the cheek. Sweet, simple. No big deal.

But my pounding heart tells a different story.

In an effort not to appear overeager for whatever it is Addison has planned tonight, I force my strides to slow. I'm taking a circuitous route around the inside perimeter of the property, instead of walking in a straight line across the lawn and to the garage off the side of the house. Two families are out enjoying the early evening light, playing a game of bean bags and chatting. Drawing attention or unwanted questions from them isn't something I'm interested in.

The truth is, I'm pretty eager to learn what Addison has in mind for our evening. I spent the hours between that kiss on the cheek in the pantry and leaving my cabin to meet her in a state of anxious impatience. I sort of watched a soccer match on my iPad. I kind of took a half-hearted nap. My dad called and I can't remember much about our conversation, because I was only partially present.

Addison confounds me. She's a study in contrasts. She's passionate, that I know for certain. The first time I met her, she read me the riot act. She was incensed about the interest I showed in her while wearing that ring. If I was married, acting like that would make me a scumbag, but Addison's response was so strong that it makes me wonder.

Whatever it is, it probably has to do with why she left Chicago. Was she married? Did he cheat? It seems likely, given her reaction to the ring on my finger. Maybe he was a liar, too. She wasn't inclined to believe me when I said I wasn't married. Not the first time, and not the second time either.

So that's it then. She was married to someone who cheated on her and lied about it.

I twist my lips and look up to the main house through the trees, wondering which window belongs to Addison's bedroom.

A thought slams into me. What if Addison was involved

with a married guy? Maybe he lied to her about being married.

Either of these scenarios spells heartbreak for Addison.

I shake my head, trying to get rid of my own conjecture. Maybe some episodes of Lennon's mom's favorite soap opera are still floating around in my subconscious. Years of passing through the living room at Lennon's house while the drama played out on TV must've lodged itself in my brain.

Addison's reason for coming to Lonesome might be boring. For her sake, I hope it is.

I round the corner of the garage and stop dead in my tracks. Addison stands on tiptoe, wearing tiny white cut-off jean shorts. She's bent just slightly at the waist, shoving a cooler into place in the back of the Jeep.

Suddenly it feels hotter than it did a few seconds ago. Maybe I'm overdressed. I look down at my shorts and t-shirt, knowing it's not my choice of clothing.

Addison is gorgeous. And heartbroken.

So are you. I didn't come here to *meet* a woman. I came here to *forget* a woman. It's a good reminder, even though I don't particularly want it right now.

"Hey," I croak, the fight in my brain slipping out into my tone.

Addison whips around. A piece of her long blonde hair sticks to her lips and she pushes it away.

"Hi," she says, almost shyly.

Is Addison... nervous?

"Do you need help with anything?" I ask, to help her cover up whatever it is she's feeling.

She shakes her head. "Should be good to go. I packed some food and drinks, and a blanket."

I nod knowingly. "A picnic?"

Addison presses her lips together and shakes her head. "No guessing."

I grin. "I'll just have to be patient, I guess."

Addison smiles. "Something tells me you're good at it."

My smile falls a fraction, and I hope she doesn't notice. Patience should be my middle name, and that might not be a good thing. Years of loving Lennon honed the skill, but having my heart stomped on took away the good I see in the attribute.

"Are we all set then?" I ask, moving toward the car. Which puts me closer to Addison. And to her scent. Something citrusy and floral. Whatever it is, it's enough to make the muscles in my stomach tighten.

"All set," Addison chirps, holding her hand out for a high-five.

My palm smacks against hers, and there's that warmth again. Does this woman have little heaters in her palms?

The thought makes me smile, and Addison asks what's so funny.

"Honestly?" I eye her, and she nods her head warily. "I've touched your hand a total of three times since I've known you, and each time they've been really warm. I was wondering if you have tiny space heaters hidden in them."

Addison barks a laugh. "You're crazy." She reaches for my shoulders and playfully shoves me to my side of the car, then pulls her hands back quickly. "Oh my gosh, did I burn you?" She winces and makes a bared-teeth face.

I shake my head and laugh. I might regret being so honest with her.

We climb in the car and Addison backs out, stopping to point a remote control at the garage. The door descends and Addison lets off the brake, backing us all the way out of the driveway. She puts the car in drive and glances over at me as we roll forward, an excited smile tugging each corner of her lips up to her cheeks.

"I'd probably be as excited as you too, if I knew where we were going." I give her a meaningful look as I say it.

"Nice try," she sings over the rush of air flowing through the Jeep.

I smile again, looking out my window at the trees as we rush past them. So far tonight I've done a lot of smiling in a very short time. And before that? I feel like it has been awhile.

There was so much history with Lennon. Everything was heavy. Every motion, every word mattered. I was constantly watching, sussing out hidden meanings or searching for words unsaid. Anything that would put me ahead of Finn in the race for Lennon's heart.

Being with Addison right now, it just feels... light. Airy. Easy. No history to look back on. Unless I count when she yelled at me in the airport. I chuckle to myself, the sound immediately swallowed up by the rush of air.

Addison drives on, following the curves in the road. The air begins to change, smelling wet and salty. We must be headed toward the coast.

Ten minutes later, I find that I'm right. We pull into a small parking lot, and through the trees I see white-capped waves. Addison parks and we both get out. I take the cooler from the back, and Addison grabs the blanket, but she also grabs a bag I hadn't noticed before.

"What's that?" I ask.

She ignores me. "Follow me," she says, leading the way onto a path.

Walking behind her isn't the worst thing in the world, especially not with those shorts she's wearing, but I don't want to be *that* guy. Seriously though, I can't resist completely. I'm only human.

"Are you checking out my ass?" Addison calls out, peeking back at me.

I make a face. "No."

Addison laughs. "Why not? These are very short shorts. They're from high school and pretty much all my clothes are dirty."

I cough, thinking of high school Addison in those shorts, driving the poor boys crazy. "They're okay."

She throws back her head and laughs. It's in this moment that I decide I really like watching her laugh. It's the freedom, the abandonment of the hurt that plagues her, that makes her laugh so special.

We walk through the trees, and up ahead the ocean looms. Addison pauses when the forest gives way to beach, and the dirt slowly becomes sand.

"Wow," I breathe the word as I gaze out. The sound of the water crashing at the shore settles over my soul, soothing it.

Addison looks pleased at my reaction. "That's how I feel every time I come out here."

She keeps going onto the beach, walking along for a short time, her eyes roaming the space, until she settles on a spot.

I follow her there and set down the cooler. "Now will you tell me what's in that bag?"

She reaches for the canvas tote and turns it upside down, its contents spilling out.

A hand shovel. Matches... fire starter.

"We're building a fire?"

She grins and nods. "A bonfire," she clarifies, then begins scanning the tree line.

"I'm putting you in charge of gathering the bigger logs. I'll get the smaller ones."

I follow her gaze to the base of the trees. It makes me realize I've spent very little time looking at this part of them. My focus is always directly in front of myself, and that extends to every aspect of my life. Would life look different if I had looked down once in a while, or up?

"Are you going to help me?" Addison calls. She's standing beside a giant tree, already holding some smaller branches. As I watch, she bends at the waist and gathers a few more from the ground.

I'd been so deep in my thoughts I hadn't even noticed her walk away. I hustle to where she stands, scanning the ground for bigger logs. They aren't difficult to locate. The forest has given us plenty in the way of kindling. Building fires isn't in my resumé, so I feel out of depth right now. Where I grew up, fires in anything but a fireplace or outdoor pit are a very bad thing, and even those are sometimes banned.

Once we have enough gathered, we walk back over to the place Addison has chosen, dumping our wood on the ground. She gives me the hand shovel.

"Put those muscles to work." She smiles at me. "We need a diameter of a few feet, and it needs to be a few inches deep. Just to decrease the possibility of the fire spreading."

"Got it," I tell her, dropping to one knee and pushing the shovel into the sand. It takes only a couple minutes, and in that time Addison has spread out the blanket she brought and began unpacking the cooler.

"Good?" I ask, gesturing to the circular pit I've dug.

Addison gives it a quick once-over and nods. "Perfect," she announces, turning to gather the small twigs she'd collected. She lays them out on the sand first, then grabs two logs. I grab a couple, waiting for my next instruction. I like that she's teaching me something like this. It's kind of hot that she knows how to build a fire.

"Remember Lincoln Logs?" She eyes me, her eyebrows raised.

I nod.

"That's basically what we're going to build." She lays her logs parallel to one another over the twigs. "A little cabin."

"Like mine," I add.

She chuckles. "Yes. We're going to build a little cabin seven."

"No porch though."

"And no tiny Brady living inside, doing a HIIT workout."

I bark a laugh and almost drop my logs. "Circuit."

"Whatever." Addison grins as I place my logs across hers, running parallel to one another.

We keep building until we have our little cabin. Addison grabs the matches and lights one, placing the flame against the base of small twigs. We sit back, watching as first the twigs catch fire, then the flames lick upward, until the whole thing is ablaze.

"Good job," I tell Addison, offering a high-five. She smacks my hand, and this time I'm not surprised by the warmth. I'm expecting it, and it's there just like I knew it would be. We settle back on the blanket, mesmerized by the colors in the flames, until Addison begins unwrapping the sandwiches she packed for dinner.

"Thank you," I tell her when she hands one to me. I didn't realize how hungry I was, but considering that it only takes me a minute to eat it, I guess I was hungrier than I thought.

"Next time I'll make you two sandwiches." Addison looks meaningfully at the empty wrapper in front of me.

She hands me a bottle of wine and a bottle opener. "Will you do the honors?"

As she watches I uncork the bottle and pour wine into the two cups she has set out.

Our reusable plastic cups make a dull sound as we tap them against each other. I lie back, supporting myself with a forearm, and gaze out.

The sky is a darkening blue overhead, but as it dips toward the sun the shades change, paling until they meet the oranges and yellows at the horizon.

"Stunning, right?" Addison says, keeping her gaze trained on the beginning of the sunset.

I nod my head in agreement. "And so different than what I'm used to back home."

"I'm assuming you're not referring to Chicago."

I glance at her, then back to the sky. "You haven't seen a sunset until you've seen one in Arizona."

Addison settles back on the blanket in the same way I'm lying. What's left of the sun settles over her, making her blonde hair glow in a subtle way. "Tell me more."

I look out at the sky before me, but instead of seeing water, I see desert. "You can see for as far as you want, kind of like now." My hand extends, motioning from one end of the horizon to the other. "But the colors are vivid. Hot pinks, purples, intense orange. Sometimes the orange is more of a salmon color. And as the sun sinks lower, the sky gets darker, until the purple is navy blue, and the pink is maroon." I stare out, and the desert scene becomes water once more. "It's bright and feels full of potential, but it inevitably darkens."

"Doesn't everything?" Addison's voice has a tinge of bitterness to it.

"It seems to." My own voice sounds like hers. I turn to

face her, moving my forearm so that my hand is propping up my head. "Are you going to tell me what you're doing here?"

Again, Addison mimics my body position. She sips from her wine, and looks down at her hand, curling and uncurling her fingers around her cup.

"I was engaged." She glances up at me, probably to see how I react to these first three words. My face remains in a careful mask of non-surprise. "But then..." She pauses, takes a deep breath, and continues. "It was almost a year ago. We were walking downtown, after work one night. We'd just eaten dinner." Addison's face softens, and her lips tug into a sad smile. "I wanted Mediterranean, but he was craving spicy table-side guacamole. He let me win, and I knew he would, because that was what he always did. We were on our way back to our apartment. A guy was flying toward us on his bike, not paying attention." Addison's eyes fill with tears, and I want to reach out to her, but I keep my hands to myself.

Her tears subside, and she continues. "I'm still not sure if I jumped out of the way or if Warren pushed me. The guy on the bike hit Warren, and they both went down. At first, Warren seemed fine. A cut on his arm, but that was it. The other guy apologized over and over, even though his face was busted up. When we got home we laughed, saying that he'd learned his lesson the hard way and would probably need a plastic surgeon."

"Before bed that night, Warren seemed off. He complained of a headache, and he dropped a glass of water on the ground beside his nightstand. He played it off, but I had been standing nearby, and I saw him reach out as if the nightstand was there, and let the glass go. I was worried, but Warren brushed me off." The tears that receded once are back, slipping from her eyes, running across the bridge of her nose and dripping sideways down her cheek. "I was keyed up, so I went to watch TV on the couch and eventually fell asleep. I woke up a few hours later and went to our bedroom. I checked on Warren, but he... he..." Addison gulps, her breath coming in shaky gasps. "He wasn't breathing. I called 911, and after that everything was so confusing. I stood against our bedroom wall and watched them work on Warren, and then they took him away." Addison sits up, reaching into her purse for a packet of tissues. She removes one and blows her nose. "He'd slipped into a coma while I slept in the other room."

"Addison," I say, reaching for her hand, but she pulls it away. She doesn't want to be consoled.

"Is he still in a coma?" I don't want to ask outright if he passed away, although I'm assuming that's how her story will end.

She shakes her head and a short stream of air comes from her nose. "They don't call it a coma anymore. It's been so long, now it's called a persistent vegetative state."

Shit. Her situation is nothing like I'd been imagining.

"I'm... sorry." It's so little to say to a problem so substantial.

Addison's head bobs up and down slowly. "Me too."

I don't want to pry, but I'm curious to know more. "Can I ask you a question?" I sit up, criss-crossing my legs.

She looks up at me, and I can see in her eyes she's considering telling me no. After a beat, she nods.

"What have you been doing this past year? After the dust settled, and Warren's" —I pause, searching for the best word to use— "*state* became persistent. You stayed in Chicago, right?"

"At first, I was by his side all day and all night. I left only to shower. But I had a bakery to run, and when it became clear Warren wasn't expected to wake up, I threw myself into my store. Quiet, early mornings in the kitchen in the back were my refuge. Ashton, my main employee, would arrive at seven with coffee, and until we closed for the day she'd be the only person I talked to." Addison's eyes shut and she tips her chin to the sky. "Before the accident I was always behind the register, chatting and discussing the news with customers. But not after. The everyday happenings seemed trivial, and I couldn't pretend like they mattered." A few more tears slip from her eyes.

Addison surprises me then, sitting up and scooting forward on the blanket, settling beside me. Her head drops onto my shoulder and my own head tips until it rests gently on top of hers. From her body language I can tell she is done talking about what happened.

The final swaths of color dip below the horizon, leaving behind a sky the shade of a fresh bruise.

"We're quite a pair, aren't we?" I ask, my eyes casting downward, but I can't see much of her aside from the top of her head and the tip of her nose.

It takes Addison a moment to answer, and when she does, her voice is full of something I can't name. "Quite a pair, Brady. Quite a pair."

10

ADDISON

I HAVE A VULNERABILITY HANGOVER.

Is this how Brady felt when he shared his heartbreak with me?

I've been rolling around in my bed since I woke up at five, trying to figure out if I said too much. Which is funny, really, because I didn't say as much as I could have.

I didn't tell him about the nightmares that plagued me for months, or the accusatory looks on Shannon's face. She, it appeared, didn't share my uncertainty about where to place blame.

There's so much more I could've said, but last night I'd had enough. I'd peeled back the Band-Aid and revealed my wound, exposing the injured flesh to the world for just as long as I could take. Brady would've listened until I'd ran out of breath, but I couldn't keep going. It all *hurts.*

I know he'd be the right person to tell everything to. He's sweet and kind, caring and compassionate. He's a genuinely good person. Now that I've seen past the mishap of our first meeting, I can see it as clearly as if these qualities were tattooed on his forehead.

Last night he'd referred to us as a 'pair', and I found that I liked it. For so long I've felt alone, since almost the exact moment Warren's family ran into the hospital waiting room. I'd grown close to his mom and sister before the accident, I'd thought they loved me, and then *Wham!* A door slammed shut in my face. Gone were the excited conversations about wedding planning and sly comments about when Warren and I would give them a baby to love on. We went from warm to icy in an instant.

The problem stretched on and on, every day that Warren didn't wake up. I'd had no one to lean on, and I needed them, but they turned inward, leaning on each other and leaving me out in the cold.

And then came the final blow: the bakery. Warren's parents had rented the space right before we got engaged, and I was paying them what I could for rent until the bakery turned a profit, while they paid the full rent to the mortgage company.

A few months into Warren's coma, the bakery began making money, and I could afford to pay them full rent *and* make a decent living for myself.

Yesterday Charlie mentioned that contest, but I'm not so sure about it. Is that really what I want? To run another bakery? I loved it when I did it in Chicago. Constantly surrounded by mouth-watering smells, and watching customers become regulars, made me happy. While Warren laid in his bed, first in the hospital and then in the long-term care facility, going to the bakery was a time when I could switch off the mess my life had turned into. I'd stand in the kitchen in the back, rolling and kneading dough, braiding challah, shaping scones and boiling bagels. I let my brain immerse itself in work, and the pain fell away.

Maybe I could have that again, here in Lonesome. I

wasn't planning on making this my home, but then again, I wasn't planning much of anything, one way or the other. And it's not like I have a good reason to return to Chicago. What was once there for me is gone now.

I wasn't planning on making a friend like Brady, either. That's what we are, right? Friends? It certainly feels like it. Especially after yesterday at the restaurant, and last night at the beach.

I push aside my curtains and peek out the window, telling myself I'm not looking for a certain tall, brown-haired man, but deep inside I know I am. It's not like I want to make him my boyfriend or anything, it's just that it's nice to be around a man again. Brady's presence is reassuring, like Warren's was. Like somehow, just by being around them, I know everything is going to be all right.

I feel a pang thinking of Warren. The pain of losing him hasn't faded. It's always there, lurking in the background, like the creeks that run beyond the trees. You don't see them, but of course they're there.

I don't see Brady outside. He's either still at his cabin, or he's already downstairs. I get out of bed and dress, then head to the bathroom across the hall. It takes me longer than usual to brush my hair and teeth. I think it's nerves. Blame it on that vulnerability hangover.

I make my way downstairs, and I hear him before I see him. His laughter climbs the stairs as I descend, meeting me halfway and swirling around me, caressing my bare legs.

A smile pulls at my lips as the first floor comes into view. I scan the room for Brady, spotting him at the breakfast table. He sits with his back to me, engaged in conversation with an old couple who checked in a couple days ago.

He can't see me, so I take the chance to study him on my walk into the kitchen. He has strong, wide shoulders, the chair he sits on dwarfed by him. His hair is messy this morning, not total bedhead but like maybe he used his fingers as a comb before heading up here.

I pour my coffee and lean against the counter, slouching slightly to keep an eye on him. He's talking animatedly with the Andersons, and I wonder what it is they're discussing. Mr. Anderson laughs, and Mrs. Anderson looks at Brady with rapt attention. She's probably thinking about who she knows who needs a man like Brady in her life.

The thought makes me uneasy. I turn my back on the chatting threesome and gaze out the window over the kitchen sink. Brady's heart is still broken from his friend back home, but one day he'll move on.

Will I ever do the same? Warren's face fills my mind as I wrap my hands around my mug, the warmth sinking into my skin. He had a sly smile, one that snuck up on me. His sense of humor was dry, and it took me some time to get used to it. Once I did, it became another piece of him I fell in love with.

It's not easy to remember him this way. A year of silence, of not moving, of *nothing*, slowly became all I could picture when I saw him. He's not dead, but he's not alive either. He's in a waiting place, and so are the rest of us who love him.

Until recently, anyhow.

I wasn't a quitter, no matter what Warren's family called me. And they had called me plenty of terrible names and accused me of horrible things. I let them throw their shade, because I was the only person available for them to take their grief out on. Did it make it okay? Hell no. But shooting back at them wasn't going to help the situation.

I blink, tears escaping my eyes. A year ago I was planning my wedding. I was in love. I was operating a bakery that bore my name on its sign. And now here I am. Hiding in the kitchen at Sweet Escape, teardrops falling into my coffee.

I'm a mess.

"Hey there." A deep voice comes from close behind me.

I jump, one hand flying to my eyes in an attempt to swipe away evidence of my upset. "Hey," I respond, trying hard to sound like I've just been standing here enjoying the view this whole time.

"You okay?" Brady leans on the counter beside me.

I feel his gaze burning into the side of my face.

I nod, looking at him. He's so handsome. How could that woman have chosen anyone over him?

"Just thinking," I say, biting the inside of my lower lip.

Brady leans back a little more, so that now his elbow rests on the counter behind him. It reminds me of last night at the beach, and how we had lain on the blanket until there were stars overhead.

"You going to tell me what you're thinking about? Or do I need to pry it out of you? I'm patient, remember? I can pry for hours."

His words make me smile. "I was just thinking about a year ago. How I was planning a wedding." I take a deep breath. "Our wedding would've been June twenty-ninth."

Brady makes a pained face. "That's only a couple weeks away."

"Yeah," I whisper, agony darting through my chest, cracking away at my battered heart.

"I'm sorry you're going through this, Addison. You don't deserve it."

"What if I do?"

Brady's eyebrows draw together. "Why would you think that?"

I shrug. "I don't know. Nothing truly bad had ever

happened to me, until that night. The universe was too good to me. It forgot to give me some awful hardship, so it made up for it." I glance at Brady. "I just hope it's finished with me for a while."

"I don't see the universe as vindictive like that."

I shake my head, searching for a better way to describe my feelings. "Not vindictive. More like checks and balances, I guess."

"Either way, I don't agree with you. I think good things happen to good people. And you" —he leans in closer, and my breath sticks in my throat— "you are a good person, Addison."

He doesn't pull back, and the air between us fills. What is that it's full of? Something sweet and gentle. And maybe... anticipation? Of what?

Brady reaches for me, his hand covering the palm I've laid on the counter. He doesn't speak, but his eyes say all that needs saying.

"Thank you, Brady," I whisper, and fight the urge to flip my palm over and slip my fingers through his.

"Hey, you two," my grandma says. I whip around, guilt blooming in my stomach. But what do I have to feel guilty about?

"You look like you're sharing secrets," she says, walking to the fridge and opening the door. Instead of looking at the contents, she keeps her steady gaze on us.

"We're just over here gossiping," I respond, trying to push away the guilt.

I turn back around and sip my coffee, making a face when it hits my lips. It's barely lukewarm.

"Let me," Brady says, taking the cup from my hands. He empties the remains of the coffee into the sink and walks to the coffeemaker, pouring me a fresh cup.

My grandma's eagle eyes have been trained on him the whole time, and she hands him the bottle of creamer just as he turns to her. He pours in a little and stops, looking up at me.

"Do you prefer a little cream with your coffee, or some coffee with your cream?" He smiles and winks.

"A dash of cream is good," I tell him. He hands me the new cup and I thank him, aware we're being watched. My eyes flash over to my grandma, and just like I thought, she's watching. She realizes I'm looking at her, so she sticks her nose in the fridge, finally turning her attention to whatever it was she came in here for.

Her attention might no longer be on us, but apparently that doesn't mean she's moved on, because from inside the fridge I hear her say, "The Andersons sure seemed to be enjoying their conversation with you, Brady. Mr. Anderson looked disappointed when you said goodbye and hustled into the kitchen."

I meet Brady's eyes and he shrugs, unembarrassed to be called out. His confidence is admirable.

"Anywho, I'd better get back out there." She pulls away from the fridge with the butter. "I'd say it has taken me far too long to grab the extra butter."

Grandma closes the fridge with her hip and rounds the island. A moment later I hear her call, "I'm coming with that butter, Mr. Cooper. Sorry for the delay."

"Do you want to grab a cup, Brady?" I hold up my coffee to show him what I mean. "I'm sure it's gorgeous outside, and I'd like some fresh air."

Brady pours a cup for himself, no cream, and we leave the kitchen. We have to walk through the living room and dining area to reach the back door, and I'm hoping nobody makes a thing about the two of us walking out together.

Thankfully nobody does, but I feel eyes on me. Certainly my grandma's, and probably other pairs also.

"Where do you want to go?" Brady asks, falling into step beside me.

"Just for a walk. The kitchen was feeling a little small."

"Was it—"

I shake my head, knowing what he's getting at before he even has a chance to say it.

"No. That was..." I trail off, thinking of the charged moments in the kitchen, filled with a crackling, confusing electricity. "That was nice." Such a lame word for how good that felt. "It's been a long time since I felt something that made me feel even a little bit good inside."

"That's sad."

"I know." I shrug. "But it's the truth."

"You shrugged your shoulders." Brady lifts his shoulders and drops them, the motion demonstrating the word. "People who really don't care usually accompany a shoulder shrug with a dismissive expression." He demonstrates this too, with one side of his mouth pulling back and the slightest shake of his head. "But most people who shrug actually care, and the shrug is a show, an attempt to hide what they're really feeling."

Suddenly I feel exposed. I reach for a sweater to pull tighter over my chest, but my fingers touch only bare skin. I don't have a sweater, only the desire to cover myself. Frowning, I say with more attitude than intended, "Since when are you an expert on reading people? I thought you were a lawyer."

"Good lawyers learn how to read facial expressions and mannerisms. People might withhold their thoughts, but their behavior often gives it away."

I come to a halt. Brady stops a second later, his eyes questioning my sudden stop.

Crossing my arms, I ask, "What am I thinking right now?" I'm straining to make my face unreadable, and I wonder if he's picking up on that, too.

He regards me with a cool expression. "You want me to stop being so invasive."

My pointer finger lifts into the air and makes little circles. "We have a winner."

Brady smiles a little and nods, his hands tucking into the pockets of his shorts. "Point taken."

I nod, happy he's understood. I feel too raw to be looked at so closely.

We start walking again.

"Can I ask you a question that skims the surface?" Brady asks.

The hope in his voice makes me say yes.

"Why did you hesitate when Charlie asked you about the baking competition?" he asks, wasting no time after I've given the go-ahead. "If you were a baker B.S.E., I mean."

I look at him, my eyebrows drawing together. "B.S.E?"

"Yeah. You know, Before Sweet Escape. B.S.E."

I smile at his acronym. I like it. "I'm not sure I'm up for running a bakery again. I didn't have the best experience the first time around." I don't elaborate, and he doesn't push.

We walk on, quietly, and before long I realize we're headed to the same spot beside the lake where we saw each other before. When we reach it, Brady takes a deep breath and gazes out at the sparkling water. I settle onto the ground and watch him take in his surroundings. It's nice to watch someone enjoy something I hold so dear.

"I think my soul needs water," he says, and his face looks peaceful. He picks up a rock and slings it. We watch it skip over the surface once, twice, three times before sinking below. He turns around, and when he sees me sitting he walks back and sits beside me.

Taking a deep breath, I say, "I waited for ten months after Warren slipped into the coma. I don't know what I was waiting for. We were told he probably wouldn't wake up. But how does a person move on from something like that? Things were bad for a little while. Constantly crying, and then that turned into darkness. This weird nothingness. I felt like a robot. I made the motions every day, but nothing went below my surface. Warren would've hated it. So, I started trying. There's nothing so brave as getting back up, Brady. Nothing."

Brady nods in encouragement, but he must sense I'm not finished, because he doesn't say anything.

"When Warren's family saw me getting better, they became angry. I think they knew what was coming, and they knew it meant one more part of Warren's life was going to slip away. But what was I supposed to do?" I shake my head, still unable to believe the way they treated me in the end. "Right after Warren and I were engaged, Warren's parents came to me with a business proposition. They offered to purchase an empty space and turn it into a bakery, if I would run it and pay them rent after it started turning a profit. It was my dream set-up. Very little risk for me, and it seemed as if there was only upside. It was going well for awhile, but after the accident, things went downhill. I told them I was going to spend some time in Oregon, visiting my grandma, and that the store manager would be perfectly capable of running things in my absence. They called me a coward and said I was a disgrace to their son's memory. They closed the store without telling me. The *For Lease* sign in the window and the padlocked front door did the talking for them."

A soft, incredulous sound slips from between Brady's lips.

Oddly, I feel defensive. Maybe it's really Warren I'm defensive of, because his family is an extension of him, a representation. "I know it sounds awful. It wasn't right for them to do what they did, but they were hurting too. I was an easy target for their anger and sorrow."

Brady's forearm brushes mine as he shifts and draws his knees into his chest. I like the feeling, like there's someone else beside me now. I was an only child and wished desperately for my parents to change that. That never happened, and eventually good friends stepped in and filled the void. Then I met Warren, and he occupied every space my friends couldn't fill. And in an instant, my Warren vanished.

"It's the little things," I say, lifting a handful of rocky sand. I flip my hand over and watch it fall back onto the ground.

"Like what?" Brady asks, not questioning what it is I'm referring to.

I take a deep breath, letting the memories wash over me. "He'd leave used paper towels all over the kitchen. Not really gross ones, but ones that were only a little used. He said they weren't ready to throw away just yet, but it drove me nuts." I used to glare when I'd see them, but now I'm smiling at the memory. "I like a clean kitchen, and those balled up paper towels looked like little snowballs."

Brady laughs. "I bet you never thought you'd find yourself missing that."

"Never," I agree, chuckling at the picture in my mind.

"How long were you together?"

"Two years, and then he proposed. And soon after..." My sentence trails off into nothing. I don't want to cry, but I can't help it. All the crying I did in the beginning was over Warren. And all the crying I'm doing now? That's for me.

I close my eyes and lift my face to the sky, letting the sunshine fall over me, inviting warmth into my sad, bleak heart.

Then I feel his arm, heavy and firm, across the top of my back. His hand slips over my shoulder, cupping it. His fingers squeeze gently, conveying his message.

He knows how it feels to be left behind.

11

BRADY

For a guy who likes taking action, sitting back and watching Addison cry is tough. I want to help her, but how? There is nothing I can do that will make this situation any better. The most I can do is be there for her, but that feels like so little.

On our walk back to the main house she said she's considering the idea of entering the contest. She seemed hesitant, but I encouraged her. What better way to get her mind off Warren?

Speaking of, I can't figure out what to call him.

Is he her ex-fiancé? Her current fiancé? How do you officially break up with someone in that state? If they were married, she'd have to legally divorce him. Relationships aren't binding, not legally anyway. They certainly are binding in many other ways.

Addison's life is in shambles, but I don't mind it. Maybe that's because my own chaos recognizes the chaos inside her. We are both so broken, so lost.

Today at the lake she'd raised her face to the sky, and the sun shone through her tears, lighting them up as they slid down her cheeks. Each drop turned translucent, and in them, I could see her grief.

I don't cry over Lennon the way Addison cries for Warren, but I won't deny that I've shed some tears. I'm lucky though. Lennon is still alive, still vital. She's down there in Arizona, helping Finn care for his uncle. She's smiling for Finn, and laughing at his jokes, teasing him when he broods the way he does. She's lying beneath him at night, *in their bed*, and the I love you's on her lips are meant for him.

I'm here in Oregon, running from a life I don't recognize, because it hasn't gone the way I expected it would. All I ever wanted was Lennon. I didn't get her. All I ever wanted was to be a lawyer. I got that, and it wasn't anything like I thought it would be. How can my expectations be so different from reality?

My phone rings and I look to where it sits on the porch railing of my little cabin. It's my mom. Sighing, I reach for it. I don't want to answer, but she called yesterday, and I let it go to voicemail. Honestly, I'm surprised she left me alone for this long. I haven't talked to her since the day before I left Chicago.

"Hi, Mom." I sit back in my chair and cross a knee over the opposite leg.

"Brady!" My mom's relieved voice comes through. "Oh, good. I'm glad you answered."

"Everything okay?"

"Yes, why?"

I'm thankful she can't see my eye roll. My mom has a tendency to make everything seem like a big deal. Apparently me not answering yesterday qualifies as such.

Instead of answering her question, I ask how my dad's doing. Since retiring from the bench, he spends his days golfing and napping.

"He's good. Finished with his morning round of golf and now he's sleeping on the couch. He was going to sleep by the pool, but it's too hot."

"It's June, Mom. Isn't it time for you to leave Agua Mesa? You've got to be the last snowbirds there by now." I grin, knowing how my mom gets irritated when she's called a snowbird. I don't know why it bothers her. My parents are the exact definition of a snowbird. They spend the winter in Agua Mesa and the summers in Chicago. It doesn't get any more snowbird than that.

"We're leaving for Europe at the end of this week, and then we'll go back to Chicago. I was calling to see if I could talk you into coming with us across the pond." She draws out the word *pond*, trying to make it sound enticing.

And it is. I consider it for all of three seconds before I shake my head. "No, thanks, Mom. I'm doing my thing here."

She snorts. It's not a sound she makes often. Too indelicate for her. "In Lonesome, Oregon? Brady, please."

Her *please* is not a request but an exasperation.

"I'm serious, Mom. I'm good here."

"You only have that place for a little while longer, Brady. What, less than two weeks?"

"I can extend if I want to. Besides, I'm not planning on going east from here. If I go anywhere, it will be on a plane flying north."

"Will you call me if you change your mind? You can join us wherever we are."

"Yes, of course."

My mom goes quiet, and I know why. At this point, I'm just waiting for her to ask. The seconds tick by in silence, then she says cautiously, "Have you heard from Lennon or Finn?"

Covering the phone with my hand, I turn my head to the side and sigh quietly. Into the phone, I say, "I've spoken with them both recently. They know where I am."

"I take it Lennon's firm in her choice?"

The tinge of hope in my mom's voice irritates me. If Lennon showed up here right now on the doorstep of cabin seven telling me she'd made a mistake, I'd... I'd... well, I don't know. I like to think I have my pride. And that her doing something like that would be not only the last nail in the coffin of our three-way friendship, but the first and all the others needed to slam it shut for good.

"Mom, you've seen them together. You know how right they are for each other. If I can admit that, maybe you can too."

"Hmph," she grunts petulantly. "I'll never understand how she chose Finn over you. Finn's great, don't get me wrong. He's your best friend for a reason. But you're... well, you."

I laugh. I can't help it. "You're biased, but that's okay. You're supposed to be."

"Such is the role of a mother. You'll understand one day when you're a parent. Speaking of dating..."

I lower the phone and give it a dirty look. That was the most obvious transition in the world. I put the phone on speaker and turn down the volume, then lay the phone on my lap and close my eyes. My mom's talking away and I'm *uh-hmm*'ing where it seems appropriate.

"Brady!" My eyes fly open at the loud call of my name. Addison's walking across my little yard, a smile on her face and the bottom of a sundress skimming the middle of her thighs. She looks gorgeous and completely recovered after this morning's walk to the lake.

I stand quickly, forgetting my phone. It falls to the floor of the wood front porch.

"Brady, who is that?" I hear my mother ask.

Addison must hear it too, because she makes a face and mouths, "Oops."

I wave a hand at her. "It's okay," I mouth back, bending to pick up the phone. I stand up in time to see Addison walking away.

"Addison, wait," I call out.

"Who's Addison?" my mother's voice floats into the Oregon air.

Addison creeps closer. She points at the phone and whispers, "Is that Lennon?"

I hit the speaker button to turn it off, and with my eyes trained on Addison, I lift the phone to my ear. "Mom, it's a friend I've made here."

Addison's chest expands with a big breath when she hears me say *mom*. Hmm. Interesting. Why is she relieved to know it's not Lennon?

"Brady, put me on speaker," my mom commands.

"You were on speaker," I protest. I don't like where this is going.

"Turn it back on." Her voice is no-nonsense.

I can either fake a sudden case of poor reception or listen to my mom.

Ever the parent pleaser, I lower the phone to the railing and hit the speaker button. Now I'm really wishing I'd let the call go to voicemail.

"Am I on speaker, Brady?" My mom's voice rings out into the open air.

Addison smiles, and I silence a groan.

"Yes, Mom."

My mother wastes no time. "Hello, Addison."

Addison's eyes are an unlikely combination of apprehension and amusement as she looks at the phone. "Hi, Mrs. Sterling."

Her gaze flies to me, and now she looks worried. "Is that her last name?" she mouths.

I nod. I'm less concerned with propriety and more worried about where my mother is going with this.

"Brady says you and he have become friends?"

"That's correct," Addison says, her shoulders relaxing. She stands on the other side of the porch and lifts her elbows onto the railing, resting her chin in an open palm.

"How old are you, Addison?"

I roll my eyes again, but Addison grins. "Twenty-seven."

"The same age as Brady." Her voice is smooth, approving. "And how did you two meet?"

"My grandmother owns the B&B where he's staying. I came from Chicago to help her."

"That's nice of you. It's always good to spend time with loved ones." This time my eye roll stays on the inside. Her comment is a compliment to Addison, but a complaint for me.

Addison thanks her, then my mom says, "Well, Brady, I guess I can see now why you refused my offer."

"Mom—" I start, but she cuts me off with a laugh.

"I wasn't born yesterday, Brady."

Addison laughs, and it joins up with the laughter coming from the phone.

"I'm glad everyone thinks I'm so funny." I give Addison a playful stink-eye.

Picking up the phone, I tell my mom I need to go.

And then, just when I'm kicking my own ass for answering her call at all, my mom says, "Brady, are you two"

—she pauses, and I picture her grasping for words— "what's it called? Benefits? Oh, that's it. Friends with—"

"Bye, Mom." I hit the end button before she can finish her sentence or say goodbye.

I slip the phone in my back pocket and let my gaze rest on the ground. I really don't want to look over at Addison, but I know I have to. Slowly I lift my gaze, and when I spot Addison, my eyes grow wide. Tears are falling from her eyes, but they're not sad.

She's laughing so hard it's soundless. Her shoulders quake and her hand covers her mouth.

I shake my head, my fear that my mother terrified Addison abating and the hilarity of the situation taking its place. I laugh alongside Addison.

"Your mom is really funny," she says, recovering her voice. She smiles up at me, her arms crossed and dangling lazily over the railing.

I lean down, resting my forearms on the railing beside hers. "She's not usually that funny. I think she's happy. What happened with Lennon worried her. And she thinks—" I stop suddenly, aware of what I was about to say.

Addison gently knocks her shoulder into mine. "She thinks you have yourself a friend with benefits to help you get over it?"

I'm not one for blushing, but right now I think I might be. "Yeah."

"There's no harm in letting her think that."

"I'll set her straight the next time I talk to her."

Addison lifts one shoulder, then drops it. A half-shrug. It makes me think of our talk earlier. "Doesn't matter to me one way or the other. If it eases her worry, you can let her think you're getting laid."

"How charitable of you."

"I've been known to be charitable from time to time."

I eye her. "You let the mothers of random men think you're sleeping with them?"

"Not random men. Only guys I've known for a week who sleep in cabin seven." She raises her gaze to the porch ceiling. "Duh."

"Hah," I bark a laugh at her joke. She grins at me, and the breeze shifts, lifting a section of hair from her shoulder. The smell of something sweet and floral overwhelms me. I stand upright quickly, needing to be out of that scent. It's not right for me to be enjoying that incredible, feminine smell coming off her. She belongs to someone else.

Right?

Or, no?

Shit.

Addison's eyebrows knit together. "You okay?"

I rub my eyes. "Yeah, yeah." I clear my throat. "Why did you come by? I don't think it was to hear my mom ask ridiculous questions."

Addison's hands join. Her forearms stiffen, and she bounces up on her toes, a nervous excitement making her blue eyes shine.

"I came to ask you if you wanted to hang out with me while I bake?"

"Does this mean you're going to enter the contest?"

She nods, a small, nervous grin on her lips.

"So you're staying here, then? In Lonesome?"

Addison's weight falls back on her heels. The excitement in her eyes decreases, but it's not completely gone. "I'm not sure where I'm going from here, but I don't want to eliminate a possibility simply by not trying."

I've only known Addison for a short amount of time, but I feel oddly proud of her.

"Let me grab my shoes." I turn around and walk inside, slipping my feet into a pair of sneakers, and grab my wallet and the key to the cabin.

"After you," I tell Addison, motioning with my arm once I've locked the front door.

Addison bounces along beside me, telling me about the treats she used to bake. It's the happiest I've seen her. I can't imagine how happy she was in Chicago, back when she was engaged and running a bakery.

In this moment, maybe she's a little taste of the person she was before everything was ripped from her.

12

ADDISON

I FEEL GOOD. I FEEL READY.

Maybe it's because I'm wearing my grandma's apron. The front reads, *Life is short, so lick the bowl.* Who wouldn't feel ready wearing something like that?

Or maybe it's the person sitting at the island.

Brady smiles reassuringly at me when I look at him. His long sleeve baby blue tee is pushed up, squeezing tightly around his muscular forearms. There's a soft dusting of hair just barely visible. I know it's soft because earlier this morning it brushed against me. And, despite the innocence of that swift contact, guilt rushed in.

How can I find Brady attractive? Worse, how can I be attracted to him? It's irrational. Insane, really.

Or maybe the insane part is entering this baking contest. Isn't that the very definition of insanity? Doing the same thing twice and expecting a different result the second time? My parents warned me about culinary arts school. They wanted me to get a 'real' degree first, then I could dabble if I wanted. They said a degree in culinary arts wouldn't pan out (pun unintended, I'm sure).

Well, they were right, but not for a reason they could've possibly foreseen.

And here I am, giving it a second go.

Yes, insanity. That's the best fit word.

"Do you listen to anything while you work?" Brady asks, fiddling with his phone.

"Podcasts, sometimes." I look over my ingredients with the intention of double-checking them, but then I catch sight of Brady out of the corner of my eye. He's dragging the pad of one thumb over his lower lip. A long-lost sensation starts up in my stomach, and my mouth feels oddly dry. My tongue turns a circle, attempting to moisten the inside of my mouth. "We can listen to whatever you want," I manage to say despite the desert my mouth has turned into.

This is what I don't understand. My heart was busted into what felt like a million pieces when I first left Chicago. For heaven's sake, I yelled at Brady in the airport bar. And then I come here and a week later I'm being enchanted by a rippling, muscled forearm, and an angular chin and a smile that belongs on Captain America.

What is my problem?

Baking. That's where my focus should lie. In a couple weeks Brady will be out of here and on to his next destination, wherever that may be.

And I'll go back to the most familiar place I know: heartache. It's a place I know well, and I've been in it so long it's oddly comforting. When I'm there, I know just what I'm getting.

Brady turns on music I don't recognize, but something tells me it's probably a song a majority of the world knows. It has the catchy beat and witty lyrics of something popular. If it's not, it should be.

"Do you mind if I read while you bake?" Brady asks. "I don't want to be a weirdo and stare at you."

For a second I freeze, remembering the ocean and walking in front of him in those tiny shorts. I wasn't lying when I said they were hold-overs from my high school days. And I knew he was staring at my ass. I could feel it in my bones. Or, ass, I guess.

"Sure, read." I smirk. "I don't want you staring at me either."

He looks up from his phone and gives me that smile, the superhero one. "What are you making?"

"Salted Butterscotch Blondies."

"Mmm." Brady's moan reverberates through my chest. "I get one as payment for keeping you company."

"If you do a good job, you get two."

I turn around and get to work, and Brady goes back to reading whatever it is he's reading on his phone. The song ends and a new one starts.

Browned butter is my secret weapon, so that's what I do first. It's what turns *Oh, that's yummy* to *Oh my god, I'll take a dozen*.

Once that's finished, I start my dry ingredients, peeking back at Brady as I stir. He looks up as if I've called his name, and winks.

I turn my attention back to my task, afraid his winking will make me spill my flour. Next up I add brown sugar to my brown butter and stir. Once it's combined, I add the remaining wet ingredients, then add that to the dry, and stir. Finally, it's time for the butterscotch morsels.

But they're not on the counter. After a quick look in the pantry, I don't see them in there either.

"What the hell?" I murmur, standing in the pantry doorway and looking out at the rest of the kitchen. Brady looks up, swivels his head to look for me, then finally locates me.

"How's it going over there?"

I shake my head slowly, still looking around. They were here before I went to get Brady from his cabin. I took them out of the pantry and set them on the counter myself. "It appears I'm missing an ingredient."

"Can you substitute something?"

"They won't be butterscotch without the butterscotch." My chest deflates a little. It would've been nice if these had gone off without a hitch.

Grandma walks into the kitchen, her little red toolbox in her hands. "Something sure smells good." She pats Brady on the back and walks over to the glass mixing bowl, peering down. With a devilish grin, she pulls a utensil from a drawer and spoons a bite of batter into her mouth. "Raw egg can't hurt me," she announces.

"Grandma, do you know what happened to the butterscotch morsels I had out on the counter?"

She wrinkles her nose. "Those things were so old, they may have been older than me. I threw them away."

I nod, disappointed, but also a tiny bit relieved to know I won't be making anybody sick with a badly outdated ingredient.

"I was surprised to come in here earlier and see all the baking stuff on the counter." Her spoon makes a loud, clanging sound as she tosses it in the sink.

"There's a thing for Lonesome Day. A baking competition that I'm entering. It's not a big deal—"

Grandma's eyes flash. "I know about that competition, and don't you dumb it down. It's a big deal. I'm proud of you."

I smile at her, but I feel bad. I came here to help with

Sweet Escape. If I win the competition, I'd be leaving her in a lurch.

"Thanks, Grandma, but I don't have to enter. I haven't officially put my name in the hat yet. I know I said I'd help you here and that will be my priority."

Grandma waves her hand around as if shooing away my words. "Don't be ridiculous. What do you think I do the rest of the year when you're not here?"

"Hire a part-time college kid?"

"Exactly. And I can do that again."

I look to Brady and he shrugs and lifts his hands, telling me he's staying out of this one.

"Smart guy," Grandma says to him. "Are you Addison's baking assistant? What's that called? A sous chef?"

"Something like that," I say, and at the same time, Brady shakes his head.

"I don't go near baking or cooking. Addison asked me to keep her company while she worked."

Grandma looks from me to Brady, and it's not hard to guess what she's thinking. She can be so transparent when she wants to be. I know she wants me to move on. I just don't know how to take that first step.

"Can I have your Jeep keys, Grandma? I need to run to the store."

Brady pushes back his chair and stands. "I'll drive, if you don't mind? I might forget how to if I don't practice every once in a while."

I smile at his joke and Grandma pulls her keys off the hook she keeps inside a cabinet. She tosses them to Brady.

"I'll back it out and meet you out front," he says to me.

I'm untying my apron when Grandma speaks. "I say you should go for it."

"Thanks, Grandma," I say, relieved even though I was

certain she would support me. "I just want to bake again, I don't necessarily need to win."

Grandma shakes her head quickly from side to side. "I wasn't talking about baking, Addison."

I hand her my apron and plant a quick kiss on her cheek as I pass her. "I was."

Grabbing my purse from the table, I hurry out the front door and to Brady, waiting in the idling Jeep.

BRADY AND I SPLIT UP WHEN WE GOT TO THE GROCERY STORE. I went to the baking aisle and Brady to the other end of the store for shaving cream. I'd noticed his five o'clock shadow had grown to be more of a ten o'clock, but I kind of liked it that way. The look suited him more out here in the forest than the clean shave he'd sported the day he arrived.

I spot the butterscotch morsels and grab them, heading to the end of the aisle. When I don't immediately see Brady, I start for the personal hygiene section. As I get closer, I see Brady talking with someone, his head bent to hear what the other person is saying.

I round the corner and find him talking to an elderly man. The man is wearing a pageboy news cap and a wrinkled, khaki-colored linen suit. In June? He must be sweating a ridiculous amount. I come closer and see a sheen of sweat on his forehead. Is it even good for someone so old to become overheated? I come to a stop beside Brady. He looks at me, his eyebrows pulled together in confusion, then back to the old man.

"...I'm not sure exactly the name of the product, but I'm really sick of looking for it. Been using it for a long time, ya know? Why would they discontinue it?" He removes his cap and wipes his forearm across his forehead, presumably to mop the sweat gathering there.

Brady nods slowly, showing no signs of irritation or impatience. "Yes, sir. That's aggravating. Maybe we can ask an employee for help."

The man waves his hand flippantly. "Bah! They're no help. I've already asked them and they're useless." He starts to shuffle to the side, but his balance isn't good and he stumbles. Brady and I reach for him, but thankfully he's already steadied himself on the closest shelf. A few bottles fall over and hit the ground, rolling away from him.

"I'm going to walk you to your car." Brady falls into step beside him.

The man scowls at Brady. "That won't be necessary."

Brady stops and takes a step back. I'm surprised he has given up so easily.

"You have a good day, sir," Brady says to the man, his voice respectful and kind.

The man keeps going, his shuffle step taking him at a very slow but steady pace.

"You're letting him go?" My voice is a whisper-hiss.

Brady scrunches his face and shakes his head. "Hell no. I'm letting him think he's on his own." His eyes keep track of him, and he says, "When he first walked up to me, he asked me if I could point him in the direction of the automotive department."

My eyes grow wide. "What did you tell him?"

"That I didn't think this grocery store had that department. He looked around and clued in a little, then he began raving about soap they no longer carry. That's when you walked up."

My lips twist. "That's so sad."

"Yeah," Brady agrees, the word trailing behind him as he

walks forward. I slip along behind him, and slowly we trail the man through the store and out the automatic doors. He never stops, never looks around. His gaze remains forward as if he's in a lane he cannot deviate from.

He stops outside the doors, and we come to a halt just a few feet away. He makes a displeased face as he scans the parking lot.

"Dammit." His frail-looking fist swipes at the air. "Car got stolen again. What do I have that those thieves want so badly?"

Suddenly he looks at us, and I feel Brady stiffen beside me.

"You," he says, pointing at Brady and shuffle-stepping over to us. "Do you have a phone I can borrow? I need to call my son and tell him my car was stolen."

"Sure thing." Brady pulls his phone from his pocket and unlocks it. With his finger poised over the screen, he looks up and asks, "What's your son's number?"

The man frowns. "It's... uh... well, I don't recall at the moment."

"No worries," Brady says confidently. I hope the old man feels reassured by his strong voice. "What's your son's name?"

"Paul Bendrop." The name is quick to roll off his tongue, and the crinkling beside his eyes conveys the pleasure he takes in that.

I smile politely at the old man and look over at Brady's phone, quickly scanning the results from the internet search he conducted in the last few seconds.

Brady looks up at the man, his finger poised over the screen. "Is your son a lawyer?"

"Damn straight," he growls, pride in his voice.

Brady grins. "Can I call you Mr. Bendrop?"

"You can call me anything, just don't call me late for dinner!" Mr. Bendrop cackles at his joke. I think he's happy now that he thinks we're going to help him. Or maybe he's already forgotten about his car.

Brady brings the phone to his ear and waits. Thankfully, there's a quick answer on the other end.

"Yes, hi," Brady says after listening to the short welcome from whoever answered the phone. "I'm looking for Paul Bendrop."

He's quiet, and he absentmindedly runs his thumb over his lower lip.

I can never, ever tell him how sexy that is. Besides, I'm sure someday in the not-too-distant future, someone will. Someone who isn't broken like me, and someone who's totally available. Both are qualifications I do not currently fulfill.

"Paul, hi. Brady Sterling here. Listen, I'm in front of" — Brady squints up at the sign— "the Shop n' Save with your dad, and he believes his car has been stolen."

There's a muffled response and Brady says, "Uh huh" over and over. Then he hangs up and tells Mr. Bendrop that his son will be here shortly.

"Lucky thing his office is only a couple blocks over." Brady grins at Mr. Bendrop and gives him the gentlest squeeze around the shoulders. Brady spends the time waiting on the son to show up asking Mr. Bendrop random questions.

"Where were you in 1980?" he asks.

"Probably at one of my sons' baseball games. They all three played."

"I played too, in high school." Brady goes on to make small talk until a sleek silver sedan pulls up alongside us.

A man somewhere in his mid-thirties with a slight

paunch hurries from the car. "Dad," he says, relief coloring his voice. He walks to Mr. Bendrop with his arms outstretched.

Mr. Bendrop waves him away. "I'm fine. It's my car we should worry about. Call the police."

"Let's get you home and let me deal with the police."

Mr. Bendrop doesn't put up a fight about it. He allows Paul to help him into the front seat of the low-slung car. When he's situated, Paul closes the door and comes to us, extending a hand to each of us in turn.

We shake and make quick introductions. Brady gives Paul a quick re-cap of events.

"Thank you for helping him out. I mean it. When I think about what could've happened to him..." He trails off, shaking his head. "I'll tell the nurse to keep a better eye on him." There's a trace of barely contained anger and annoyance when he says this. I don't blame him. I would feel that way too.

"Do you need us to stick around while you call the police?" I ask Paul. "We didn't see anything, but if we can help we certainly will."

Brady grabs my hand, winding his fingers through mine. The touch is so sudden and unexpected that it causes my heart to beat faster. Brady leans down slightly, so his mouth is close to my ear, and murmurs, "On the phone Paul told me Mr. Bendrop doesn't have a car. He had his license revoked years ago."

"Oh," is the only response I can manage. My gaze flies to Paul.

He tucks his hands in his pockets and rocks back onto the heels of his black dress shoes. "He's not well, obviously. But who is at that age?" For a quick second, I see the weight he carries around on his shoulders. The next second it's gone, covered up and tucked away. The way we all do.

Paul thanks us again and leaves. Mr. Bendrop doesn't look our way as they drive off. I wonder if he's already forgotten us?

"Come on," Brady says, tugging on my hand. Which makes me realize he's still holding it. He leads me back through the store and doesn't drop my hand until we reach the aisle where the old man first approached him. He gathers the items we dropped there in exchange for our secret mission and walks to the register to pay.

He drives us back to Sweet Escape. At long last, I add the butterscotch to the blondie batter and put it in the oven. While it bakes, I get out a deck of playing cards and Brady and I play War until the oven timer beeps.

When Brady sinks his teeth into the blondie, he doesn't say a word. He closes his eyes and lets out a long, slow, pleased sigh. Then he finishes it and immediately eats a second.

"That," he says, holding up his hand for a high-five, "was the best thing I've ever eaten. If you don't win the baking competition, I'm pressing charges against all the judges."

I laugh and smack my hand against his. When I go to pull my hand away, I find that I can't. Brady's fingers have slipped through mine and captured my hand. He flips it over, and for a moment I think maybe he's going to kiss it.

But he doesn't. He stares at it, then reluctantly lets me go. He meets my eyes, picks up a third brownie, and tells me he'll see me in the morning.

13

BRADY

I DIDN'T BRUSH MY TEETH LAST NIGHT. GROSS, I KNOW, BUT I wanted to keep tasting those incredible brownies. Addison's brownies.

Who knew the crazy woman who yelled at me in the airport is actually a sweet as hell, little bit sassy baker?

It's morning now, and the delicious taste in my mouth from last night has turned into more of an unpleasant, cottony aftertaste. I'd love to lie in bed and think about Addison and how cute she looked in that apron, but the situation in my mouth has me hauling my ass from bed and into the bathroom for a thorough cleaning.

I'm wide awake now, and my mouth is bursting with invigorating peppermint. A run sounds like a good idea, and then I can go through my workout.

In Chicago, I made good use of the gym on the first floor of my building. Here, I have to get creative.

I change into running clothes and shoes, and tuck my phone and cabin key into my pocket.

The early morning air is cool and crisp. Trails zig-zag around the property, and I really don't know where I'm going. The map Louisa gave me on my first day here sits on the dresser in my cabin, unused after that day I followed it to the lake.

It only takes a minute before I decide how much I prefer running here in Oregon to running on a treadmill in a stinky, four-walled room in Chicago. Gulping in the fresh scent of the fir trees, I run on, alternating my speed between sprinting and jogging.

The sun is higher now, sending its rays through the trees, the shadows from the tree branches creating odd shapes.

In the near distance, I see a clearing in the trees. I slow as I get closer, until I come to a full stop at the top of what looks to be some kind of stage, and rows of seats, like bleachers, but made of concrete. An amphitheater? I step down the concrete stairs and run my hand over a row, brushing aside the blanket of fir needles.

When I was a kid, I went to a summer camp in Northern California that had a space just like this. We'd write and perform skits and plays, and on the final night, we played Charades. For six years I looked forward to the week I knew I'd spend there, but it was always hard to leave Lennon and Finn. Lennon wasn't allowed to go to any camp that wasn't the Bible camp her stepdad's church put on, and Finn didn't have the money to go to any camp, especially not one that required airfare.

I sit in one of the spots I've cleared of needles, and look down at the stage. For one week out of the whole summer, I lived with a bunch of other boys my age, and we became brothers for the week. Maybe it was proximity that initiated the immediate closeness, or maybe it was sharing a bathroom and cafeteria. Whatever it was, we attached ourselves to one another in a life that didn't include school or organized sports. It was a life separate from the real one we lived the other fifty-one weeks of the year, and that detachment made it easy to share secrets without consequence. My bunkmates knew all about Lennon and Finn, my desire to protect and care for them, and the weight of responsibility I felt to be the good kid for my parents.

I haven't thought of camp, or the boys I shared those weeks with, in years, but this amphitheater brings it all back. Maybe on some level that's why I chose Lonesome. My subconscious knew it resembled the place I spent idyllic weeks of my life, and it was searching for that time, yearning for the moments when I wasn't Brady the star baseball player, Brady the perfect son, or Brady the caretaker.

With a last look at the stage, I stand and take the stairs two at a time, then jog at a steady pace back the way I came.

Except I'm pretty sure I don't know where I'm going. When I get to the point where the trails intersect, I pause and pull out my phone.

Oh, wait. I'm in the woods. The internet won't load, the little bar across the top stopping about one-third of the way across the page.

I let out a growl of frustration, then a laugh trickles into the air around me.

I know that laugh.

My head snaps up and swivels around. About ten yards away Addison bounces from foot to foot in running shoes, her blonde hair swinging in a ponytail. She wears soft-looking black shorts and a matching sports bra. A long sleeve shirt is tied around her waist, and she's smirking at me.

"Don't look so pleased," I tell her, embarrassed at my lack of an innate sense of direction.

She laughs and walks closer. Her chest heaves with her

previous exertion, a lifting and falling that makes it hard to look away. Using all the strength I can muster, I rip my gaze from her chest and back up to her eyes.

The smirk is still on her face, but her eyes narrow. I've totally been caught.

"Fine, I'm lost. I admit it." I'm hoping the admittance will distract her from my obvious ogling.

Addison steps lightly onto one foot and pivots. She turns back to look at me, motioning with her hand. "From now on I'll be known as Sweet Escape Search and Rescue. Follow me." She bounds away before I can come up with a response that will reinstate my man card.

There are a lot worse things I could be doing than following a bouncing Addison through the trees. The path is wide enough for both of us, so I lengthen my strides and soon I'm beside her. She grins and says a breathy, "Hey you."

I tip my chin in acknowledgment and smile back. Addison is still the leader of this run, so when we come to other places where the paths intersect, I fall back slightly and let her lead.

By the time we reach the central path, we're both panting hard. We slow our pace and then stop completely when we reach the lawn in front of the main house. Both of us bend over, our hands on our knees as we slow down our breathing.

"You don't take many breaks when you run, do you?" I ask her when I can breathe long enough to string together words.

Addison lifts her arms above her, then bends to one side to stretch her side-body. "Usually I do. But you didn't seem like you wanted to stop, so I didn't."

I hang at my waist, stretching the back of my legs, and look up at her. "Next time, let's take breaks."

Addison pretends to salute me. She's red-faced and out of this world gorgeous. She looks relaxed. Maybe it's the endorphins. Whatever it is, it's great to see her this way.

"Have you had breakfast yet?" she asks, a flattened palm shading her eyes from the sun.

I shake my head. "I woke up early and went out." My stomach growls at the idea of food. "I'm starving now though."

Addison makes a mock scared face. "Are you going to eat enough for two grown men again?"

I bark a laugh. This woman is funny. "Maybe I will," I tell her, reaching out and poking her in the side. It's only a fingertip to bare skin, but *damn* it does things to that place in my stomach where desire sleeps coiled like a snake.

She squeals and hops away, then whirls around and points a finger at me. "Watch it, mister. I'm embarrassingly ticklish."

I return her salute. "I'll be very careful from now on."

She grins and turns, starting for the main house. "Let's eat."

I fall into step beside her and nudge her arm with my elbow. She nudges me back.

I'm well aware we've stepped into flirting territory now.

"Here you go," Addison chirps, placing a plate on the table in front of me. I look up to tell her thank you, but the mischievous gleam in her eyes makes my eyebrows pinch with suspicion.

Looking back down at my plate, I see the reason for her impish expression.

"A carrot muffin," I say slowly, swallowing my immediate

revulsion. I don't want to offend anybody whose palate might be very confused and actually likes vegetables in a muffin.

Addison claps her hands together and beams. She's enjoying this too much.

"I made them this morning. Eat up."

To make matters worse, she stays rooted in place across from me, standing beside Mr. Anderson. She has pulled on the long sleeve shirt that was tied around her waist, but she's still in her running clothes. Her eyes stay glued to me, waiting for me to behave and eat the damn muffin no matter how much I hate it.

With a fake smile plastered on my face, I peel off the paper wrapper and lift it to my lips. The first thing I notice is the scent. It doesn't smell like the carrot muffin from the other day. Warm, spicy cinnamon automatically kicks my salivary glands into working order.

I'm not so scared to take a bite now. And when I do, it's so good I hurry up and take another one. And then a third, and just like that the muffin has disappeared.

"Addison." I look at her with reverence and clutch my chest. "Will you marry me?"

Addison rolls her eyes, but the corners of her lips turn up into a pleased smile. Mr. Anderson cackles an old man laugh and Mrs. Anderson's eyes widen.

"Don't you go making any lasting decisions, Brady. I've got a granddaughter I want to introduce you to."

"Yes, ma'am." I nod at her. I'm not interested in meeting their granddaughter, and I'm not too worried about ever having to say that directly. The Anderson's will only be at Sweet Escape for two more days.

Now that Addison has completed her mission of watching me eat the muffin, she leaves me with a wink and goes back to the kitchen. Louisa comes out a moment later to refill the mini-jams she keeps in a basket.

I watch her smile and laugh with the guests, chatting about their plans for the day and suggesting hikes or activities. She seems to be genuinely happy during breakfast when her home is open to all the guests. I wonder how she feels the rest of the day when the place is mostly quiet and the guests are all out enjoying their vacation?

Louisa pats another guest on the shoulder, and then the door opens and the family with the teenage boys comes in. She glances at the spread on the buffet table against the wall, then greets the newcomers and hustles toward the kitchen.

Pushing back from the table, I pick up my plate and cast a glance at the Anderson's across from me. "I'm going to see if I can help the ladies in the kitchen. Enjoy your day, Mr. and Mrs. Anderson."

As I'm walking away, I hear Mrs. Anderson say, "Don't tell me to stop meddling. He'd be perfect for Britt."

Laughing softly to myself, I round the corner and come into the kitchen. Louisa's holding a large bowl and Addison is spooning scrambled eggs into it. "Those boys eat like, well, just what they are. Teenage boys." Louisa passes me, the steam from the hot eggs wafting around her, and says, "If only rice were a breakfast food."

She keeps going and disappears around the corner.

"Need any help in here?" I ask Addison. She's standing at a long griddle set up on the counter, flipping bacon.

"Please," she says, nodding gratefully. "Watch this bacon and make sure it doesn't burn." She hands me a pair of tongs. "I need to get the muffins out of the oven."

"Nice move with those muffins, by the way." I push a slice of bacon with the edge of the tongs. I'm not really sure what I'm supposed to be doing here. When I offered to help, I'd hoped I'd be given the job of cleaning or carrying something.

Addison grins proudly while she slips her hands into big, black oven mitts and opens the oven. She pulls out two pans with fresh carrot muffins and slides them onto the cooktop.

The scent is phenomenal and overpowers the smell the scrambled eggs left behind. I turn my attention back to my task.

"How exactly do I avoid burning bacon?"

Addison gives me an exasperated look. "Brady, have you seriously never cooked bacon?"

I shake my head. "I've hardly cooked at all."

She sets one hand, still encased in an oven mitt, on her hip. "Who did the cooking at your house?"

"My mom and dad both cook now, but when I was a kid, we had someone come in and prepare meals."

Addison gapes. I don't blame her. I know how posh it sounds. "My dad worked all the time, and my mom was constantly busy doing charity work and whatever else it was she did." Come to think of it, I didn't pay much attention to what she spent her time on. I was too busy getting good grades and staying out of any and all trouble.

"What did your dad do for work?" Addison asks as she uses a fork to gingerly lift each muffin from the tin and place it on the tray.

"He was a federal judge until recently. He's retired now."

Addison pauses to glance at me, her eyes wide. "Your dad was a federal judge? That's a really big job."

I nod. "Yep."

Addison's mischievous smirk is back. "Did he ever use his pull to get you out of trouble?"

I press my lips together, thinking about a situation with Lennon's stepdad.

"Once, yeah."

Addison's face lights up. She sets the last of the fresh muffins on the tray and lifts it.

"Hold that thought. I want to hear all about it." She hustles out and I look back down, remembering I had a job to do.

Oh shit. I think the bacon might be burned. The sides are tinged a darker brown than they should be, and the smell is more bitter than mouth-watering.

I use the tongs to gather all the strips at once and drop the bacon onto a plate. Pushing aside the pieces, I inspect them. They might be salvageable. I was a teenage boy once, I don't think I would've been deterred by too-crispy bacon.

Addison comes back in, scoops up the plate with the bacon, gives me a 'one-minute' sign with a single finger, then leaves again. She's back quickly, throwing herself into a chair at the island and setting two carrot muffins onto the counter.

"They won't miss two," she tells me, pushing one over into the counter space in front of the open seat beside her. "And they aren't carrot muffins." She peels off the wrapper and takes a bite. "Not really, anyway. They're carrot *cake* muffins. More cake-y than muffin-y." She bobs her head from side to side as she says it.

She's so damn cute.

"So," she says, swallowing her bite. "Come eat a muffin and tell me your story."

Pulling out the seat beside her, I sink down into it and inhale the muffin.

"You're going to make me gain weight," I tell her, wiping my hands on a napkin.

"I hear getting lost on long runs is an excellent antidote to calories consumed." Addison smiles and drinks from a glass of water that was on the counter.

"That was my water," I tell her, even though it wasn't.

"I don't care about your germs." She takes another sip just to make her point. "And it was mine. Quit stalling and tell me how your dad bailed you out of jail."

Alarm widens my eyes. "How did you know—"

Addison's mouth drops open in astonishment. "I was right?"

I shake my head. "Not totally. I was questioned at a police station when I was eighteen. So were Lennon and Finn, but none of us were booked. Technically, it was my dad's reputation that kept us out of jail. That and a lack of evidence." I think back to that night. "And our family lawyer."

"What?" Addison's voice is an assertive whisper. "Why were you questioned?"

"Lennon's stepdad died and they thought something about it was odd. Her mom overheard us talking and reported it to the police."

"Her mother?" Addison hisses, eyes even wider now.

"I know." I nod in agreement. "But she's dead now too."

"Oh." Addison's face falls. "That's sad that Lennon lost both her parents."

My head shakes, thinking of Lennon's childhood. "You wouldn't think that way if you knew them. They weren't good people."

Addison shifts in her seat so she's facing me. "Suddenly I'm really feeling that sheltered life I told you about." Her face darkens. "Other than, well, you know."

Without thinking, I reach for her hand and give it a light squeeze. "We all have our own troubles, Addison."

She seems to recover, because the light comes back into her eyes. "I seriously cannot believe you've been questioned at a police station. And for a suspicious death, too." Her eyes narrow as her words hit home. "You're not a murderer, are you?"

I laugh. "We were let go for a reason. We were innocent. Even my dad can't make something like murder go away. Nor would he, I don't think." Even as I say the words, I'm not sure of their truth. My dad made a lot of my sister's shenanigans disappear, but that was petty stuff. Nothing like taking a life.

"I believe you," she says, then yawns. "Sorry, I was up early making the batter for the muffins. My grandma cooked the first batch so I could get in my run."

"No worries," I assure her. "I'm tired, too. Maybe we should take a nap and then later would you want to—"

A loud ring fills the air.

"Oops, sorry." Addison takes her hand from mine and digs into her pocket. "I was listening to music before I ran into you earlier and I must've turned up the ringer along with the volume."

She frowns at the phone, and I can see it's a number she doesn't have stored, but it's an area code we both know.

Chicago.

Why does the sight of it shoot nerves straight into my chest? I know the answer to that, and it's incredibly selfish.

It can't be what I'm thinking anyhow, because surely she'd have Warren's family's number stored in her phone?

My thunderous thoughts have caused me to miss the first few sentences of her conversation, but now I'm tuned in.

Addison's expression, which was so happy and carefree before the call, is not only sad, it's anguished.

"I don't need the venue anymore. I—"

She pauses, and the person on the other end speaks.

"No, it's not that it didn't work out. It's... it's..." Her eyes blur as she struggles with her words. "It's just not needed anymore. Thank you for checking in."

She hangs up, setting down the phone and slowly sliding it away from her, as if creating distance can decrease the pain stirred up by the call.

"Addison?" I say her name softly.

She turns to look at me, her blue eyes bright and a tear stuck in her lower lashes. "That was a wedding venue I filled out an interest form for last year. They wanted to let me know they'd had a last-minute cancellation if I was still interested in having my wedding there." Her voice is raspy, and so, so sad.

"I'm sorry," I whisper. My hand rubs slow circles on her back.

"I don't know what to do." She closes her eyes. "Everything is confusing. I have so many thoughts and emotions, and they all feel so wrong." Her eyes open and she looks at me.

I wish I could take it all away. All the pain and sorrow. I want to take it all away and replace it with something good.

"Addison?"

She finishes wiping a napkin across her eyes and looks at me.

"I have an idea. Are you in?"

She eyes me for a moment, then nods.

"Let's take showers, then meet me at my cabin when you're done. Dress like we're going on a walk." I stand up.

"Thanks, Brady."

"I haven't done anything yet."

She catches my hand. "Yes, you have."

Without thinking, I lower my lips to her temple and quickly kiss her. It's not a big deal. It's an act of kindness, a human touch offered to another person in need.

Except it's not.

And I think we both know it.

14

ADDISON

My hand is raised, poised to knock, but it remains suspended in the air. I don't know what Brady has planned, and I'm nervous.

The call from the wedding venue earlier really threw me.

Is any of this a good idea? Should I be spending time with Brady?

Am I even single? I mean, yes, I am single. For all intents and purposes, I'm single. Warren's family made certain I knew that if I was leaving their son behind in Chicago, then I was closing the door on ever being a member of their family or marrying their son at all.

As if there's any chance their son will wake up. I researched, I read, until my eyes were bleary. Here's what I learned: Warren has a snowball's chance in hell of waking up.

Still, everything feels unfinished.

Warren's family thinks they've cut the cord for him, but only Warren and I can do that. And at this point, only *I'm* capable of doing that.

And I have. Sort of. At least, I thought I had. I came to Lonesome under the impression that I was closing that chapter in my life. But then I met Brady, and the attraction I know we both feel confuses the hell out of me. Because alongside the attraction is guilt, and it sits heavy on my chest like an anvil.

The door to cabin seven swings open, even though I didn't knock. Brady smiles, but it's not a warm, welcoming grin. Restraint keeps his lips from really curling upward, and his eyes are wary.

"You okay?" he asks tentatively.

I nod. Truthfully, I'm not okay, but I need to be. And I will be. Eventually.

Brady surveys me for a moment, probably determining the level of truth in my answer. He must decide it's enough, because he steps out of the cabin and turns back around to lock the door.

Brady glances down at my feet. Is he checking my footwear?

"We're going on a walk, back to where we ran into each other this morning, and then further back from there." Brady pulls out his phone and studies something on it.

"Do you know where you're going?" I know I teased him earlier about getting lost, but I'm asking right now out of genuine curiosity.

Brady's gaze shifts to me as I walk beside him down the steps and out to the trail. "I know where we're going."

"And we need a backpack for it?" I raise my eyebrows at the small black pack he's toting.

"Water, snacks. Bear spray."

"Ah." I nod. "All good things."

Brady leads the way this time. He must've really studied a map or something, because he makes turns without hesitation. Maybe he's doing some weird guy thing where he redeems himself for getting lost before.

We're quiet the entire walk, and I'm good with that. There aren't many people a person can be with in a comfortable silence, and probably far fewer who can be that way after knowing each other a short time. Apparently Brady and I fall into that category.

We come to the spot where I saw him huffing and growling this morning when he realized he didn't know which way to go. Brady turns left, and I catch on to where he's taking me.

Soon we reach the amphitheater, just like I thought. It's an old place, an artifact from a youth summer camp adjacent to Sweet Escape's property. It closed down some time ago when the owners grew too old to run it.

Brady looks so excited I don't have the heart to tell him I already know about this place.

"Wow!" I look around, doing my best to feign excitement.

Brady frowns. I must be really awful at faking it.

"You know about this place?"

His disappointed face is probably the cutest thing ever.

I scrunch my nose and nod. "I can still pretend it's a surprise."

Brady grunts his answer. His eyes search the area, and I'm about to ask what he's looking for when he finds the object still unknown to me. Leaving me on the top step, he walks down and to the center of a row, reaching down and lifting a smallish branch.

"This," he says, his tone suddenly serious. "Is the branch of truth. Whoever stands on the stage and holds this branch is free to say what they think without persecution or judgment."

I can't help it. I laugh. Brady's serious face and tone are too much for me.

Brady breaks from his role and smiles. He comes back down the row, and I walk forward to meet him.

"I went to a summer camp when I was a kid, and we used a branch of truth as an exercise. It was actually pretty cool. Liberating."

Hmm. It sounds interesting. There are plenty of thoughts I'd like to release from my mind, if only to lessen the hold they have on me.

"You go first," I say, nodding my head at Brady. I'm feeling a little shy at the notion of baring my soul, even though I'm sure it will feel good.

Brady walks down the steps and I follow, breaking off to sit front and center in the second row while he goes on to the stage. It's only a foot or so off the ground, so we're on nearly the same level.

Brady steadies his gaze on me, and I don't see playfulness in his eyes anymore. As I watch, his chest expands with the deep breath he takes, and slowly contracts as he releases it. Holding the stick in his fist, he begins speaking his truth.

"I'm still angry with Lennon for not choosing me, even though I think she made the right choice. I'm mad at Finn for not backing away all those years ago when he realized I liked her too. Sometimes I think if he were a real friend, he'd have given up his dream for mine. It's the epitome of selfish, but it's true. In that same thought, I suppose I could've given up my dream for his." He looks down, shaking the stick in his hand, and glances back up to me. "Truth stick, right?" His raised eyebrows lower and he keeps going. "I think maybe it's a good thing Lennon didn't choose me, because if she'd picked me she might've chosen incorrectly, and what if she'd realized her mistake somewhere down the line, and it ruined our friendship?" Brady pauses, his free hand coming up to pinch the space between his eyes. "I can't believe I'm at a point in life where I'm looking for myself, when I've spent my whole life certain I knew exactly what I wanted. Who is this person who quit the job he couldn't wait to have, just to embark on some journey without an end, or a specific destination? I'm afraid I don't know myself like I thought I did." He looks deep into my eyes, and in his gaze I see his yearning, his belief in what he's about to say. "More than anything, I'm afraid I'll never get what Lennon and Finn have. All I've ever wanted is to love deeply and profoundly, to share a life with someone whose soul matches mine. And after what happened with Lennon, after it turns out my whole life was a mismatch, I'm afraid I never will."

My fingertips graze my lips as I absorb Brady's truth. I long to pull him into my arms, to tell him one day it will all work out, even though I don't know that to be true. It just seems as though, for someone like Brady, it has to be.

He steps off the stage and walks to me, truth stick extended.

I reach for it cautiously. Baring your truth is terrifying.

"I'll give it a shot," I say, faking bravery. I reach for the branch, my fingertips brushing against his. For the shortest second I leave them there, and when I feel the weight of the stick in my palm, I turn away toward the stage.

Brady takes my place in the second row. He props his feet on the row in front of him, grasping his hands and placing them on his bent knees.

"I'm not sure how to begin," I tell him, shrugging, then remember what he said about shrugging. He's totally right.

"Start small," he suggests. "A food you hate, a smell you dislike. Something you love most about your grandma. Once you start, sometimes it's hard to stop. You'll see."

I take a deep breath. "I hate tomatoes. I like tomato sauce though, and salsa. I can't stand putting gas in a car because the smell of gasoline disgusts me. And people who like the smell of gasoline scare me."

Brady's shoulders move with suppressed mirth. I wasn't trying to make him laugh.

"I'm just being honest," I tell him.

He nods and gets control of his quaking shoulders, making a motion for me to continue.

"I don't like how Warren's parents or his sister treated me, even if I do understand it. And I'm mad at his sister, because before the accident happened she was my friend." A small piece of the anvil on my chest breaks off and floats away. "I don't know how I'm supposed to move on from here. I'm single, but I'm not. I'm followed by his ghost, except I'm not, because he's not dead. I have this guilt inside me for being alive when his life is given to him by machines. And I'm mad at him for being human and getting hurt. And I'm mad at myself for not being the kind of person who never leaves his side. It sounds selfless, like something from a storybook. Does it make me selfish that I wanted to go to Oregon, that I needed a break from all the hurting? I stayed in our apartment and I was surrounded by his things. And it was all so painful." It's coming off my chest, piece by piece, but there's a chunk still there, the worst truth of all. Before I can shove it down, this dark and shameful thought, I let it free.

"There's a part of me that's relieved I'm not marrying him." As I say it, I can't believe it's me talking. This truth is one I've pushed away, hidden deep down under the grief and sadness.

"There were things about him I wasn't sure I could live with forever, and that terrified me, because I loved him. How can you love someone and also be unsure about them at the same time?" My whole body feels like it's going to give out, even with the weight off my chest now. I sink down slowly onto the dirty concrete, the truth stick falling from my grasp. "I'm a horrible person."

Brady's there in an instant, gathering me into his arms. He pulls me to his chest and holds me. I cry until the tears run out, until there is nothing left inside me. His fingers caress the length of my arm.

"You're brave, Addison."

There's one last piece of anvil on my chest, one last morsel of truth, and I'm either brave enough or crazy enough to release it.

"Brady?"

His chin dips and he looks down at me, his blue eyes deep, searching.

"Do I need the stick to tell you one more truth?"

A smile tugs at one corner of his mouth. "No."

"I like you, Brady Sterling."

Brady stills, his face suspended over mine, as my words sink in.

Then he lowers his face, or maybe I'm lifting mine. I can't tell.

His lips press against mine, a gentle caress. A reassurance that my truths are safe. His mouth isn't taking, but giving. My fingers wind into his hair, and I kiss him back with more force than I mean to.

After all this time hurting, all this time confused and lonely and sad, Brady's kiss is everything.

15

BRADY

I SWEAR THAT KISS WAS NOT WHY I BROUGHT HER HERE.

I wasn't expecting anything, hoping only to give her a respite from the sadness that plagues her. Honestly, I wasn't sure how she'd respond to the truth stick. It was just something silly my camp friends and I did when we were younger, but I remember how much better it made me feel after my turn with it. That was before I was a full-fledged teenager and would've scoffed at the idea of sharing my feelings so openly.

Addison embraced it, and I loved watching her find her voice. She was timid at first, but it didn't take long before she was letting it all go.

Her willingness to be so vulnerable was incredibly sexy. Not that I find upset, crying girls sexy, but it was her absence of fear. Lennon loves me and Finn deeply and unconditionally (and differently, as I recently learned), but she's not free with her emotions the way Addison is. And before meeting Addison, I didn't even know that was something I liked in a woman.

I kissed Addison.

She kissed me.

And it was perfect.

She's still in my arms, sighing softly against my neck. I gulp as the warm air from her sped up breathing decreases slowly. She palms my chest, and I feel her chuckle.

"Your heart is racing."

"Your. Fault." The sentence is broken into two words because I'm running after my frantic heart, trying to reign in its beats.

Addison pulls back slightly and looks up at me, her eyes wide. "I cannot believe that just happened."

"Which part?" I'm picturing her with the truth stick, then the feel of her lips against mine.

She sits back on her butt and shakes her head, her hair falling down around her shoulders. "All of it."

"Do you regret any of it?" My chest tightens as I steel myself for her answer.

She keeps me in suspense for a second that feels like an eternity. Slowly she shakes her head back and forth. "No."

I blow out a breath of air I didn't know I'd been holding and look up at the blue sky studded with cotton ball clouds.

Addison laughs and leans forward, sliding her arms around my neck. "Here, let me show you."

She kisses me again, harder this time. Her lips part and allow my tongue to sweep inside, tasting her.

My hands encircle her small waist and running up her ribcage. I feel her intake of breath. She pulls her mouth away and sucks in a loud, dragging breath.

"Brady, my god." She breathes the words.

"I've never been called a god before," I tease, breaking into a smile.

Her eyes roll up to the sky and she playfully shoves my arm.

A somber expression takes over her face, as if a thought has just occurred to her. "We should head back soon. I have a list of things my grandma needs help with." She climbs to her feet and stretches her arms above her.

I stand too, watching her shirt ride up her torso and show a small stretch of her skin. I saw her in a sports bra earlier, so this shouldn't be a big deal, but now I know what the inside of her mouth tastes like, and that makes a minor peek of skin even more tantalizing than it would have been before.

"I can help you with that list," I offer.

She turns me down with one simple swivel of her chin. "You're a guest, Brady."

"Do you make out with all guests?" My raised eyebrows challenge her.

Addison's hands fall from the top of her stretch to her backside. She brushes off the seat of her shorts, reminding me I should probably do the same, and says, "Yep. I finished a session with Mr. Anderson just before I came to your cabin for the mystery walk."

She grimaces even before she completes her sentence.

I laugh, following her lead and wiping off the backside of my shorts. "Never play Bullshit. You're as bad as Lennon."

Curiosity flames in Addison's eyes.

Crap.

I take Addison's hand in mine and lead the way up the amphitheater steps, hoping she'll let the comment slide.

"Is it hard that she's still your friend?"

My hope vanishes.

We start back onto the path, our pace slower now.

"It's... different. She has been my best friend since we were little kids, and I can't cut that off. I don't want to. But we're in a weird place right now. Normally, if a person chooses someone else over you, the relationship is over. But when that person is your best friend? There is no *over*, not unless I want the friendship to be over also. We're navigating something very confusing."

"Like on the roadmap of life, you've landed in a place where the lines are blurred and the paths are one amorphous blob," she says knowingly.

I squeeze her hand. Of course she knows exactly how I feel.

She continues. "At this point, I'm certain the only way past it is to go through it."

"You're very wise."

"Hard things will make you wise."

"Hard things give you the opportunity to become wise. You have to be intelligent enough to step back and see the lessons available to you."

Addison pokes my side. "Now you're the wise one."

The walk out takes longer than the walk in, mostly because we stop three times to make out. I can't help it. Addison tastes like sunshine and sugar. She has hair my fingers want to curl up in, and soft skin my hands are begging to touch.

When has this ever happened to me? Never. I loved Lennon and had she chosen me that would've been it for me, but she was never new to me.

Addison is a discovery, and each layer I peel away has me more hooked than the previous. Lonesome was a stop on my way to somewhere else, but now?

I'm not so sure.

I've been looking around, finding some things I want to do in the area. None of them can be done without a vehicle, and I'm not going to keep borrowing Louisa's Jeep. I want something of my own, and I think I've found it.

To get it, I need to borrow the Jeep one more time. And for that, I need to go to the main house and ask Louisa. Which means maybe I'll get a glimpse of Addison. And, if I'm lucky, maybe I can sneak a kiss.

We said goodbye at my cabin without a touch. No kiss, no embrace, not even a high-five. Anybody could've seen us, and since we hadn't discussed what we're doing, what this thing between us even is, we parted without any physical contact.

Such sweet sorrow.

I open the back door and step into the main house, looking around for signs of Louisa or Addison. From a small hall that shoots off the main room, I hear the rumbling sounds of a washer or dryer. I'll check there first before calling out for anybody or ringing the bell Louisa keeps on the table in the foyer.

I know she's the proprietor, and I'm technically a guest because I'm paying to stay here, but ringing a bell to get her attention bothers me. She's a grandma. Addison's grandma.

As I approach the laundry room, I hear hushed voices. My mouth opens to let whoever it is know I'm there, but then I hear my name, and my mouth snaps closed.

"It was just a walk in the woods, Grandma."

"You're already lying to yourself, Addison. Don't lie to me, too."

"Grandma," Addison half-scolds, half-whines.

"Brady doesn't seem like the type to run around laying his lips on women for no reason."

"I know," Addison concedes in a soft voice I have to strain to hear.

"Are you ready to move on with your life?"

"I'm here, aren't I?"

"Don't sass me, Addison Louisa West."

Addison laughs.

"I've been on this planet long enough to have learned something, and here's what I know. Good things have something in common with bad things. They come whether you're ready for them or not. You just have to be brave enough to grab on to them."

I'd like to say I feel guilty for listening in on their conversation, but I don't.

Backing up a few feet to the living room, I take a breath and call out for Louisa.

She pokes her head through the doorway, tucking a strand of gray hair behind her ear as her gaze darts back into the room behind her.

"Hey, Brady," she says, straightening and walking closer. "What can I do for you?"

Tucking my hands into my shorts pockets, I roll back onto my heels and ask, "Can I borrow your car? This will be the last time, I promise."

Addison's head appears in the hall. "Why for the last time? Are you leaving?" Her voice is high-pitched, her eyebrows squishing together and her head flinching back a little, as if her concern has caused her physical pain.

"No," I assure her, one hand extending into the air between us.

She steps all the way from the laundry room. Her eyebrows have returned to their normal position. "Good," she says, her voice taking on a forcibly relaxed tone.

"Would it upset you if I left?"

Addison's gaze flits between me and Louisa. There is laughter in Louisa's eyes, and though I'm lacking the mirror that can affirm my suspicion, I'm certain my smile has turned into more of a smirk.

"If you left, who would eat the products of my adventures in baking?"

My mouth waters at the thought of those carrot cake muffins and butterscotch blondies. "Everyone, Addison. That's why you're going to win the competition and be the proud new owner of the bakery."

"That's right," Louisa adds, making a fist and pumping it into the air. "Brady, you can borrow my car if you stop at the store and grab strawberries. Addison's making strawberry shortcake for me tomorrow."

Louisa shuffles from the room. As soon as she's gone, Addison moves in closer. "For a second there I thought you were pulling the dine-and-dash version of a goodbye."

I grab her hip and pull her in closer. Her surprised inhale catches in her throat.

"Never," I growl. "There's a truth I forgot to share with you earlier."

She tilts her head back, her tongue darting out to moisten her lips. "Oh yeah? What's that?"

I lean closer, so my lips brush her ear and her scent fills me. "I like you, too."

A slow smile takes over her face. "Those are words I like to hear."

"Here you go," Louisa calls out. Was she perhaps doing what I'd done just a few moments ago? Maybe she'd heard our conversation and backed away.

Addison steps back, her blue eyes holding excitement.

I turn to Louisa, taking the keys from her outstretched hand. "I'll make sure this gets back to you in one piece."

Louisa waves a hand. "It would be hard to hurt that beast."

With a wink at Louisa and a wave to Addison, I leave the house.

"HEY, MAN." I TOSS THE BAG HOLDING THE REQUESTED strawberries into the passenger seat of the Jeep and turn, offering a hand to the guy approaching me. He looks to be in his mid-forties, and he's wearing a short-sleeved plaid shirt and khaki cargo shorts. "I'm Brady Sterling. Nice to meet you."

"Ralph Henson. Nice to meet you too, Brady." He shakes my hand with exuberance. "I have to say, I was surprised when you called. Haven't had a single call about this truck in three weeks."

"I guess the timing was right," I tell him, running my hand along the top edge of the truck's tailgate.

He looks over the vehicle. "She's old, but she runs well."

"Does it have power steering?"

Ralph gives me a look that's part surprise, part embarrassment on my behalf for not automatically being able to tell just by looking. Like cooking, I lack a general knowledge of vehicles.

"Uh, yeah, it does." He nods as he speaks, doing a good job of covering up his surprise.

"Would you mind if I did a quick test drive?" I crane my neck and look around the parking lot of the grocery store where we agreed to meet. "Just around the block?"

Ralph pulls his keys from his pockets and works a single silver key with a black rubber cover from the key ring. "Here ya go," he says, dropping it in my open palm.

The test drive is quick, and everything seems to be in order. The truck runs well, and it doesn't require an exorbitant amount of my energy to turn the wheel. I don't need a smooth ride with top-of-the-line speakers, in-dash navigation, and a rear back-up camera. I just need something I don't have to ask Louisa to borrow and can get me where I want to go. And, if she says yes, can get Addison out on a date with me.

"It seems good," I tell Ralph as I slow to a stop and hop out. "I need to run over to the bank and bring you the cash."

"Take your time," he says, opening the passenger door and lowering the glovebox. "I'm just going to make sure this is cleared out. My buddy's on his way to help out."

I rub my chin and try not to look confused. Help out how?

Ralph must notice me flailing internally, because he explains. "You have two vehicles to drive back to that B&B you're staying at, right? You can drive the Jeep, I'll drive your new truck, and my buddy will follow. That way you don't have to have someone bring you back here to get the second car."

"Right." I nod slowly. What is my problem? Where has my brain gone? *Perhaps my focus has been trained on a certain blonde baker...*

I set off across the parking lot to the bank on the corner. When I get back, there's another man standing at the back of the truck talking to Ralph.

Ralph spots me and waves. "Brady, this is my friend Paul." He gestures to his friend as he turns around.

I smile at the man I met in this same parking lot a few days ago. "Paul, how's your dad?"

Ralph looks between us. "You two know each other?"

Paul nods. "This Good Samaritan helped out my dad

when he was having one of his senior moments."

I hand Ralph the envelope with the money. "Happy to help."

"You staying here in town, Brady?" Paul asks.

"I'm out at the Sweet Escape B&B."

Recognition lights up in Paul's eyes. "Is that why Addison West was with you the other day?"

My chest tightens. What does this guy want with Addison? I check his left hand. *Married.* "She and I were running errands for her grandma."

"Is she single? I have about four different friends who would love to know she's back in town."

I gulp down the urge to lie. "She's single," I say, the truth slipping between gritted teeth.

Paul cracks a smile and pats my shoulder. "Get in line, buddy. Addison West has had the guys in town tied in knots since she started showing up here every summer."

His non-threatening demeanor doesn't do much to relax me. I've been in fierce competition recently and I'm not dying to enter into another one.

Before I can say anything, he keeps going. "You must be staying for a while if you're buying this hunk of metal."

I think back to earlier today, and the feel of Addison in my arms. "I don't have a game plan. All I know is that I need to have the freedom to come and go when I want, and I don't want to ask Addison's grandma if I can borrow her car."

Both the guys laugh, then Ralph asks where I'm from.

"Chicago. I was a lawyer there." I say this directly to Paul, because I know he's a lawyer too.

"Didn't suit you?"

"I like the work. I just don't like how much work there is to do. I don't want to lift my head up from the desk one day and find life has passed me by."

A look comes onto Paul's face, one that I recognize. It says, *I'm stuck on a hamster wheel of my own making*.

"The missus tells me I work too much." Paul sighs, looking down at his wedding band. "She's right. I'm the only lawyer this town has though. Unless," he draws out the 's' sound, his eyebrows lifted optimistically.

My hands dart in front of me, palms out and agitating the air. "I'm not here for that."

Ralph whacks Paul on the back. "Quit trying to lure in the new guy. He came here to save old guys and take away other people's shot at Addison West." Ralph winks at me to let me know he's joking. "I don't even know who she is, but she must be something."

"You wouldn't know her," Paul informs him. "She was closer to my youngest brother's age." He looks at me. "I'm pretty sure she didn't know who I was a couple days ago."

Ralph nods. "She came around long after my time chasing skirts. I was probably off serving the country when she was starting kindergarten."

This piques my interest. "You served? What branch?" I'm genuinely curious, plus it steers the topic of conversation away from Addison.

Ralph straightens, his shoulders pulling back as if a puppet master has pulled his strings. "Marines," he answers in a deep, proud voice.

"Thank you for your service," I tell him. Every chance I get I thank the men and women who serve our country. I didn't choose to serve, and a part of me regrets it.

Ralph accepts my gratitude with a single, solemn head nod.

"I think," Paul says, reaching out and resting a hand on my shoulder, "that we should take our new friend out for a beer sometime. I'd like to properly thank you for what you did for my dad."

Ralph looks down at his watch. "It's just about drinking time right now."

"MaryAnn made some kind of complicated dinner." Paul clears his throat and shuffles his feet. Under his breath, he says, "Something about the anniversary of our first kiss."

Ralph howls and Paul shoots him a death glare. When Ralph sees Paul's dirty look, he shuts up.

"Sorry, bud. I didn't mean anything by it." He shrugs. "Hell, if we'd celebrated the small things maybe Jaclyn and I wouldn't have ended up on the wrong side of the divorce statistics."

My head's spinning from all I've learned about these guys in the last two minutes. They certainly aren't the stereotypical, keep it all on the inside type of guys. It's kind of nice to be around. Finn's my best friend and always will be, but getting him to talk about feelings is sometimes harder than pulling teeth. Lennon could always extract his emotions, though. Once again, here I am thinking maybe she knew what she was doing when she chose him after all.

Ralph and Paul decide two nights from now works for them, and obviously it works for me. I don't do anything at night except warm up my dinner in a microwave and stream a movie on my iPad until I fall asleep. The only exception was the one evening I spent with Addison at the beach.

I hop in the Jeep, hoping this will be the last time I have to drive it. Ralph follows in my new-to-me truck, and Paul is behind him.

We pull into the circular dirt drive at Sweet Escape and get out. Ralph hands me the truck key.

"She's all yours," he says with a grin.

I take the key and shove it in my pocket. Behind us, a

door opens.

"Brady, did you get the strawberries?" Addison steps out. Her hair is piled on the top of her head and a smear of what I'm guessing is flour decorates the front of her apron. She looks gorgeous.

I walk over and hand her the bag. Her eyes dart from me to Ralph and Paul. She waves politely, then looks back to me and asks, "Are you throwing a party?"

"Nope." I back away and walk to the truck, laying my arm on the side of the bed. "This is my new truck."

Addison laughs. "The Jeep wasn't cutting it?"

"I don't want to keep asking to use it."

Addison eyes me playfully. "Good, because I have some places I'd like to go and I hate driving that Jeep." She grins, says goodbye to Paul and Ralph, and goes back inside, the bag of strawberries swinging.

Ralph eyes Paul, then they burst into laughter.

"What?" I ask.

"You're so wife'd," Paul answers through his laughter.

"What the hell is that?"

"She has you picking up strawberries and taking her places," Paul explains, grinning knowingly. "Wife'd."

I roll my eyes at the noun turned into a verb. "She's just a friend, guys." Technically, it's true.

"Sure, sure," Ralph says, placating me. "We'll see you in a couple days for that beer." He and Paul get into Paul's car and drive away.

After I pull Louisa's Jeep into the garage, I park the truck in a parking spot designated for guests and head for the main house to return Louisa's keys.

Knowing Addison is in there has my heart beating just a little faster than normal.

A little too fast for someone who's just a friend.

16

ADDISON

I WAS TWO SECONDS AWAY FROM CANCELING ON CHARLIE, BUT now I'm glad I didn't. Girl time was something I didn't know I was missing until I arrived and met Charlie's friends. They're nice and funny, and the conversation that started out polite is deepening with the aid of a glass of wine. And getting raunchier too.

My life doesn't look anything like theirs right now, but I can follow along and appreciate the drama that comes with kids and a husband and all the trappings of domestic life.

So far, I've decided that Amanda, the loudest of the bunch, is the de facto leader. Her voice is husky, and she has a sarcastic, sharp wit, which she gears mostly toward herself. To her friends, she's supportive and funny.

Samantha is less exuberant, and she seems happy to let Amanda have the spotlight. She's a little crunchy too, based upon her recipe for a homemade stretch mark cream that she gave to Liz, who just had a baby three months ago and is probably going to be the first to bail because she looks exhausted.

And, of course, there's Charlie. She's sipping a mocktail, something bubbly and pink the bartender put together for her. She smiles at me as she takes a drink, then squints her eyes, her forehead coming forward slightly. I can tell she's asking if I'm doing okay in this group of women I hardly know, and I give a small nod, my eyes flicking over to the person who's talking.

"I've had two kids on the tit for what feels like longer than the Queen's been on the throne, and now that the last one is weaned, Jacob thinks it means I'm open for business again." Amanda, the only brunette of the group, makes a horrified face and motions toward her chest. "I don't want anyone touching the girls again for at least two years."

"Just be happy you have tits," Samantha declares, the corners of her mouth turning down. She runs a flattened palm down her front, as if running it along a wall. "Mine are gone. Gone!"

"Why?" I ask, unable to comprehend how boobs just disappear.

With her wine glass poised at her mouth, Amanda says, "Because she met Rory and let him put his penis in her. Now she's paying the price with deflated balloons."

I press my lips closed to keep from spitting out the sip of wine I've just taken.

Charlie's laughing so hard she starts coughing.

Samantha gives Amanda a side-eye. "You let Jacob poke your hole and you kept your boobs."

"That's what happens when you have fauxbs," Amanda responds.

We all stare at her. "What are fauxbs?" Charlie asks.

It clicks in my head just as Amanda says, "Faux boobs. Fakies. Breast implants," she says, reluctantly using the medical term with a face that conveys how much of a drag we all are that we forced her to say it.

"Oohhh I want to see them," Samantha squeals.

"Me too," Liz pipes up. Dark circles sit below her lower lashes, but now her eyes are brightened by her piqued curiosity.

"Let's go," Amanda says, inclining her head toward the ladies' room.

Samantha and Liz stand up, giggling and saying they can't believe they're doing this. Amanda sweeps her arm in the air like it's no big deal.

"You girls keep our table safe," she says to us, then walks off with Samantha and Liz.

"Oh my gosh," I say, turning to Charlie when they're gone.

She grins. "I told you they were fun. Tonight may be a third glass kind of night. They went through that first glass faster than usual. I think they're excited to have a new friend."

"I like them. They seem nice. And funny. Amanda is—"

"Addison?"

I turn to the voice I already know by heart. Brady stands beside the two guys I saw him with outside Sweet Escape a couple days ago. I know one of them is Paul, the son of the old man Brady helped, but I don't know the second guy. He looks like he's about twenty years older than us.

"Brady, hi. What are you doing here?" Memories of our walk in the woods assail me. I've seen him since then, and each time my thoughts are dominated by the feeling of his lips on mine.

My tongue darts out to moisten my lips and I tuck a strand of hair behind my ear. My nervous grooming annoys me, so I force my hand to wrap around my wine glass.

"Just grabbing a beer. You remember Paul?" He gestures to him with his thumb.

"Yes, hi. How's your dad doing?"

"Fine, thanks." Paul smiles politely.

Brady redirects his thumb to the other guy. "This is Ralph. I bought the truck from him."

"Hi, Ralph. This is Charlie," I say, since we're making introductions.

They say hello and Paul looks over his shoulder. "I'm going to grab that booth while it's still available. Ralph, come on."

They amble off across the place, but Brady doesn't take his eyes off me. He sinks down into the empty seat beside me. Taking my hand, he turns it over and traces the lines in my palm with his fingertip.

"You look beautiful tonight," he says, the compliment spoken under his breath.

"You don't look too bad yourself." Roughly translated, *too bad* should really mean *hottest man to ever step foot in this place*. Brady shaved after he picked up the razor, but it's been a couple days since then and his scruff has regrown. It only adds to his appeal, along with the navy blue tee he wears that has turned his blue eyes even bluer.

His fingertip on my palm is so potent, he might as well be stroking a totally different part of me. I press my thighs together and let my fingers curl into my palm, halting his progression. I meet his gaze, and it's like I can read his mind. First he's confused, then understanding dawns, and the look in his eyes becomes hungry.

"This is supposed to be ladies' night, but someone as handsome as you might be allowed to join us." Amanda's throaty voice breaks through the moment.

Brady quickly gets to his feet. "I'm sorry, did I steal your seat?"

Amanda slings an arm over his shoulder as if she knows him. "And he's polite too? Keeper!"

She lets him go and walks around the table to her chair. I stand up and make quick introductions, then turn my attention to Brady. As much as I'd like to attach myself to his hip right now, we both came here with friends. "Do you want to meet me for a run tomorrow morning-ish?"

Brady smirks. "Ish?"

Lifting my glass, I explain, "This is my second glass. Which means I'll want to sleep later than six."

"How about nine?"

"Perfect. I'll smuggle some breakfast down to you and we'll run after you eat."

Brady leans in, his hand on my hip and his lips at my ear. "I hear you have an extensive male fan club in this town."

I honestly don't know what he's talking about, but even if I did, it wouldn't matter.

"Are you a member of said club?" I whisper back.

"I'm the president." His words are a growl that vibrates my ear.

"That's all I care about," I assure him, letting my lips graze his earlobe.

He pulls back, that dark, hungry look in his eyes once more. "See you in the morning."

"See you tomorrow," I murmur, pivoting and turning my attention back to the girls.

For a second I feel him looking at me, then the feeling vanishes.

"Uh, yeah." Samantha looks around the table. "Anyone else ready to go home and screw their husbands after watching those two?"

"And get pregnant again? No thanks." Liz's answer is accompanied by a lip curl.

"Your mouth can't get pregnant, Liz," Amanda says loudly enough to draw attention from the table of older women nearby. I duck my head and look away.

"Anyway, can we please talk about that walking sex machine? I'm going to call him that because that's what I want to call him," Amanda informs me, but she stares at me, making it clear I'm supposed to respond.

"I cannot confirm your new name for him. We're just friends." I think. Friends who kiss. I know that's a thing. What about friends who hold truth sticks and say the worst things they feel? And *then* kiss.

"You won't be for long." It's Charlie speaking now, which takes me by surprise. "That tension was" —she holds a fist in front of her and makes slashing motions— "thick enough to cut. You'd better hop on that stool before someone else gets there first."

I shake my head, wishing I could sneak a peek at Brady without being obvious. "Brady's getting over something very significant."

"He has a broken heart?" Samantha asks, her tone doing this half-simper, half-maternal thing.

I look around at their faces. A moment ago they were going to go home and pretend their husbands were Brady, and now they all want to take him under their wings and place a cartoon-themed bandage on his heart.

"Can we talk about something else, please?" I drain the contents of my glass. I don't want to spend any more time talking about Brady, or me and Brady. I don't know what I have to offer, I don't know what he's capable of offering, and it's all too much for me right now.

Liz yawns loudly and grabs some money from her wallet.

"I'm going to have to move on completely, ladies." Amanda moans like a whiny child, which prompts Liz to say, "I have to get up with a baby at least twice tonight." She points to her breasts and makes a moo'ing sound.

After she leaves, I ask, "Is it really that bad?" I've always wanted a family, but tonight I'm getting introduced to the dark side of the dream, and it's frightening.

"Nope," Amanda says, popping the 'p' sound. "Kids are the best. Sometimes they're assholes, but name somebody who isn't every now and then. It comes down to this," she taps the tabletop with the tip of her fingernail. "A kid will fill a hole in your heart you never knew was there."

I blink. Amanda has been forthcoming all night, but something about what she just said feels incredibly intimate.

Charlie claps her hands. "I'm so excited to meet this little guy!"

"Don't wish these days away," Amanda warns. "Once he's here, you can't put him back."

Charlie starts asking questions about childbirth and infants, and I only half-listen. Someday this will all be fascinating to me, but right now I'm more interested in my current issues. Specifically, the *issue* sitting across the room from me. I'm dying to turn around and find him, but I don't want to get caught.

"Does anybody want another drink?" I ask, interrupting Samantha. "Sorry," I tell her, placing my hand on her forearm.

The group consensus is that another round is needed. I wave away offers of cash and insist this one is on me. I'm a nice person, but this run for more wine is really so I can locate Brady without craning my neck.

I walk to the far end of the bar and place our order, then lean back against it while I wait, casually (at least, I hope it looks that way) scanning the place. In a corner booth, Brady sits facing me. Our gazes lock, as if we're magnets.

"Hi," he mouths.

"Hey," I mouth back, my stomach doing back flips and my fingers curling into a surreptitious wave.

Suddenly, his face darkens. I'm confused, but the reason for Brady's look is cleared up almost instantaneously.

"You look like you could use some company."

My gaze swivels to the voice coming from right beside me. A dark-haired man stands too close, smelling of whiskey and arrogance.

"I'm good," I tell him, my voice cool and calm. "I'm here with my friends."

"I noticed," he says, leaning in further. I refuse to back away, even an inch. I get the feeling he likes intimidating women, and I don't plan on giving him an ounce of what he likes.

"You're not with them now," he drawls, his words slow. "They haven't even noticed you're gone. Bet they wouldn't miss you if you slipped into the bathroom with me for a few minutes."

I look him dead in the eyes. "Leave me alone." My voice is clear, my tone firm.

He leans in farther and my mind races with what I should do next. "How'd you know I like a challenge?"

"Get the fuck away from her." His voice is a low, menacing growl. If I didn't know the owner, hadn't felt the warmth of his hand and the gentleness of his kiss, I'd be terrified.

The guy shifts his slow, lazy gaze to Brady. "Fuck off,

bro." He turns to leave, and for a brief second I think he has given up, but as he's turning he snatches my hand, yanking me to him. The force is too much, causing me to stumble, and I catch myself on his chest.

"Look at that," I hear him say, but I'm positive his words are meant for Brady. "She can't wait to fuck me."

Two seconds later, the guy is on the ground. I'm not sure exactly what happened, but the grip on my hand is gone and I'm standing on my own two feet, looking down at the guy. His chest is rising and falling, but he's out cold.

I raise wide eyes to Brady. "Did you—"

He nods. We both look around, but it appears what happened didn't grab the attention of very many people. The bartender catches my eye and loudly says, "That guy arrived hammered. I've been wondering how long it would take him to pass out drunk like that." He pushes the three glasses of wine and one mocktail closer to me. "These are on the house," he says in a lower voice. "You shouldn't have to put up with that shit." He comes out from behind the bar and looks down at the guy still slumped on the ground.

"You get one side, I'll get the other," Brady says, bending down. "Let's get him to that booth over there."

They work together and lay the guy on the empty booth.

Brady shakes hands with the bartender, who goes back behind the bar like nothing happened.

Brady comes to my side, running two knuckles down my arm. "You okay?"

"Are you?" I ask, instead of answering. He's the one who hit someone.

"I'm good. The bartender said he knows someone who's friends with this guy. He's going to call and tell him he passed out here and needs to come get him." Brady looks down at his hand, straightening and flexing his fingers. "I'll have to call Finn tomorrow."

"Why?"

"We got in a fight a long time ago and, afterward, he taught me the right way to throw a punch. He'll be happy to know I finally had use for his lesson."

I gape at him. "Why did you fight your best friend?"

Brady eyes me. "It was over Lennon. We were young. In middle school, I think."

I nod once, slowly. "I see."

I'm starting to feel curious about this Lennon person. Apparently she's pretty great, since she had two guys in love with her at once.

"Can I help you carry these to your friends?" He tips his head toward the drinks still sitting on the bar.

"Sure."

We each grab two. I lead the way over to the table, and Brady smiles when Amanda asks where the hell I've been.

"Some guy was giving Addison trouble. I helped her out," he says modestly. I like that he's not bragging about knocking someone out.

"And he fights for the lady's honor as well!" Samantha throws a hand into the air. "Is there anything you don't do?"

"I have plenty of faults, don't worry," Brady assures her. He turns to me. "I'll see you tomorrow, okay? Unless you need a ride home tonight?"

"Charlie's my designated driver, but thank you."

I brush a kiss onto his cheek and when my lips touch his skin, a jolt of electricity shoots down my body, making everything inside me stand at attention.

"Have fun," he says, backing away. "Try not to attract any more assholes."

"I promise not to leave this table alone again."

He turns, and I watch him go back to his table. I sit back down and am enfolded into the conversation as if I never left.

And even though I'm surrounded by interesting, funny women, I feel a pang in my heart.

I miss Brady.

17

ADDISON

I'M GLAD I TOLD BRADY NINE-*ISH*. WIGGLE ROOM IS NEEDED when *someone* had three glasses of wine the night before.

I feel okay, not great. I made sure to drink lots of water while I was there and when I got home. Still, I have a niggling, dull headache.

Hopefully the breakfast and run will banish it. I've packed ham, egg and cheese croissants, fruit, and coffee.

My grandma gives me a curious stare on my way out of the house, but since she's engaged in conversation with a guest, I don't have to answer any questions about where I'm going or who I'm going to see.

I still can't believe Brady hit that drunk guy last night. He seemed so calm and collected, so level-headed. Maybe it wasn't out of character for him. Maybe it was another facet to him, one that is adjacent to his extreme dislike for injustice. I can add it to what I already know about him, like a brightly colored stone being placed in a mosaic.

When I get to cabin seven, I find the front door propped open.

"Brady?" I stay on the threshold and peek my head in, peering around.

"Just a sec," he yells from the bedroom. He comes out wearing running shorts, pulling a shirt over his head as he walks. For the two seconds of time it takes for the shirt to clear his face, I get to appreciate his midsection without getting caught.

Without the interference of a porch screen, I can see clearly what a drool-worthy midsection it is. Defined muscles, even all the way down to the lower portion, and disappearing beneath the waistband of his shorts. He's lean but not skinny, muscular but not bulky. In a word, perfect.

If I were better at checking out guys, I'd have gotten away with my gawking, but I'm substandard in that area. That particular skill isn't one I practice, and Brady catches me. Big time.

"If you want me to run shirtless, I can," he offers, lifting up the bottom of his shirt just enough to reveal a thin line of smooth skin. He breaks into a grin, enjoying the look on my face. If I'm reflecting in my expression what I'm feeling on the inside, it's complete mortification.

"I brought breakfast," I announce, ignoring him and walking inside.

"Let's eat on the back porch. The air smells so good right now."

"Is that why your front door was open?" I walk past the little living room and kitchenette and through to the back porch. "It's pre-rain air." I unpack the food and pour coffee into paper cups.

Brady grabs a croissant sandwich and takes a bite. "You're always hungry," I tell him, grabbing the second sandwich. Today, I'm probably as hungry as him.

Brady nods at me while he chews, agreeing with my observation.

We finish off the food and coffee and Brady leads us both through some pre-run stretches. I don't usually stretch before a run, even though I know I should, but I follow along.

Brady locks the front door on our way out, and we start off. We run at a slow jog so we can chat. He tells me about his night with Ralph and Paul, skirting around the whole rescuing me from the drunk guy incident, and I tell him about Charlie's friends.

"Apparently no matter how old women are, they still go to the bathroom together," Brady comments. He's only slightly winded, even though we've been jogging without a break for fifteen minutes.

Remembering the fauxbs, I laugh as best I can while being short of breath. "They went to the bathroom so Amanda could show them her breast implants."

Brady stops short. By the time I've slowed, I'm a few feet in front of him.

"Seriously?"

I laugh at his wide-eyed expression. "Yes. It's not that uncommon."

"I know implants aren't uncommon. My mom has them. I just didn't know girls went around showing them to other girls."

"Oh, Brady." I walk closer and throw my arms around his neck. "Girls share *everything*."

"Is that right?" Brady winds his arms around my waist. "What did you tell them about me?"

"Nothing."

He arches an eyebrow. "Why not?" He sounds a tiny bit offended.

My tongue slips over my lips in anticipation, knowing that what I'm about to say will be taken as a challenge. "There wasn't much to tell."

Brady's eyes narrow. He pushes his body weight into me, walking me backward until my backside meets the solid shape of a tree trunk.

"I'm going to give you something to talk about," he says against my hair, his deep voice tickling my ear.

He pulls back a few inches, his steady gaze traveling over my face. My lips part, my stomach muscles contract, the breath in my throat suddenly has weight, as if it has been mixed with something hot and sweet.

Brady gathers my hands, lifting them above my head and pinning me against the tree by my wrists. His free hand traces its way up my rib cage, pressing gently against the fabric of my sports bra, and over my chest, coming to rest at the base of my throat. He leans in, kissing first the hollow space above his hand, then up my neck and over my chin. When he gets to my lips, he pauses before taking the tiniest bite.

I exhale a quick breath, surprise and desire coursing through me. Brady's lips crash against mine and he swallows my surprise, inhales my desire, devours *me*. We are lips and limbs, kisses and ragged breathing, bodies pressed close and at the same time not nearly close enough.

"Brady," I moan against his cheek, dragging in a breath, more winded now than from our run.

"Addi—"

Overhead, the sky booms like a cannon. We look up, and above the green trees, I see a bruised sky, heavy with moisture.

"I think it's going to—"

He doesn't get to finish this sentence either, because there's another loud crack, and the sky opens.

Brady lets go of my wrists, only to grab ahold of my hand and pull me onto the path. We start back, and now we're running, not jogging. The rain pours down, the water soaking through my clothes, rivulets entering the top of my sports bra and sliding down through the valley of my breasts.

We reach Brady's cabin and climb the steps to the covered porch, finally out of the downpour. Brady shakes his head, and water droplets from his hair go flying. He runs a hand through his hair a few times, and although it's messy, his hair looks relatively dry. Me, on the other hand...

"Can I use your bathroom?" I rub my palms on my forearm. It's not actually cold outside, but I feel cold anyhow. "And maybe borrow some dry clothes from you?"

Brady leads me inside, and I grab a towel from the linen closet and begin drying off. It's a standard-issue Sweet Escape sage green cotton towel. I may have even been the one to fold it.

"I'll be right back," Brady says, disappearing into the bedroom. He comes back a minute later with a button-up shirt and shorts, his expression apologetic.

"You'll probably have to roll the shorts up a lot, if they even fit at all."

"I'll make do," I tell him, taking the clothes and walking into the bathroom. I close the door behind me and peel off my wet clothes, laying them on the edge of the bathtub.

I dry off and get to work on my hair, toweling as much water out of it as possible and then attacking it with Brady's brush. The tangles make the whole process take longer than usual. Grabbing Brady's shirt, I slip it over my head, breathing deeply as it passes over my face. It smells like him.

I grab the shorts, holding them up to see just how big they are. They look huge. I'm pretty sure they won't fit me even with multiple rolls of the waistband.

I look in the mirror, my gaze drawn to my lips. I run my fingertips over them, remembering Brady's kiss, the feel of his hips pressed to mine, the bark of the tree digging into my back.

Reaching down, I unbutton one more button of his shirt, so it falls open even lower, and roll up the sleeves until they're almost to my elbows. I take a deep breath, gazing at myself in the mirror, then open the bathroom door and walk out.

Brady's sitting on the couch. He's wearing a dry set of clothes and paging through a magazine about the Oregon coast. He looks up when I get closer, and understanding dawns in his eyes.

"Addison, don't do anything you're not ready for."

But that's the thing about Brady that I can't seem to fathom. When it comes to him, I feel ready for *everything*.

I keep going, walking until I'm standing between his knees. My fingers find the button located between my breasts and get to work, until every last button is undone. The shirt falls open, and Brady's eyes rake over my skin, his gaze burning into me.

"You're beautiful, Addison," he says, dragging his stare up to my face.

I place one bent leg on either side of him and sink down onto his lap. "Give me more to talk about at girl's night, Brady."

In reality, I'd never share private, intimate moments, but it's fun to pretend.

Brady kisses me, his lips hungry and searching. And then he does just what I've asked of him.

Skilled hands give me a story to tell.

Lips and tongues make certain the tale is scorching.

And somewhere in the tangle of limbs and toe-curling pleasure, our hearts collide, setting us up for something that will either deliver what we want most, or leave us more broken than when we arrived.

BEFORE I OPEN MY EYES, I KNOW WHERE I AM. IT TAKES A FEW seconds to orient myself but I'm aware of him beside me. The heat of his skin warms me, and his scent tickles my nose. At some point we made it back to his bedroom, and after all the exertion we fell asleep.

Eyes still closed, I allow my mind to wander. What happened after our run was hot and intense, not awkward and fumbling. We were experts in a field for which we'd never studied. Our bodies fit perfectly, our movements practiced as if we'd been in that position a hundred times, and at one point I thought *why is this so easy for us?*

My sample size isn't large, so I don't have a lot to draw on, but with Warren—

Warren.

Shame licks its way through me, lapping at the bubbles of happiness I feel inside.

I didn't think about Warren even once. Shouldn't he have been on my mind? A fleeting thought, at the very least?

I know it's over. The accident was like the blade of a guillotine, its effect swift and eternal.

Guilt is a fucked up thing. I would have felt it if I thought of Warren while I was with Brady. And right now, I feel it because I *didn't*. Damned from all angles.

I tense as something touches my face, then relax as the finger continues, brushing hair from my cheek.

I open one eye first, then the second.

Brady. Messy hair, from both the rain and our time. A lazy smile creeps across his face.

"I can think of a lot worse ways to wake up." His husky, sleepy voice curls over me, disappearing beneath the sheets and awakening the part of me that took control after our run.

"Me too," I say, curling myself into his body, pressing myself against him. I grin slyly and look up.

He chuckles. "There's no hiding how I feel right now."

My tongue moistens my lips as my heart beats faster. "How I feel isn't worn on the outside of my body. Instead, I'll have to show you."

Once again, everything is smooth and effortless, no hesitance or bashfulness.

Maybe, after all the pain we've endured, we are more than ready to be seen.

"Farewell," I say dramatically, placing the back of my hand against my forehead and pretending to swoon.

"I'll write," Brady jokes, leaning on the front door of his cabin.

He's still rumpled from our nap, and, well... other things.

"Are you sure you don't mind taking me into town?" Today's the last day I can officially enter the baking competition.

Brady grins. "I'm more than happy to drive Miss Daisy."

I stand on tiptoe to kiss his cheek. "I'll see you soon." With at least three backward glances on my walk out of his cabin, down the steps, and across his small yard, I finally turn a corner and stop, dragging in a long breath.

Overwhelming feelings threaten to consume me. Being in his presence fills me with the highest high and being apart from him makes me feel depleted. I shake my head, a physical attempt to clear the mental fogginess and keep going toward the main house.

I freeze the second I open the back door. My grandma sits at the dining room table, steam swirling up from a cup of hot tea on the table in front of her.

"That was quite a run you went on," she says, leveling her knowing gaze on me. "In the rain, no less."

Walking to the table, I grip the back of a chair and say, "It started pouring while we were on the trail. I ducked into Brady's cabin to get out of it."

"Is that right?" A smile tugs a corner of her mouth, causing the wrinkles around her lips to fan out.

"Housekeeping is doing a good job. The place was clean and the linen closet was stocked with fresh towels." Every afternoon a team of ladies shows up and tidies the rooms. My grandma used to do it, but the labor became too much for her. I tried to tell her she could also pay them to wash the sheets and towels, and she was offended by the very notion that she could be too old to do something so basic, which of course wasn't what I was saying. Attempting to get her to understand what I meant was futile. Instead, I try to get to the laundry before she can.

She smirks. I can tell she won't be deterred by my report of the cabin's cleanliness. "And tell me, Addy, how were the sheets? Soft? Comfy?"

I sigh, lifting my hands off the chair only to lean forward and rest my forearms. "Grandma..."

Her shoulders shake with her chuckle. "Don't blow

smoke up my ass, granddaughter. I know a sated face when I see one."

A blush warms my cheeks.

She lifts her tea to her lips and blows across the top of it. "How are you feeling about it?"

"I was feeling great about it actually, until a moment ago. Now that I'm away from him," my forehead meets my cupped hands, my weight supported by them, "I'm starting to feel like it wasn't such a good idea."

Grandma's chin tips to the side. "Why not?"

"Warren." I feel a little stab as I say his name. "I wasn't thinking about him at all while I was with Brady, but then on the walk up here, I just..." I trail off, shrugging. "I don't know."

"You came back down to reality?"

I nod.

Grandma shifts in her seat, leaning forward. "Does the way you're feeling right now make you want to hop on the next plane to Chicago and rush to sit beside Warren?"

My arms cross in front of my body, my hands gripping my skin. I feel uncomfortable.

Grandma keeps her expectant gaze on me, and because she's waiting for me to answer before she continues, I say, "No."

"Tell me then, what good is feeling guilty doing for you?"

"Warren deserves a person to feel guilty. A person who feels like it's wrong to move on. He didn't deserve what happened to him."

"Nobody deserves what happened to Warren. Not him, not his parents or his sister, and certainly not you. So now you get to make a choice." She raises her palms into the air, lifting one higher than the other. "Do you lie down and give yourself over to a lifetime of pain," she lowers one palm and raises the other "or do you let yourself continue on with the same things you once enjoyed?"

I know what the right answer is, I just can't seem to make the words leave my mouth.

"Do you still like reading a book in the sunshine on a warm summer day?" Grandma's expression is an odd mix of stern and gentle.

"Yes," I answer.

"Then go do it and don't feel guilty because you're alive to do it. Do you like what it feels like when Brady touches you?"

I nod.

"Then, my god, let him touch you and don't feel wrong for it. Of all people, you know how precious life is and how it can change on a dime. Don't deny yourself another day of misplaced indentured servitude. And" —she points a stiff finger at me— "you'd better get your behind into town and sign up for that baking competition or so help me I will drive there and put your name in the running myself."

For the first time since stepping foot in the house just now, I feel myself smiling.

Grandma straightens, pride etching its way onto her features. Her talk worked.

"Don't worry, Grandma. Brady's driving me into town after a while, so I can add my name to the list."

She makes a fist and punches the air in front of her in excitement. "That's my girl. You fall down seven times, you get back up eight, Addison. You're last name might be West thanks to your father, but you're a Craft in spirit, and Craft women don't belong on the ground."

I come around the table and wrap my arms around her. "I love you, Grandma."

She pats my arm. "I love you, too. Why don't you go take

a shower and get ready? You smell like sex and you look like a bedraggled kitten."

I pull away, laughing. "You don't always have to say what you think."

"That's one of the joys of getting old. You get to relax your filter and everybody attributes it to old age."

I kiss the top of her head and go upstairs, heading directly for my bathroom. I peel off the damp clothes and step under the hot spray of the shower.

My grandma is right. I can't use what happened with Warren as a crutch, allowing it to keep me from living. I thought I wasn't sure how to take the next step forward, but then I made it here to Lonesome, befriended Brady, and had a baking competition fall into my lap.

While my mind was busy freaking out, my heart was doing exactly what it knew I needed.

18

BRADY

"THERE," ADDISON SAYS PROUDLY, BOUNCING ON HER TOES and beaming. "I did it." She tucks the pen into her purse while I look at the piece of paper on the cork-board at the bakery.

Addison West scrawled in her loopy handwriting. I take her hand and bring it to my lips. "It's in the bag," I murmur against her fingers.

"Your biased, but thanks for the vote of confidence." She walks to the display case and bends, perusing the treats. Straightening, she tells the girl behind the case, "We'll take a chocolate eclair and a sticky toffee bread pudding. And a blueberry muffin." Twisting to look back at me, she winks and says, "Research."

We sit down with our food and Addison grabs a fork, but instead of taking a bite she dissects everything but the blueberry muffin. When she's done with them, they resemble the leftovers of a messy toddler.

"I left the muffin for you. Those are easy." She places a tiny bit of filling from the eclair on her tongue, then runs it along the roof of her mouth before closing her lips and swallowing.

She must see the curiosity burning in my gaze, because she says, "I'm trying to get a feel for what the customers expect in terms of flavor. What if I'm into vegan baking and I show up and take over the place using cashew cream instead of custard? That's not what people expect when they come here." She looks around. "This place is cute, right? I love how it looks like a little home. The front door needs a new coat of paint, and maybe I could put a couple small tables with chairs on the front porch. The homier it feels, the more time people will spend here."

I grin. I love watching her talk about her passion. She's not only incredibly talented when it comes to baking, she has a good head for business. Too bad her ex-fiancé's family couldn't get past themselves long enough to see that. Their loss, my gain.

The bell above the door chimes and in walks a woman with black hair and a purposeful gait. Maybe it's the severe bun at the nape of her thick neck, but her energy is palpable and off-putting. She marches to the counter and thunks her flattened palms on the surface beside the register.

"I'm here to sign up for the baking competition." Even her voice is harsh. This woman gives off the general sense that she doesn't take an ounce of shit from anybody. Ever. I think she missed her calling in law enforcement.

"Oh-kay?" the poor girl behind the register stammers. Compared to the woman in front of her, the girl looks like an innocent dove.

Tearing my gaze from the situation, I glance at Addison to see if she's aware of what's happening. Her gaze is glued to the woman also, her eyes scrunching slightly.

"Well?" the woman demands. "How do I sign up?"

The girl stays silent but points at the cork-board on the wall above the offered utensils and napkins. The woman twists her thick neck to see what the girl is pointing to. From my seat, I can see a portion of her face, enough to know she has bushy eyebrows and a permanent frown.

She looks back at the girl, nodding once at the case. "I'll take a blueberry muffin."

Addison and I look at each other. She's as astonished as I am at this interaction. The woman takes her muffin and stops by the board, using a pen to write in the space below Addison's name. She settles at the table beside us, facing me, and just when I think the spectacle is over, it's not.

"Too much sugar," the lady declares, after taking a bite. And then I realize she's talking to me.

"Don't you agree?" She's pointing at the blueberry muffin sitting in front of me.

I look down at the completely intact muffin. "Oh, uh," is all I manage to say.

"Too much sugar," she repeats, and I see a smear of blueberry across one of her front teeth.

Addison swipes the muffin from in front of me and takes a bite. She shifts her upper half in her seat so she can directly address the lady. "I don't think they're bad." Her gaze flits over to the girl behind the register, who I'm certain is listening to our conversation. It would be hard not to.

"I'll make a better one," the woman says. "I've entered the competition, and I'll win. I've been a baker my whole life."

Addison smiles serenely. Unlike the harsh woman, she does not have blueberry smeared on her teeth. "Good luck," she tells her, turning back around to me.

"Let's go," she mouths, gathering the dirty plates and placing them in a bin on a shelf above the trash can. Grabbing the poor muffin, I nod my head at the woman and follow Addison out the door.

I take a bite of the muffin on the way to the truck. "Tastes okay to me."

Addison glances at me. "Beatrice was right. It has too much sugar."

"Beatrice?"

"Beatrice Connelly, according to the sign-up sheet. I looked when I was putting away our dirty plates."

I nod my understanding and finish the muffin, using a balled-up napkin from my pocket to wipe crumbs off my lips.

"I've had the world's best blueberry muffin," I tell her, climbing into my truck. Addison clicks her seatbelt and stares at me expectantly.

"It was from a little bakery in a town in northern Arizona. Brighton. That's where Finn and Lennon are living right now, with Finn's uncle." In my mind, I see the cabin Finn built, the road into town, and the quaint street with the bakery. "The window literally has a sign that says 'World's Best Blueberry Muffins', and they sell out of them every weekend by mid-morning. The place is like an institution."

Addison grabs her phone and starts typing, pauses, then her fingers are scrolling. She glances at me triumphantly. "Got it!" She presses a button and puts the phone on speaker, holding it sideways so the part with the microphone is closer to her mouth.

Ringing fills the truck cabin, and then a pleasant voice answers, "Lady J bakery."

Addison's excited, nervous gaze meets mine. "Hi," she says, her eyes still on me. "Can I please speak with the owner of Lady J?"

"You already are. This is Jane. What can I do for you?"

"Jane, my name is Addison West. I live in Lonesome, Oregon, and I used to operate a bakery in Chicago. My friend Brady was lucky enough to eat one of your famous blueberry muffins recently, and he was raving about it." Addison's fist clenches as she speaks. "I'm in a baking competition here in Oregon and the prize is a bakery."

"That's quite a prize," Jane says. "But I don't quite see what this has to do with me."

Addison glances at me, then back to the phone, as if willing the person on the other end to give her what she's after. "I think my competitor is going to make blueberry muffins. We're supposed to make three things, and I want one of the things I make to be blueberry muffins that blow hers out of the water. And to do that I need—"

"My recipe?" Mild amusement trickles through Jane's voice.

"Yes, I know it's a weird request, but..." Addison taps her knee with a finger and looks at me. "I really want to win."

I try not to show her my surprise. I thought she was entering just to enter, to have something to fill her time. When did it go from reluctant interest to something she'd set her sights on?

Jane laughs, a quiet, easy sound. "You seem like a nice person, Addison. How old are you?"

"Twenty-seven." Hope shimmers in Addison's voice.

I think it's a good sign Jane is asking Addison a question. Perhaps she has a daughter and she's thinking of her. Maybe that will tilt things in Addison's favor.

"I use one tablespoon of lemon zest, and I mash a quarter of the blueberries and mix them into the batter," Jane says. Addison turns a wide-eyed stare at me, and smiles so huge that it pulls her skin taut.

"Also," Jane continues, "the remaining blueberries

should be coated in flour and then folded in. It keeps them from sinking to the bottom."

"Oh my gosh, oh my gosh, thank you so much!" Addison gushes.

Jane laughs again, but the sound isn't pure happiness. Somewhere in there, I detect a sliver of sadness.

"You said your friend was in Brighton recently?" Jane asks, the sadness now gone.

Addison brings the phone closer to me, urging me to speak.

"Hi, Jane. This is Brady. I'm the one who's guilty of bragging about your bakery."

"Well, thank you, Brady. Word-of-mouth does seem to be the best form of advertising. When were you in?"

"About eight months ago. My friend just finished building a cabin there. He and his...girlfriend live there." I glance at Addison. Did she notice the change in my voice at the reference to Lennon?

"Are you talking about Finn?"

I grin, the pleasant, surprised feeling of knowing the same person running through me. "Yes, exactly. Finn has been my best friend since I was a kid."

"He's probably one of my best customers. If he's not in here for his uncle, he's in here getting something for his girlfriend. She came in with him yesterday. They're just about the sweetest couple I've ever seen, and she's finally showing."

Showing? Showing what?

Addison's eyes widen in alarm.

My mind scrambles, trying to understand, and then the fog clears and the meaning of Jane's words click into place. Lennon is pregnant.

An uncomfortable tingling sensation starts in my chest, blocking any words from exiting my mouth.

"I bet she's just the cutest," Addison says, her tone not giving away the worry in her gaze as she looks at me.

"Yep," Jane agrees happily. "Well, listen, I have to get back to what I was doing. You use that recipe, and call me when the competition is over. I'd like to know how it works out."

"Will do."

Addison says goodbye and hangs up. She's quiet. I'm looking down, studying my hands as they rest on my thighs, the light skin a contrast to the dark blue of my shorts.

How can Lennon be pregnant? I know how, but *how?* And why haven't they told me yet?

I know the answer to that question. Telling me isn't something either of them are looking forward to. I know them well enough to know they'd rather bury their heads in the sand than face me and tell me something they know will upset me.

"Brady?" Addison's voice is cautious. Her hand snakes its way over my thigh and onto my hand. Her fingers slip into the empty spaces between my fingers. Her hand is warm.

"How are you feeling?" she asks.

It's hard to choose from all the emotions floating inside me, but there is one feeling that dominates. "Confused. I should feel blindsided, and I do, but I'm not devastated. I'm shocked, but it doesn't hurt like I'd thought something like this would." I shake my head, sighing. "Maybe moving on is supposed to feel like this. Surprising, but not painful."

Addison's free hand touches my head, her fingers running through my hair and down my neck like a trickle of warm water. I turn to look at her. Beautiful Addison, so gorgeous both inside and out.

"I understand." Addison's fingers reach for my hair, retracing the path, stroking me.

I look into eyes that hold empathy. "You do, don't you?"

She nods, and it's right now, in the cab of this used truck that still smells like its previous owner, that what I felt for Lennon turns opaque, the way a memory should.

Here is Addison, sitting beside me, living, breathing, giving me her next steps.

And here I am, wanting to give her my next steps too.

19

ADDISON

I've done it.

I grab my phone and text Brady, unable to wait for him to show up at the main house on his own time.

Come up here. You need these in your life.

I take a picture of the blueberry muffins and hit send, but it won't go through.

Brady shows up ten minutes later, a look of anticipation on his face.

"Here," I announce proudly, grabbing a muffin off the cooling rack and presenting it to him, along with a kiss on his cheek. His face falls, which makes my face fall.

"What?" I ask, worried.

"When you said I need *these* in my life, I thought you were talking about something else." His eyes lower to my chest, and with a glance around to be certain we're alone, he uses a fingertip to follow the hem of my V-neck tee.

"First," I say, giving him a stern look, "you need to eat this muffin. And then—"

"I can eat another muffin?"

I give him an exasperated look, but it's mostly an act. If

sex with Brady is a drug, consider me addicted. I haven't slept in my own bed in three days, not since Brady got the news about Lennon.

I was afraid he'd pull away after that, but it only seems to have caused him to double-down on me and whatever it is we're doing here, which we've yet to discuss. At some point we'll have to, especially considering I'm now a contender in a bake-off that will keep me in Lonesome if I win.

"Fine," I say, crossing my arms and looking away playfully.

Brady tips up my chin with one finger, leveling his lust-filled gaze on me. "Don't act like you don't love it. Last night you said—"

"Okay, okay." I hold up my arms in defeat. "I can't be held accountable for what I say when I'm in the throes."

Brady laughs. He takes the muffin from me and makes it disappear in two bites. He lifts his eyes to the ceiling. "God, that's good."

I watch him chew and swallow, then hand him a second option. "Okay, now, try this one."

Brady eyes it. "I thought you were going with Jane's recipe."

"It is Jane's recipe, but with an Addison kick. I don't want to copy her exactly."

"The topping?"

I nod, my hands urging him on.

He takes a bite, closes his eyes again, but this time he sighs deeply. "Heaven," he says simply.

A mixture of joy and relief swim through me. "Yeah?"

He nods solemnly and takes a drink from my water cup sitting on the island counter. "There's no way you won't win that competition, Addison."

I make a face. "It's only a couple weeks away." I glance at

him, a sudden feeling of nervousness coming over me. Grabbing the dirty bowl, I take it to the sink and run water into it. Without looking at him, I say, "Your stay is ending soon. Where do you think you'll go after Lonesome?" I work to make my voice nonchalant, but on the inside it feels like all my organs are squeezing together.

It's only been a couple weeks since I decided I liked him. Too soon to care this much. And even though I know that to be true, even though I can hear and feel the practicality of these words, my heart rejects them.

I came here thinking good things weren't in the cards for me.

And then, along came Brady.

And, according to the calendar where my grandma writes her bookings, in a few days, there he'll go. The notion twists my stomach into knots.

The bowl has filled with water, so I turn it off and spin around, my lower back resting on the edge of the sink.

Brady's eyebrows are drawn in confusion. "After Lonesome? I thought..." He pauses, running the pad of his thumb across his lower lip. "Maybe I read us wrong, Addison. If I did, I'm sorry." He pushes back from the island where he's been leaning.

I stick out a hand as he turns to go. "Brady, what did you think?"

Brady looks at me, his hesitance plain on his face. He's just come from a terrible rejection. Telling me how he feels now must be terrifying.

So, I put on my big girl panties and walk closer to him. I don't feel brave, but I can damn sure act like it.

"You already know I like you, Brady. But what you don't know is how much I'd like you to stay in Lonesome. I know we're not meeting in a typical, easy way. We're both coming into this with some baggage. But, if you're willing to push through the fear and give this a shot, then I am too."

Brady's eyes roll back and he looks upward. "Thank you," he says to the ceiling.

I laugh, closing the space between us and molding my body to his. He kisses the space beneath my ear and murmurs, "I talked to your grandma this morning and extended my stay through the summer."

I pull back and glare at him. "Why didn't you just say that?"

His grin is playful and fiendish. It makes my toes curl, because I've seen it before, and good things usually follow it. "I wanted to hear how you feel about me."

"Oh yeah?" My eyebrows lift in defiance. I can't pull it off completely because a smile tugs at my lips. "Do you want to hear how I feel about you at this exact second?"

"Nope. Come on."

Brady grabs my hand and leads me out of the kitchen. He stops when we get to the living room, craning his neck as he searches for somebody who might spot us. Namely, my grandma.

"Let's go to your cabin," I whisper-hiss against his back.

He shakes his head. "No time. I won't make it. I'll end up taking you on the lawn and then we'll get arrested."

I laugh into his back until I have to gulp in air, and when I do, his manly, clean scent fills my nose. It's so overwhelming it makes me want to rip off my clothes and risk being walked in on. Now I understand what he means about not making it all the way to his cabin.

When he's decided we're in the clear, he leads me through the living room and to the stairs. He takes them two at a time and I have to speed up my climb to keep up with him. He pauses at the top and looks back at me, making me realize he doesn't know which room is mine.

I dart around him and to the third door on the left, pulling him inside and locking the door behind us. Brady is all over me the second the lock clicks into place.

There goes my shirt.

My shorts are pooled at my ankles.

He's wasting no time today. That's okay with me, because last night he acted like time was the very last thing on his mind. I don't think I could take it if he did that again so soon.

Brady drops to his knees, dragging a trail of kisses up the inside of my thigh. "I don't know what you've done to me, Addison, but I don't want it to stop." His words invade my heart, and yet I also feel them on my body, their heat searing the delicate skin at the apex of my thighs where his mouth hovers.

"Brady," I groan, quickly slamming a hand to my mouth to cover the sound. I'm too late, though, and the hand covering my mouth is there for no reason.

Except, it's not.

Brady gives me every reason to keep my hand in place.

Twice.

AFTER THE DAY IN MY BEDROOM, WHATEVER WALLS WE'D constructed to keep what was happening between us at bay crumbled as if they were made of sand. Wherever one of us was, the other was sure to be nearby. Brady helped me with the never-ending laundry, though I'd had to show him the proper way to fold a towel. I didn't ask, but assumed he learned towel-folding from the same person who taught him to cook: nobody.

And even though I didn't want it to, even though I willed it away with all my strength, the day came anyway. My fervent whispered prayers didn't slow its approach.

June 29th.

My would-have-been wedding day. I've been *wouldhave-been'ing* all day long.

I *would have been* getting my hair done right now.

I *would have been* drinking champagne before getting into my dress.

Warren *would have been* trying to peek at me before the ceremony.

My grandma must somehow know the turmoil inside me, because she's asked me to take her into town to eat lunch. Leaving Sweet Escape is something she does so rarely, the unusualness of the request jolted me from my despondency.

"Thank you," Grandma says as the server sets down her food.

"Is everything okay?" I ask, taking a bite of my salad. "It's not often you ask me out to lunch."

"All good," she says cheerfully. "Let's talk about you. Let's talk about what today would've been."

I push aside the mixed greens with my fork. "You really know how to get right to it."

"No use in beating around the bush. You've been moping around all morning."

"I know," I sigh. "Do you think Brady noticed?"

"Well, yes. He's not blind. Did he mention anything to you?"

"No." My fork clatters to my plate and I catch my head in my hands and groan. "Why is this one day such a big deal? It's no different from yesterday, or every other day before it."

"Addy, this was supposed to be your wedding day. Of course it's different from every other day."

I lift my head. "But the circumstances are the same. I know today what I knew yesterday. My Warren is gone."

And he took with him our entire future.

A little thought digs at me, poking, forcing me to acknowledge it. Would I have married someone I wasn't one hundred percent certain about? The answer scares me. I'd like to think I would've either decided I was all in or been brave enough to back out. I guess now I'll never know.

"None of this matters anymore, you know that, right?"

I flinch. Grandma's tendency to cut through the bullshit can sting.

"Of course I know that. Warren's not coming back, obviously."

"So how long are you planning on letting it hurt you?"

"How does someone *let* something hurt them?"

Grandma snorts. "Easily. You either allow the emotion to affect your thoughts and actions, or you don't."

"Maybe not everyone is as iron-willed as you."

She shrugs and takes a bite. "Their loss."

I can't take much more, so I move the conversation to the mundane and Grandma doesn't stop me. We finish eating and pay. I pause a few feet from the outside of the restaurant, turning my face up to the summer sun. The air conditioning had been turned on so high I'd had goosebumps for most of lunch. The sun's rays permeate my skin, and I'm busy enjoying it, until a harsh, gravelly voice interrupts me.

"Are you Addison West?"

Even though I've only heard it once, the voice is unmistakable. Reluctantly, I turn to look at Beatrice. She looks just as intimidating today as she did in the bakery the first and only time I've seen her.

"Yes," I confirm, waiting to hear what she has to say.

"Why didn't you tell me that day at the bakery when you saw me adding my name to the list?"

I make a face. I don't know what kind of face it is, I just know that I can feel my cheeks scrunch. This woman is a few bricks shy of a load. Either that or her frontal lobe never fully developed.

"I didn't view it as a vital piece of information, seeing as how I'd never met you."

The woman makes a sound, kind of like a *hmph.* "I hear you owned a bakery in Chicago."

Instead of answering, I ask, "Are you checking up on all the entrants?"

"Yes." Her face is even, her lips in that permanent scowl. "It's prudent to know one's competition."

Even if her baking is so good it makes a man of the cloth denounce religion, there's no way she can take over the bakery. Her people skills are terrible.

"Okay, well, bye." I scoot around her. "Nice seeing you again."

I don't know if she answers, because I don't stop. Grandma is in step beside me, and I can feel the curiosity coming off her in waves.

"She's my competition," I explain, rolling my eyes.

"No she's not," Grandma quips.

"She's in the contest."

"Right. But she's no competition of yours."

I grab Grandma's hand, bringing us both to a stop, and hug her tightly.

Sometimes, a person really just needs to have someone in their corner. Lucky me, I have two someones.

"Grandma, I'm going down to see Brady. He asked me to visit when we got back." He probably wants to know what was up with me this morning. I told him only once, at the very beginning, about the day when I was supposed to be getting married. I'm sure he doesn't remember.

"Bye, hon," she responds, walking off to her office.

On the way down to Brady's I notice for the first time since I arrived this summer how beautiful this place really is. The wide, sloping lawn of green grass, gently giving way to the trees, and beyond them, the guest cabins. Sunlight filters through the trees, dappling the ground I walk over.

Maybe, for the rest of my life, this day will be a sad one for me. Or maybe this year will be the hardest, and each subsequent year will feel easier, until there is no longer pain but only a memory.

I round the corner to the front of Brady's cabin, quickly climbing the steps and knocking on the front door.

"Hi." Brady opens the door only partially, just enough for his large frame to fit through. He steps out, his body pushing me back a couple feet.

"Brady, what is going on?"

"Here," Brady says, ignoring me and holding out what looks like a t-shirt that has been rolled up length-wise. "Turn around."

"Is that a blindfold?" I ask, doing as I've been told.

Brady slips the fabric over my eyes and pulls tightly. I can feel him tying the knot at the back of my head. He gets a couple stray hairs tied in too, and I wince in pain. When he lets go of the knot, the pain ceases.

"Can you see anything?" he asks.

I squint my eyes, trying to see through the fabric, but I really can't. I shake my head.

"Good," he says. "Now, let me guide you."

He stands behind me, gripping my forearms and propelling me forward.

"Step," he says, and I assume we're at the front door. It's weird to take a step when you can't see, and so I'm certain I've lifted my leg too high. It makes me think of how I'd walk if I were wearing clown shoes.

He instructs me where to turn and helps me sit down. I sit with my hands in my lap, excited and impatient. I'd love to rip this thing off and see what he's doing.

I feel something being placed on my head and automatically lift my chin.

"Put your head down," Brady instructs.

I feel something slide against my scalp on top of my head, like the teeth of a comb. Brady mutters to himself, then takes a deep breath.

"Okay," he says, the excitement in his tone barely contained.

His fingers work at the back of my head, and he gently pulls off the blindfold.

I gasp when I see it. When I see it *all.*

"Brady, I..." My fingers trail over my lips as I try to come up with something, *anything,* to say that will be appropriate.

Brady sinks down into the chair beside me at the table. He watches me closely, gauging my reaction.

"I don't know what flavor you would've chosen, but I hope this is something you like." He points at the small two-tiered cake sitting atop a silver cake stand. *Grandma's cake stand.*

"It's lemon cake with vanilla buttercream."

Finally my ability to speak comes back to me. "It sounds incredible. Where did you buy it?"

"I made it."

"You made it? *You*?"

He nods. He looks proud but nervous.

"Brady that's so sweet. Why did you make me a cake?"

He licks his lips and purses them. "It's a wedding cake."

I stare, unable to speak. I reach for a finger on my left hand, seeking out a ring I'm not wearing. Speechless. Breathless. Rendered immobile. Brady's gesture has reached down into the deepest part of me and filled me.

"Look on your plate," he motions at the spot on the table in front of me.

I look down. A square gold box sits on a dessert plate.

"Can I open it?" I ask, reaching down.

Brady nods, giving me the go-ahead. Gently, I lift the top off the box and peer down. Nestled in cloth is a sapphire blue picture frame. There is no picture in the frame.

"That's your something blue and your something new. And the veil is borrowed and old." Brady watches me. "It was the best I could do."

Oh my gosh, a veil. I'm wearing a veil. I didn't even feel it. I lift my hand and capture the fabric on my back. I pull it to the side, rubbing the gauzy fabric with my fingers.

"This was my grandma's," I say incredulously. "You... you're... giving me a wedding day."

Despite the joy I feel inside at the kindness and compassion inside this man, I begin to cry.

"I'm sorry," I sputter, as Brady leans forward and wraps his arms around me.

"Don't worry. I think it's normal for brides to cry on their wedding day."

His joke stops the tears and I laugh.

"I can't believe you would do something like this for me." I pull away and look at him. "Actually, I can." I kiss him, long and deep, hoping he can taste my gratitude. "What did I ever do to deserve someone like you?"

"You existed." Brady kisses the tip of my nose. "You deserve everything good, Addison."

I kiss him again, until I run out of oxygen and I have to pull away, gasping for breath.

"There's more," Brady says, getting up from the table. He goes to the small fridge and comes away with a bottle of pink champagne.

I feel happier now than I can remember feeling in so long. It's warm and snuggly, this happy feeling. I want to stay in it forever.

Brady cuts the cake and pops the champagne, and I cheer.

"I want a big slice," I tell him, moving the box with the picture frame.

He places a monstrous slice on my plate. We toast, and I recognize the champagne glasses from my grandma's stemware cabinet. Clearly she was in on it. Which explains the lunch she wanted to go out to.

"To many more good things," Brady announces, clinking his glass against mine.

I tip my glass to his, echoing the sentiment and hoping fervently that his words come true.

20

BRADY

My phone's ringing. For some reason, I know who it is. I don't know how to explain it, other than a lifetime connection.

Lennon.

Addison sees the name flashing across the screen and starts to lift off my chest.

"No, no, stay," I tell her, placing my palm on her back.

She gives me an uncertain look but settles back down onto me.

I hit the button and Lennon's face comes into view. She's sitting on the couch in the living room of her place. Her smile falters.

"Brady, hi. And hello to you," she says, addressing Addison. I can tell immediately that Lennon is sizing her up.

"Hi," Addison chirps. "I'm Addison."

"Nice to meet you," Lennon responds politely. She looks off screen. "Finn, come say hi to..." She looks back at the screen, taking in the image of Addison's head on my chest, "Brady's friend who looks like more than a friend."

I feel Addison's chuckle.

Finn appears in the background, leaning over the back of the couch, his head next to Lennon's.

They really do look good together. I've thought that before, but this is the first time the thought hasn't hurt.

"Hi Addison, I'm Finn."

"Nice to meet you, Finn. I've heard so much about you guys."

Finn laughs, but Lennon looks disgruntled.

Addison continues. "All good things, of course. Brady loves to talk about the fun you had growing up."

Lennon's face relaxes a little. Perhaps she was afraid I'd vilified her in my retelling of our story. I'll admit, it's a tricky story to tell.

Finn nudges Lennon, and she glances at him. She looks nervous, and I bet I know why.

"What's going on guys?" I ask. "Lennon, are you pregnant or something?"

Lennon's eyes bug out. Finn smirks. Nothing fazes the guy. Nothing except for Lennon, of course.

"How did you know?" Lennon asks, her voice wobbly.

"Just a hunch," I say, winking at them. I don't want to throw Jane under the bus.

"Congratulations," Addison adds. "How far along?"

"Fifteen weeks," Lennon responds, happiness finally dawning on her face. "It's a boy."

Finn beams and pumps his fist into the air in front of them. "I made a boy."

Lennon gives him a look. "*We* made a boy," she corrects him. To us, she says, "He keeps saying that."

Addison laughs again. Lennon asks her how she and I met.

"Well..." She gazes up at me, and I brush a kiss onto her

forehead. "Technically, we met on the flight from Chicago to Oregon. But I thought he was married. Then—"

"Wait," Lennon interrupts. "Why did you think he was married?"

"He was wearing his grandpa's wedding ring."

Lennon's gaze turns quizzical. She doesn't say anything, but I know she smells bullshit.

I try not to act like it's a big deal, but inside I'm sweating bullets. "Just keeping it safe during travel. I didn't want to put it in storage and I didn't have a good place for it." I shrug, acting like it's not a thing.

Which it totally is. I wore that ring because my heart had been obliterated and the person I thought was my soulmate had chosen someone else. I was playing a stupid game of pretend. Just for a blip in time, I wanted to walk around like I was a person lucky enough to have found my other half.

"What are you guys up to this evening?" I ask brightly, steering the conversation away from Oregon and into Arizona.

"Usually someone would be going to sleep in a few hours," Finn looks over at Lennon and she grins sheepishly. "She says the baby makes her tired."

"He *does* make me tired," she confirms. "But tonight we're going on a double date. Finn hit it off with the handyman who has been coming out here to help with random things. Finn's into learning everything about... well, everything, and this guy, Connor, has been showing Finn what he does when he's out here so Finn can do it himself."

Finn rarely makes new friends so easily. Maybe having Lennon has made him an all-around calmer, more easy-going person. "Is my best friend status in jeopardy?"

"Yep," they both answer, looking at each other and

laughing. Their heads are so close that they can't help but nuzzle for a second.

"Ugh." I pretend to be sick. "You two are nauseating."

For the briefest second Lennon looks stricken, but then she realizes I'm kidding and sticks her tongue out at me.

"What are you two up to?" Finn asks.

Addison shrugs, but I say, "We need to get a good night's rest. Addison doesn't know it but I'm taking her somewhere in the morning."

She peers up at me, surprised. "Where?"

"The rodeo."

She sits up. "Are you serious?" She's shocked, but her cheeks are pulling up, telling me she's also happy.

"I thought it seemed like something you'd like."

"Um, yes!" Her fisted hands open exuberantly, like fireworks exploding.

Lennon and Finn are laughing. "You two turn in early. We'll go be party animals," Lennon jokes.

We say goodbye and hang up, and I'm struck by how *normal* that phone call was.

"They seem great." Addison trails a finger over my chest as she talks. "Lennon is beautiful."

"She's a troll," I say, laughing because I know if Lennon were in the vicinity she'd kick my shin and pinch the skin on the underside of my arm.

"Brady," Addison scolds.

I cup her face, my thumbs stroking her soft skin. It probably wasn't easy for her just now, having to interact with someone I thought I was in love with.

Was I in love with Lennon? I think so. But being with Addison makes me question how I felt about anybody, ever. She's a fresh breath of air for a soul who didn't know it was being deprived.

"Addison, you are beautiful. Inside and out. Your blue eyes have little brown flecks in them. Your nose is the cutest thing I've ever seen, and I don't think I've ever thought a nose was cute before. Your lips are the prettiest shade of pink, and they're so kissable that I," I lean forward and plant a feather-light kiss on her.

"Just." Another kiss.

"Can't." A third one.

"Help myself." And a fourth, for good measure.

"Brady," Addison closes her eyes and breathes my name. "I wasn't expecting you."

"I came here to escape, Addison. But every day I'm feeling more and more... found."

A sound comes from Addison's throat, a strangled, low moan. She's on me in a flash, tugging down my shorts and pulling off her own. She sinks onto me, letting me fill her, and kisses me, long, slow, and deep.

She doesn't say anything more, and neither do I. We don't need to speak when our bodies are talking, saying everything for us.

Afterward we collapse into an exhausted, sweaty, sticky heap. Her blonde hair splays across my chest, her head rising and falling with my still-quickened breathing.

My fingers brush through her hair and I stare down at the profile of her face, the curve of her back, her long legs stretched out.

The words are there, on the tip of my tongue, but I hold them in because it's too soon.

Too soon to feel the way I do. It's impractical, inexplicable.

In a matter of weeks, this woman has taken my messy world and set it back on its axis.

I don't know what my future holds, but I damn sure know who's in it.

"YOU READY, COWGIRL?" I REACH OVER AND TAP THE BRIM OF Addison's hat. I have no idea how she managed to get a cowboy hat between late yesterday afternoon and this morning.

"Sure am," she drawls, grabbing her purse from the floorboard of my truck and winding her arm through the strap.

We meet at the back of my truck, and just like this morning when I met her at the main house, she makes me pause and fumble for words. She's wearing a bright red sundress that falls to the middle of her thighs, and matching cowgirl boots. As if her outfit isn't enticing enough, there is no back to the dress, except for two straps that run like an x. When I saw that, I'd had to bite the skin on the underside of my lip to keep from dragging her into the trees and showing her how much I liked it.

We link hands and walk through the dusty parking lot to the arena. Around us are men and women in Levi's and boots, and more cowboy hats than I've ever seen in one place. That's saying something, considering I grew up in the desert southwest.

I don't look the part. I have on jeans, but they aren't cowboy tight. My shirt is collared, and the sleeves are rolled up onto my forearms. I don't have boots, but my tennis shoes are leather. Does that count?

"Brady, we should get a hat for you," Addison says as we walk by vendors. She stops at one and picks up a tan hat, holding it up to me. One eye closes as she considers it.

"Nah," she says, replacing it and looking around. Her eyes light up and she pounces on a hat a few feet away. "This one," she declares, bringing it over.

I take the black hat from her and place it on my head. The woman working the booth comes forward with a mirror.

"Hats pick the wearer, you know," she intones seriously. "And that hat has certainly chosen you."

I look in the mirror. After I get over the shock of seeing myself in a cowboy hat, I agree it's the one. Addison does a little dance, then slips her arm through mine.

"You might have to wear that later," she says under her breath.

I hand my credit card over to the woman and turn my lips so they brush the space beside Addison's ear. "Only if you keep your boots on when everything else comes off."

"Okay," Addison agrees loudly.

"Did you say something?" the woman asks as she hands me back my credit card.

"Oh, um, nothing," Addison tells her, grinning.

"Thank you kindly, ma'am." I tip my hat to the lady.

She breaks into a smile. "And they say cowboys are only born, not created." She waves her hand as if the saying, which of course I've never heard, means little to her.

We spend the rest of the day watching bull riding, barrel races, and mutton roping. Women, children, and men show off skills and talents I could never imagine possessing.

Addison is captivated by the bedazzled chaps some of the women wear, and she claps for the kids as they rope the sheep.

"I love this," she says, leaning over and giving me a happy kiss. "Thank you for bringing me here."

I wind an arm around her shoulder and she tucks into

me, a move so practiced an onlooker might think we've been doing it for years.

As the rodeo winds down, we leave the arena and go in search of a restaurant. It's a two-hour drive back and we need to eat before we get on the road to Lonesome.

There's a kitschy place nearby, and tonight we fit right in.

I order a beer, Addison gets a glass of wine. She's talking animatedly about what she's chosen to make for the baking competition, which is only a week away, when she stops abruptly and pulls her phone from her purse. She frowns at the phone, then puts it back in her bag.

She doesn't say who it was, and I don't ask, but I'm curious.

My curiosity is heightened by the fact that now Addison can hardly remember what it was she was talking about. Gently I remind her of the desserts, but even with my reminder she can hardly string together two real sentences.

"Right... yeah. So I'll make... that topping... yeah." She fidgets with the gold necklace she's wearing. Her eyes are unfocused.

"Everything okay?" I ask, grabbing her hand and urging her to look at me.

"Um hmm," she says quickly, looking at me but not really. Her gaze might be on me, but her thoughts are somewhere else. She pulls back her hand from my grasp and grabs her wine, taking two big sips. "That was Warren's sister, Shannon."

"Did she leave a message?"

Addison looks at her phone, then shakes her head no.

"Are you going to call her back?"

"I don't want to. I prefer to keep that door firmly closed." Addison replaces her palm in mine. She attempts a smile, but it's forced.

I get up from my side of the booth and slide into hers. Pulling her into me, I kiss her temple and slide two fingers under her chin, tipping her gaze to mine. "You came here to get away from the pain that held you captive in Chicago. Don't let it follow you here."

She smiles a tiny smile, but at least it's real. "You're right." She reaches for my beer and slides it to me, then clinks her wine against my glass. "To good things."

"To good things," I echo, taking a drink before lowering my lips to hers.

21

ADDISON

THE IMAGE OF SHANNON'S NAME ON MY PHONE HAS BEEN running through my mind since last night when I let it go to voicemail. What does she want?

I woke up to a text from her this morning, but it was cryptic. *Are you available?* That's all it had said. It's been an hour and I haven't responded.

Brady stayed the night with me, waking at first light and going for a run. I stayed behind to help my grandma with breakfast. And, I suppose, to respond to Shannon.

I grab my phone off my nightstand and navigate to my messages, clicking on Shannon's name.

I begin typing.

Me: Hey, Shannon. How are you?

As if she were right beside her phone, the little dots appear instantly.

Shannon: Hi, Addison. Sorry to contact you so out of the blue. I'm having a blanket made from Warren's old concert shirts and wondered if you had any? My mom can't find them.

Oh. My heart thumps. Warren's prized concert shirts. It

had taken me months to convince him to let me sleep in them.

Me: There are some in a box in storage. The operator keeps a master key. I'll email him and tell him to expect you.

Shannon: I appreciate it, Addison. Really.

Me: How is Warren?

Shannon: How do you think?

My chest tightens. She always was on the sarcastic side, but for two seconds can't she just be some semblance of cordial? My phone buzzes again.

Shannon: Are you still at your grandma's?

Me: Yes. It's going well.

Shannon: Are you planning on coming back here?

Me: Maybe at some point.

I'm vague on purpose. I'll have to go back some time, if only to deal with the things I have in storage.

Shannon: Are you making a life for yourself there?

I blink, unsure of how to respond.

Me: I'm trying to. I have to move on.

Shannon: Is there someone you're moving on with?

There's no way I'm telling her about Brady.

Me: Life is still very confusing and I'm making the best of a horrible situation. Let me know if the storage operator gives you any trouble. I'll send you his contact info.

Shannon: Thanks.

I pull up the operator's information and send it to Shannon, then turn my phone face down on the nightstand and bury my head in the pillow. I feel sick inside.

The night it all happened comes back to me, only this time I'm seeing it differently. I'm going to bed with Warren, choosing to lie beside him and read a book. I'm there when it happens, this stroke the doctors say he had. I call for help, and they get to him in time. I save him.

I cry into my pillow, knowing this alternate reality can never exist.

The really horrible part of this is how much I want Brady to comfort me right now. I want him to hold me while I cry for someone else. How can that be?

I get out of bed and change my clothes, then brush my hair and teeth. I'll catch Brady at breakfast, and then maybe we can take a walk and I can tell him about my text exchange with Shannon.

BRADY DIDN'T COME TO BREAKFAST AT THE MAIN HOUSE.

I played my role, chatting with the new guests and fetching more food as it was needed, but I kept one eye on the door the entire time.

After the last guest left, I helped clean up, then packed a bag with items from breakfast and walked it to Brady's cabin. I knocked once and he didn't answer, so now I'm knocking a second time.

Still no answer.

"Brady?" I call, looking at my watch. He should be back from his run by now.

Walking around the back of the small structure, I peer in through the small, covered back porch. Either he's sitting still as a statue, or there's nobody inside.

Trudging up to the main house, I put away the food and pour myself another cup of coffee. When my cup is empty and I'm done paging through a magazine, I get up and rinse my cup. Really it's just an excuse to stand at the sink and stare out the window.

No sign of Brady.

I go upstairs, check my phone, and when I don't see any calls or texts from him, I take a long, hot shower. The water works on my nerves, soothing them.

Everything is okay. There's no need to be worried about him.

I dry my hair. I curl my hair. I even put on makeup. Still, nothing from him.

Downstairs, I run into my grandma in the kitchen. "Do you need anything from town?" I ask her. "I have to go do all the shopping for ingredients."

"I always need something," she says, opening the fridge and looking through its contents.

She rattles off a few things and I write them down. While she busies herself doing various things, I write out my list of what I will need to make butterscotch blondies, blueberry muffins with streusel topping, and lemon cupcakes with vanilla buttercream frosting. Brady inspired my third choice. I'm switching it up by adding lemon curd filling.

I do my shopping slowly, trying hard not to check my watch every few minutes and totally failing. It's almost lunchtime and I'm getting worried.

While I'm in town, I kill some time with Charlie, who is blessedly available when I call her.

"I'm so happy you were free," I tell her, sliding into a seat across from her at the coffee and tea shop.

"Me too," she winds her hands around a warm cup of herbal tea. "Here I thought I was getting my summer buddy back, then Brady went and snatched you up." She grins to let me know she doesn't mind that much.

Despite my concern about Brady's whereabouts, and my guilt stemming from Shannon's messages, I smile. "He's amazing, Charlie. Truly. He makes it hard to think about anything beyond being with him."

"I hope he doesn't make it hard for you to practice for the competition. I've met the latest entrant and she is a real bitch."

I choke on a laugh, surprised at the word that just came from Charlie's sweet mouth.

"What?" Charlie says, crossing her arms stubbornly. "She is."

"I know. I've met her. Twice." My lip curls at the memory. "She's going to be one of those dark horses. She doesn't look or act like a baker, and then *bam!* Her treats make everyone orgasm at first bite."

"Hah!" Charlie laughs, then coughs on her mouthful of tea. "You sound like Amanda."

"I think everyone has a bit of Amanda in them now and again." I sip my tea, a calming vanilla Rooibos. No more caffeine for me. I'm hyped enough as it is. "How are you feeling?" I look down at Charlie's belly as I ask the question.

"I can't see my feet anymore," she says cheerfully.

I laugh, glancing under the table. I don't have the heart to tell her one flip-flop is black and the other is hot pink. "I can't wait to snuggle your baby."

She raises an eyebrow. "Is that right? Are you and Brady going to start working on that?"

"It's a little soon for that," I murmur, distracted as I peer out the window we're seated beside, hoping that perhaps Brady will just appear on the sidewalk and my worries will be assuaged.

No such luck.

Charlie and I chat for a little longer, then she announces she needs to take a nap. It reminds me of Lennon.

We say goodbye and I head home. Presumably to sit around and wait for Brady to show up.

My mind wanders as I drive, and I hate where it goes.

What if something bad happened to him? What if he's trapped somewhere, with nobody to help him? He doesn't know the area very well. He could be lost.

There are a million ways he could be hurt or in danger. He could be taken from me in an instant. It's a cold, harsh truth with which I'm too well-acquainted.

A sliver of hope flashes through me as I round the bend for Sweet Escape. Maybe his truck will be parked in the guest parking. It wasn't there when I left, but hopefully he's returned from wherever he went.

My hope deflates as I pull into the driveway. He's not here. I park the Jeep in the garage and lift all the grocery bags from the back. I trudge across the yard and to the stairs, my arms shaking because I utterly refuse to make an additional trip. When I hear an engine behind me, I swing my gaze around. Brady's truck turns into the driveway. All the bags I was holding fall to the ground and I run for the truck.

I didn't know I was this upset. It's the relief. The amount of relief I feel belies the fear I hid even from myself.

"Brady," I say his name through tears.

He grinds to a stop and hops out, his eyebrows drawn. He takes me into his arms and strokes my hair. "What happened?" he asks.

"You... you were gone," I wail. "I was so scared."

"Hey, hey," Brady croons, his hand rubbing circles on my back. "I'm fine. I'm right here. I didn't want to run so I went for a hike instead, and my phone died."

He holds me until my tears subside.

"I'm sorry," I whisper, feeling silly now.

He looks into my eyes. "Never be sorry about something that affects you this strongly, okay?"

I nod and take a breath.

"Why were you so upset?" he asks, guiding me toward the house with his arm around my shoulder.

"I thought something bad had happened to you. I took breakfast down to your cabin today, but you weren't there. I went to town for groceries and noticed your car was gone. And I... I didn't know."

Taking a deep breath, I decide to be brave and tell him how I really feel. "I had no way to save Warren. I wasn't there for him at all. If something like that happened a second time, I don't know what I would do."

Brady groans. "Addison, that's an awful way to feel. You can't run around saving everyone all the time. It wasn't your responsibility to keep anything bad from happening to Warren. That's too much responsibility for any one person to ever take on."

I know his words are right, but that's completely different from believing them.

"Come on, let's get this stuff inside." Brady bends down and gathers my groceries in his hands. We walk in the house together and he helps me put them away.

"You bought a lot of stuff," he comments, eyeing the tremendous amount of butter.

"It's everything I need for two rounds. I'm going to do a trial run before I bake everything for real."

Brady, sitting on a chair at the island, pulls me to him so that I'm standing between his legs. "Can we have a little fun this afternoon before you embark on a baking frenzy?"

I think I know what he's asking, so I press my breasts against him and whisper, "Yes."

I feel his chuckle on my skin. "We'll definitely leave time

for that, too. But I was thinking of a waterfall I found about thirty minutes away."

"That sounds perfect." I need a change of scenery and some alone time with Brady. I kiss him swiftly, and even though I'm longing to let it turn into more, I control myself. "I need to change into my suit."

I start to step back, but Brady stops me, gripping my face between his hands. "I'm not going anywhere, Addison. Understand?" He kisses me, crushing his lips to mine. He takes from me every last ounce of fear, erasing all my concerns, swallowing my guilt.

He leaves to grab his bathing suit, and I run my fingers along my lips. Nobody has ever made my body, my soul, my heart come alive the way Brady does. Not even the man I was prepared to marry.

22

BRADY

I DON'T THINK I'VE EVER SEEN SOMEONE SO PETRIFIED.

After a long walk up to the top of the waterfall, Addison has decided she can't jump off. It doesn't matter that a line of people have already gone before her, including a twelve-year-old. She's refusing.

"No worries," I tell her, as she bites her lip and peers over the edge. "Are you okay walking down by yourself? I want to jump, and then I'll meet you along the trail."

She looks at me in alarm. "I don't want you to do it either," she squeaks.

I laugh, and then when I see the look on her face, my laughter stops. "Addison, it's going to be okay. I promise. See all those people down there?"

She looks over the edge at the people milling around.

"Yes." Her voice is tiny.

"They all jumped already. And they're fine."

The sounds of another splash float up to us. We both watch as the jumper surfaces, laughing and hollering, and swims to the shallow part of the water.

"See?"

Addison nods. "Can we go together?" Her tone is hopeful.

Oh, man. This is going to make her say no. "It's safest for one person at a time," I admit, carefully leaving out *why* it's safest for one person to jump at a time. There's a window of space where it's deep enough to jump, and that window *might* be big enough for two people. But it also might not. Body size, force, distance, and probably other things factor in. Bottom line: no.

"Let's just get in line. I'll go first, and then you can decide. If you don't want to, it's not a big deal. I'll meet you on the trail, okay?"

I grab her hand and pull her into line behind someone who's probably thirty years older than us. He's shirtless and ultra-tan, the kind that can only come from a bottle or a booth, with a coating of back hair.

Addison wraps her arms around me and buries her face into my chest. She makes an incoherent sound, like a little yell, into my skin.

She hides her face and I move us forward in line as a unit. When it's my turn, I tap her on the shoulder. She looks up at me.

"I'm up, Addison. Unless you want to go first?"

She shakes her head back and forth quickly. I brush my lips across hers and turn around, locating the spot in the water where people have been jumping.

I let out a yell, maybe I'd even call it a holler, because it's loud and full of vowels. For a brief time I'm suspended in the air, and then my body slips into the water. It's colder than I anticipated, and I break the surface as quickly as possible to show Addison I'm okay.

I look up and see her face, tiny from this distance,

peering over the edge at me. I wave a thumbs up in the air and turn sideways, treading water and watching Addison.

She's going for it! She yells too, more of a terrified cry than a delighted whoop, and sails through the air. Changing directions, I swim back and watch her hit the surface and then pop back up. She draws in a loud breath and says, "It's so cold." She swims to me, and I pull her into my chest. We're both kicking to stay afloat, so we can't stay attached for long.

She swims first, probably to generate warmth, and I follow.

We get out and sit in the sun, letting the rays permeate our skin.

"Fun?" I ask, running my fingers up her arm.

"So fun," she agrees, her body bouncing excitedly. "Can we do it again?"

I chuckle, planting a kiss on her wet hair. "My little adrenaline junkie."

"Let's go," she urges, standing and pulling me along with her.

We walk to the top and jump again. And again. And again. Finally, I have to be the first to quit. It was only this morning that I hiked for hours, and my legs are beginning to scream at me.

Addison pretends to pout on the way back to my truck. "What are we going to do now?" she asks, pausing in the open passenger door.

"Shower."

A devilish grin lights up her face. "Together?"

I return her smile. "Is there any other way?"

Louisa has asked Addison and me to eat dinner with her tonight. She's trying out a new recipe and wants us to be the guinea pigs.

We arrive in the main house freshly showered, and of course, freshly sexed. I'm sure it's obvious. We both look pleased and relaxed, a telltale combination.

Louisa is in the kitchen, putting together a salad. When I offer to help, she tells me to uncork the wine and asks Addison to set the table.

We all sit down, and Louisa looks excited but nervous as she sets the casserole dish in front of us. "Chicken tetrazzini," she announces, removing the foil from the top.

"It looks good," I say.

"And smells amazing," Addison adds.

Louisa dishes out portions onto our plates and I take a bite.

Oh, no. Looks good, smells good, does not taste good.

Louisa spits her bite out into her napkin. "Oh, crap," she groans, looking at us. "If you haven't taken a bite I would refrain from doing so."

"Too late," Addison and I say at the same time. Addison spits hers into her napkin, but I manage to swallow.

"How much salt did you add, Grandma?"

"Too much, apparently."

Addison laughs. "Why don't we let Brady take us out for dinner?"

"Oh, phooey. Brady doesn't want to take an old lady like me out to dinner." She says it, but she still peeks at me hopefully.

I clutch a hand to my heart and say dramatically, "It would bring me great pleasure, Louisa."

Louisa pushes back from the table. "Well, then, I'll just go get my purse."

Addison leans over to me after Louisa is gone. Strands of her hair tickle my shoulder, and the scent of my body wash comes off her skin. "Thank you for taking me to the waterfall." She kisses the corner of my lips. "You are a person worth doing scary things for."

I'd love to respond, but I can't. I'm struck silent. My whole life I've been the pursuer. Of good grades, degrees, accolades, popularity, friends, and Lennon. And then Addison happens. Every day she comes to me willingly, mangled heart open, ready to love me and let me love her in return.

Tucking her hair behind her ear, I look into her ocean blue eyes. "Addison, I—"

"You kids ready?" Louisa calls, her voice reaching us a second before she does. She walks in with her purse hanging from a shoulder.

"Crap, did I walk in on something?" Her features rearrange into an apology.

"No," I say, and at the same time Addison says, "Yes."

I push away from the table and walk to the front door, holding it open. "Ladies, your chariot awaits."

For dinner, I take them to a place with white tablecloths and hardback menus printed on heavy card stock. We're not dressed for it, but the maître d' begrudgingly agrees to allow it if we'll sit at a table in the full-service lounge.

Louisa peers over her menu at me. "I'm feeling like a fancy woman, Brady."

"You are, Louisa."

She gives me a withering look. "I'm wearing sandals."

"We all are," I remind her, taking a piece of bread from the basket in the center of the table. "Still fancy."

Addison and Louisa tell me story after story of summers

in Lonesome, and the wacky people who've been guests over the years.

"This man hardly spoke to me during his entire two-week stay, and then he came in the house and asked me if I had any" —Louisa's eyes dart around us, and Addison and I lean in to hear whatever is so forbidden she has to check out our neighbors before speaking— "weed." She holds pinched fingers to her mouth like it's a joint.

I laugh. Louisa is sweet and innocent, thinking weed is that big of a deal.

"What did you say, Grandma?"

"I told him no. I certainly wasn't going to share with someone like that!"

"Grandma!" Addison's mouth drops open.

The sip of wine I've just taken fights to fly from my mouth. It stays in, along with my laughter, and I end up coughing as the red wine burns my throat on the way down.

"Don't act like you're a saint, Addison." Louisa wags a finger at her. She turns the finger on me. "Or you, either. You two have been going at it like sailors on leave."

I cough again, thank god this time it's only water.

The rest of dinner isn't nearly as raucous. We all eat too much and are less talkative on the drive home. Our energy has gone to our stomachs.

The moment we get back to the main house, Louisa announces she's tired and goes to her room. Addison takes me outside to the set of lounge chairs on the lawn. I settle into one, and instead of taking her own, she slips between my legs and leans back against me. The curves of her body fit into the hollows of my own.

"Thank you for taking us to dinner tonight. That was very sweet of you." Addison's words rumble against my chest.

"It was fun. Your grandma is a special lady."

I stare at the top of Addison's head. Nerves build up in my stomach, twisting it into knots. I know what I want to say, I just don't know quite how to get there. I stare up at the stars, attempting to wrangle my thoughts like those kids roping sheep at the rodeo.

"I can see why you loved Lennon."

Her statement startles me. It's so far away from what I'm thinking about.

I stay quiet, trying to figure out how to respond. Addison sits up, forcing me to do the same to make room for both of us on the one seat. She crosses her legs and twists her hands in her lap.

"She's gorgeous and witty. She's intelligent, too. And loyal. She watched me closely. Like a robot scanning me for flaws. She wanted to figure out if I posed a threat to the well-being of her best friend's heart."

Addison picked up all this from a video chat?

She looks up at me and opens her mouth to continue. "It's not hard to picture you and Finn fighting over her. Figuratively, not literally. It's a beautiful, heartbreaking story, really. You both grow up loving your best friend, and then she had to choose between you two."

In the glow of the outside lights, I see a faint pink blooming on her cheeks.

"I'm jealous," she admits softly.

"Of what?" I can't fathom what there is to be jealous of.

"That you loved her."

I can't help it. I smile. She loved Warren, but of course that's not the point. She's as human as I am, and that means she can only see my situation as an outside observer. She sees a beautifully tragic love story. And it was... but it's not anymore. I have a new love story.

Reaching for Addison's hands, I wind my own through them and pull them so they're no longer in her lap but lying in the crevice our folded legs create. She lifts her gaze to mine.

Here goes nothing. "Lennon chose Finn. Did she love me? Yeah, she did. But she didn't need me desperately, all-consumingly, didn't need me like she needs air. What air is to her lungs, Finn is to her heart. I didn't understand that until I came here, Addison. Because it's how I feel about you."

Addison's lower lip falls away from her upper lip, her mouth forming a surprised 'o'.

"I've never felt like this about anybody. Not even Lennon. I didn't know what I was missing out on, because I hadn't met you yet. And I know we haven't known each other very long, but that doesn't matter to me. I knew Lennon my whole life and thought she was the one for me, and I was dead wrong." A smile tugs at my cheeks as I watch Addison absorb my words. "I want every one of your kisses and sighs and irritated looks. I want to love you loudly. I want to love you messy." Addison laughs in a soft, incredulous way, and I continue. "I won't settle for less, and less is anything that's not you. And I thank god Lennon didn't choose me. Because, Addison, I love you."

I feel lighter and more terrified, more vulnerable, than I ever have.

Addison's face breaks into a large, open smile. Until now, I hadn't fully known what it meant to say someone was *glowing*, but now I get it. Addison is radiant.

She launches herself at me. I catch her, and the momentum takes us both back against the reclined chair.

Addison steadies herself on my chest, her beautiful face backlit by the moon. "I love you too, Brady. And it all seems so crazy and totally opposite of what I saw for my life, but that's okay. Thank god someone else knew what I needed to feel complete, because obviously I didn't have a clue. When we received Warren's prognosis, I was certain my life was over. For a long time I was stuck in a waiting place, and it was hell. Finally I came here, and yes, I moved on physically, but emotionally and mentally I was in the same place I'd been in from the day the doctors told us. And then I met you. And you awakened in me something that has never been tapped, Brady. Never. Not even by Warren. And that made me feel guilty as hell. Honestly, it still does, but I'm learning how to navigate that. There's nobody I'd rather wake up beside, or bake for, or jump off cliffs with." She takes a deep breath, then says, "I love you."

23

ADDISON

I'M HIGH.

High on life. High on love. High on Brady.

Ready to move forward. Ready to be truly happy.

For the first time in so long, my soul feels at ease. The guilt is still there, but it's a fraction of what it used to be. Instead of telling myself it's wrong to feel that way, I'm accepting its existence.

Beside me, Brady stirs, tightening the arm he has wrapped around me, pulling me in even closer.

Last night, after the declaration that created this high, we went inside and quietly climbed the stairs to my room.

We laid down, and Brady pushed inside me, holding me together while I went to pieces beneath him.

I can't imagine moments more perfect than last night, but then he's beside me now, waking up, his brown hair sticking up in places, the sheet leaving behind an indentation on his cheek, and I realize I'm wrong. The perfect moments with Brady just keep getting better, like the swelling crescendo of a symphony that never ends.

"Morning, baby," Brady croons, his voice thick and sleepy, wrapping around me like rough silk.

"Good morning." I kiss the inside of his elbow, the soft skin where his forearm and upper arm join. "I wish I could stay like this all day, but" —I reach out, tapping the face of my phone where it lies on the nightstand— "we've overslept. By a lot. And I need to start the trial run for the bake-off."

Reluctantly, I roll away from Brady and stand. I look down at him and use all my strength and willpower to fight the urge to jump back in bed. A body in motion stays in motion, so I keep going. First to my dresser, where I slip on shorts, and then to my closet, where I choose a shirt that has a neon rainbow on the front of it.

"I was hoping you'd change your mind," Brady grumbles. I look at him in the mirror above the dresser.

He's sitting up, the sheet bunching around his midsection. I know from our close proximity a few minutes ago that he's naked.

Turning around, I lean a hip against the edge of the dresser. Right now, it's best to keep my distance. If I walk any closer to him, even to swiftly peck his cheek, I'll be a goner, like an insect perched on a carnivorous plant.

Unlike those insects, I absolutely want to be devoured. Which is why I have to keep my distance. I tell this all to Brady, and the smugness that crosses his face is endearing, not annoying.

"Do you promise to let me devour you later?" He gets out of bed and tugs on his clothes from last night.

"Pinky promise," I tell him, holding out my pinky from my spot beside my bedroom door. As soon as his shirt is fully on his body, I open it. I'm much more likely to follow through with my plans if it's open.

Brady winds his pinky around mine, using the union to

pull me in. He kisses me, bites gently on my lower lip, and backs off. He's teasing me.

"I know what you're doing." I step around him and start down the hall.

"Good." Brady smacks my butt, and I yelp in surprise. When I recover, I do a little shimmy just out of his reach.

"I know what you're doing," he says as we start down the stairs.

"Good," I shoot back, making him smile.

When we get downstairs, I avert my gaze to avoid my grandma's knowing stare. Not Brady though.

"Hi, Louisa," he says cheerfully. "Lovely day."

I peer out the windows, where a light rain tumbles lazily to the earth.

"Addison needed help hanging a picture in her room," Brady continues. A smile curls up one side of his mouth and his eyes twinkle.

"Bah." Grandma throws back her head. "I told you last night I know what you two have been up to." She shakes her head. "I swear, it's like every generation thinks they invented sex. How do you think everyone else in the world got here?"

Brady and I break into a fit of laughter and Grandma rolls her eyes at us on her way to whatever it is she's doing.

"Wish me luck baking today?" I squeeze Brady around the middle.

"Do you need luck for a trial run?"

"I'll take luck any day, for anything."

Brady crosses his fingers.

"Thank you." I rise on tiptoe to kiss his cheek. "After I'm finished, I'm going to take it all to Charlie's book club meeting this afternoon. Do you want me to make dinner tonight?"

"I thought you were my dinner," Brady's whisper is more of a growl in my ear.

"I'll be dessert." I wink at him and take a step back. My bedroom isn't that far away, and I need to start baking.

With a lingering look, Brady leaves the kitchen. I wait until I hear the door close, then I go to the pantry and begin assembling ingredients.

"YOU'RE OFFICIALLY THE MOST WELL-LIKED PERSON IN THIS place," Amanda announces, leaning in and grabbing a blondie. I've just removed the cover from the plastic container, amid the watchful gazes of twelve women ready for a sugar onslaught.

I move away to make room for more hands to reach in. In a matter of thirty seconds, the mound of goodies has dwindled by half.

Appreciative moans surround me.

"No offense, but my thighs hope you don't win," says a woman I haven't met yet. She takes another bite of the lemon cupcake.

Through a mouthful of blueberry muffin, Charlie says loudly, "I hope you win, Addison."

"Of course, of course," the other woman rushes to say. She looks flustered. "I didn't mean I don't want you to win. I only meant..."

I stop her with a hand on her arm. "It's okay. I know what you meant."

She smiles at me gratefully.

The book club meeting begins. I haven't read the book, but based on the discussion I might have to. Of course, if I don't leave soon, they're going to ruin it for me.

"Can you even imagine losing your best friend like that?" An older woman with a chic white bob clutches her chest.

"No," Charlie answers, shaking her head. Her eyes fill with tears. "The portrayal of grief in this book was so raw, so stark, I felt like I was the one grieving. I went through at least one box of tissues and had to open a second."

"That's because you're pregnant," I joke, helping myself to a cupcake. Quality control.

A chorus of rebuttals rings out around me. I raise my eyebrows.

"Read it and try not to cry." Amanda tosses her copy on my lap. I pick it up and look it over. The cover shows a worn dog tag, just above the author's name. *Kate Masters.* "Military?"

"Yes, and based on a true story. It's sad, but it's so much more than that. Just trust us."

"Oh-kay." I slip the book into my bag. "Ladies, I'm going to leave you to your meeting."

I spend a minute transferring the desserts to a bed of napkins and put the container in the bag alongside my new book. I bend to plant a kiss on Charlie's cheek, wave goodbye to the other women, and duck out of the coffee shop where their monthly meetings are held.

I told Brady I would make dinner for him tonight, but maybe it would be more fun if I taught him how to cook something.

Hmm. It'll have to be something basic. Then again, he taught himself how to bake. Sort of. He said he watched me and then found a few good tutorials on the internet. Something tells me he's a quick study.

On Fridays in the summer, a cute outdoor market stays open until six. I'll swing by there and grab some things for tonight. We'll start easy with pasta. A light sauce, a bunch of roasted veggies. Pre-made noodles so as not to complicate things.

The market is a collection of white topped tents and folding tables, people selling their wares. I choose organic summer squash, one green and one yellow, an orange bell pepper, and cherry tomatoes. Very colorful. I also pick up an orange blackberry jam with the idea of making thumbprint cookies. My next stop is for Sancerre. Pasta like the one we're making tonight needs a light, crisp, but not sweet wine. Sancerre will be perfect.

A memory invades my brain. A cool Chicago evening, the leaves on the trees just beginning to turn. I'm walking to my apartment from Whole Foods, carrying dinner and wine, to be enjoyed alone because Warren's state had been determined by then. I glanced down to admire my new shoes. I splurged on them. Being a baker means always wearing sensible, flat shoes. I gazed lovingly at the pointed-toe black Jimmy Choo's. I felt a pang knowing they didn't really belong to me; every month, until I paid them off, I would only own a fraction of them.

My lustful gazing at my footwear kept me from looking where I was going. I tripped, reaching out for something to hold on to, but there was nothing there in the middle of the sidewalk. I hit the ground hard, my knees bearing the brunt of it. They were a scraped mess, blood oozing onto the pavement. The wine bottle had broken, and cabernet spilled out. I watched it stream toward me, the burgundy color mixing with the bright red of my blood. People rushed over. The wine spill made it look far worse than it was. Someone handed me a napkin, and I wiped my knees. By then they'd already stopped bleeding. I'd thanked everyone around me and done my best to dispose of the broken wine bottle. The embarrassment stung more than my scraped knees. As I took my first steps away from the unfortunate incident, I saw a swish of icy blonde hair up ahead. Not many people have hair the color of a Frozen princess, but I knew one person: Warren's sister, Shannon. She walked quickly in the opposite direction, and just when I thought maybe she didn't see my fall, she glanced surreptitiously over her shoulder. Right into my eyes. She stopped, turning around and plastering a smile on her face. As she approached, she pretended to be shocked to see the angry red of my knees. I played her game, recounting the story, and she responded as if she had no idea what occurred.

It's an unpleasant memory, one I'd rather forget. I wiggle my shoulders, as if I can wring it from me like a wet towel. Warren, and his family, are gone from my life.

I put the memory out of my mind and make the rounds to each tent, hoping to come across someone with homemade pasta. I'll even settle for the dried variety, if it will mean not having to run to the grocery store.

I get excited when I find I'm in luck. And freshly made, to boot. I choose a fettuccini. I need a noodle big enough to hold up the veggies.

It happens when I reach for the bag, taking it in my grasp and smiling my thanks at the owner/pasta maker. The white-blonde flash of hair catches my eye in the twelve inches of space between tents, then it's gone.

Shannon? No.

There's no way she's here. Why would she be? Other people have that hair color too. Despite all the rationalizations, my pace speeds up. I dodge a double stroller and almost trip over the toddler walking beside it. I wasn't expecting him. Shouldn't he be *in* the stroller?

I make it around the corner and turn into the next row of tents, where I saw that hair, but now I don't see it anywhere.

A sigh slips from my lips. It was just a memory coming to life, feeling real, like when I was a kid and swore up and down a clown lived in my closet.

It didn't, of course, nor did I see hair that belongs on Shannon's head.

Ugh.

Fishing through my bag, I find the wine and inspect the top, hoping it's a twist-off. It's not.

A few yards away, a vendor sells popcorn. That'll do.

I order buttered popcorn and a cold bottle of water, then go to a bench and sit down. My frazzled nerves are slowly eking out, drop by drop.

I shake my head and let out a soft, disbelieving laugh. That was wild. I hope nothing like that happens again for a long time. It's bad enough tha—

"Hi, Addison."

I shoot from my seat, upending my popcorn, and whip around. My breath slams up my throat, choking me.

Tall. Thin. Too thin.

"How...I..." A sob mixes with a word, incoherent. I step into him, wrap my arms around his neck, and I'm careful, so careful, because he looks frail.

"Warren." His name is a whisper, a question, a statement, a *how the hell are you here*.

"Addison." My name is a reverence on his lips, but his voice is wrong. The baritone is scratched, like a cat reached into his throat and clawed him. Something else is missing, too, something so essential. *His smell.* Where is the spicy cologne, the scent of freshly washed clothing? Warren had been meticulous in his appearance. This is my Warren, *but it's not.*

White-blonde hair shimmers. Shannon stands a few feet away. The tips of her mouth turn down.

I pull back to look at him, open my mouth to ask how this all happened, but he silences me. His lips come down on mine, and suddenly he's Warren again. The pressure, the feel, down to the scruff of his chin scratching my own. His kisses always had a cadence, long at first, followed by two shorter pecks.

He might look and sound different, but this kiss is like every kiss we shared. As if he'd never fallen into a dreamlike slumber, as if the past year never happened.

My heart, stitched together only recently, breaks again.

Brady.

24

BRADY

"Brady, you have a package up here." Louisa's voice comes through my cell phone.

Confusion causes the corners of my mouth to turn down. I didn't order anything.

"Who's it from?" I ask, pulling on pants. I've just showered and the only thing I was wearing when she called was my underwear.

"I can't look right now. I left it on the table near the front door. Just come up here."

Louisa's voice has an eager intonation. It makes my confused frown deepen.

"Be up in a few," I tell her. I pull on a shirt and run a towel through my hair one more time. It's longer than usual and holds more water than I'm used to. After I've brushed it into my typical side part, I slide my feet into my shoes and head for the main house.

I use the short walk to guess what the 'package' could be.

Maybe my mother sent me something, but who knows what. She's not the cookie baking, care package type.

Maybe it's Addison, naked save for a pale pink ribbon tied around her neck. No matter how much I'd love for it to be the latter, it's obviously not. Louisa wouldn't be the one calling me.

Before I can come up with any other possible and improbable scenarios, I'm pulling open the back door and stepping into the house.

"Louisa?" I call, walking through the informal dining room and rounding the corner.

"Holy shit!" I stop short.

My 'package' isn't on the table. It's *standing* by the table. And there are two.

"Surprise!" Lennon yells, flinging open her arms and giving a couple small, excited hops on her toes.

My eyes zero in on her stomach. I can't help it. Her bump is small, probably missed by the casual observer, but to me, it might as well be a flashing beacon. Lennon is pregnant, and even though I already knew it, seeing it in person makes it real.

My shock at seeing the swell of her stomach is covered up by the even greater shock that they are in the living room of Sweet Escape. "What the hell?" I ask, dumbfounded, and step into a hug with both of them.

Lennon laughs. "We wanted to see what you had going on up here in Lonesome."

We're still hugging, so she can't see my eyebrows pinch together. There isn't a soul in this room, including her own, who believes her. She wanted to meet Addison and check on me.

I take a step back and look at Finn.

He shrugs and tucks his hands into his pockets. "What she said."

So whipped. He always has been.

"You came all this way to see what was going on in Lonesome?"

She averts her gaze and crosses her arms, knowing her motives have been brought to light but unwilling to admit it. While she surveys the living room, she asks, "Why don't you show us your cabin? And the town?"

I smirk. "And Addison?"

Lennon groans. "Fine, yes. And Addison."

"She's jealous," Finn quips, grinning. He thinks it's funny. He's so secure in her love for him that he doesn't care if she's jealous of Addison.

"I am not," Lennon argues. She meets my eyes. "Okay, fine, I am. And it's weird. I just want to make sure she's good for you. You're on the rebound, and..." Her chin dips to her chest, one hand fidgets with her earring. "It's my fault. I needed to see that you're okay. You're my best friend."

She steps into a hug with only me, wrapping her arms around my middle. Her frame is still so small in my arms, and she smells like she always has. But, unlike all of our hugs since we were old enough to be interested in the opposite sex, this one feels different. I'm not holding her and wishing for more. This is a hug between old friends. Yes, I still love her, but I'm no longer in love with her.

I didn't think I needed the confirmation, but now I'm glad I have it. My whole heart is pointed in Addison's direction, and there will be no second-guessing.

"Come here, baby," Finn says in a kind and slightly possessive voice I've never heard him use, something I'm guessing is usually reserved for when they're alone together. He pulls her from me and into him. Their embrace is different. Her arms are around his neck, her whole body molds to his.

Above her head, he mouths, "Emotional," his eyes rolling upward.

"I know what you just said." Her voice is muffled against his chest.

He chuckles, and her head bobs with the movement.

Before Finn can get himself in any more trouble with Lennon, I invite them to see my place. They follow me through the house, and I realize Louisa didn't come out to chat. She must be somewhere nearby, giving us privacy but most definitely in hearing distance. I'm sure she was curious about my visitors.

I point out the kitchen and tell them about Addison's baking and the competition, explaining that she's in town delivering the trial-run baked goods to friends.

Finn spends time looking over the main house and then my cabin. He says he's collecting ideas for their place.

"I thought you were finished," I tell him after I've completed the tour and we're standing on the little porch in front of my place.

"I think it'll always be a work-in-progress. I keep seeing things I want to add or change."

Lennon steps onto the porch, late to join us because she'd needed to use the bathroom. Something about the baby being parked on her bladder.

"Brady, you'll have to come out and see the baby. Maybe when he's born you can visit us?" Hope makes Lennon's eyebrows lift higher on her forehead.

"Of course I will. Can't keep me from my godson."

Lennon makes an annoyed noise, her narrowed gaze flying at Finn. "You asked him without me?"

His palms lift in defense. "Nope. Brady guessed." He gives me a look, asking for corroboration.

"He didn't say anything," I vow, backing up Finn. "Who else would it be?"

"Oh. Okay." Lennon looks disappointed. She'd wanted to ask me. She gazes out across the small yard and into the trees.

Behind her, Finn mouths the word *emotional* again, and this time Lennon doesn't notice.

My lips purse together to keep my laughter silent. Reaching into my pocket, I jingle my car keys. "You guys want to head into town? I can show you some places and maybe find Addison?"

"Yes!" Lennon exclaims, clapping her hands together twice. She leads the charge down the steps and back across the yard. Finn and I follow.

The three of us, back together. It feels good, but now there's a missing spot where Addison should be.

Hopefully we'll see her in town, and that spot will be filled.

"You bought a truck?" Lennon eyes the vehicle. "I guess you're staying here awhile?"

"I bought it a couple weeks ago because I wanted a way to get around, and I was planning on giving it to the owner of Sweet Escape when I left, but now..." My sentence trails off, but my meaning is loud and clear. Addison has changed everything for me.

Lennon pokes my side before climbing into the back seat. "Brady's in lo-ove," she sing-songs.

I nod, pulling my lower lip between my teeth and biting down. "That I am, guys." Going around the front of the truck, I get in the driver's seat and Finn gets in the passenger seat.

Lennon meets my eyes in the rearview mirror. She is happy for me, truly happy, and seeing me move on eases her guilt. She doesn't need to verbalize any of this. Communicating without talking has always existed between us, and I'm pleased to see it still does, at least for now. Someday, it will probably wane. She'll become a mother and a wife, I'll become a father and a husband, and what we once shared will have to fade so we can nurture our new roles. But we'll always be best friends. Always.

Suddenly I'm relieved and overjoyed Lennon and Finn decided to surprise me. I needed their visit, even though I didn't know it. I needed to know that I could do it, that I could move on without reservation.

I put the truck in drive and head into town. I'm ready to find Addison. Ready to pull her into me and show her off to my best friends. They're going to love her. How could anybody not?

I point things out to them as we drive through town. The grocery store where I helped Paul's dad. The bakery I'm certain will soon be Addison's.

"And that place," I say with a note of pride at Finn, pointing at the bar. "Is where I finally put your punching lesson into practice. I knocked a guy out who wouldn't leave Addison alone."

Finn laughs and lightly shoves my shoulder. Lennon, who I thought wouldn't like that story, grins. "Classic Brady. Defending the honor of a lady."

"Always," I declare, pretending to bow as much as I can with the steering wheel in my way.

"Ohhh, what's that?" Lennon asks excitedly. Her hand reaches into the front seat, pointing ahead.

"An outdoor market, I think." I haven't seen it before, but I'm guessing based on the white tents lined up in rows.

Lennon taps my shoulder. "Can we stop? An outdoor market in the summertime sounds so picturesque."

I get what she means. In Agua Mesa, markets are held in the late fall and spring. Nobody wants to shop or sell outdoors in the intense heat of an Arizona summer.

Without answering her, I pull into the next parking space I find.

Finn offers Lennon his hand, helping her out of the truck, and she rewards him with a big kiss. We walk around the market, and Lennon picks out a few things. Finn reminds her they'll have to take it back in their carry-on, and she pats her belly and cheerfully tells him the homemade jam and freshly baked bread will probably be eaten long before their return flight.

He kisses her in this sweet way that is completely appropriate, but I get the sense they're sharing something deeply personal. I look away.

What the fuck?

A fist sails into my gut. Not a fist made of flesh and bone, but one of anguish and sorrow, burrowing deep into my core. The fist climbs north, grabbing ahold of my heart.

"Brady, what's wrong?" Lennon's concerned voice sounds far away, at the end of a tunnel.

I am in the tunnel too, unable to see anything but what's happening ten yards away.

Addison, in the arms of another man.

His lips pressed firmly to hers.

Her hands, hanging limply at her sides, rise, palming the man's chest.

And I know, I don't know how, but I do, I know this is

Warren. Somehow, some way, he came back from the near-dead. He has come for his fiancée.

Beside them, a woman with hair so blonde it's nearly white, eyes me. She takes in my expression, whatever it is I don't know because I can't get a firm grasp on the hundreds of emotions flying around inside me right now, and then she smiles.

She fucking smiles.

Like a victor.

I know what I've lost, but what has she won?

"BRADY." LENNON'S VOICE POKES THROUGH MY JUMBLED thoughts. "Was that... Addison?" I hear in her voice how much she doesn't want to be right.

I say nothing, which probably confirms her suspicion. She and Finn follow along behind me as I make my way back through the tents. How happy, how carefree, how blind I was when we walked through here only minutes ago.

We're silent on the drive back to Sweet Escape. I leave Finn and Lennon in the truck, slipping around the side of the main house to avoid Louisa.

Twenty minutes later, I emerge from cabin seven. My duffle bag is heavy on my shoulder, and my suitcase catches on the thick grass.

When I reach my truck, I toss both in the bed, beside Finn and Lennon's luggage.

I guess it's still just the three of us after all.

25

ADDISON

I PUSH AWAY FROM HIM. GENTLY, THOUGH. SO CAREFULLY. I don't want to hurt him. Physically, or emotionally.

Warren cups my cheek, stares into my eyes.

It is his gaze, the one I fell in love with. But it's all wrong.

I'm looking into brown eyes, and longing for blue.

"Warren, I—"

"Addy!"

Shannon wraps me in a hug, and I can taste her fraudulent friendliness. Because we're in front of Warren, I play nice. And also, I'm too shocked to form an intelligent argument against her, to do anything except go along with her.

She looks smug, and I don't know why. A moment ago she looked upon Warren and I with disapproval.

Warren sways, blinking hard and slow a few times, and Shannon jumps into action, leading him to the bench I'd been on when I saw him. I follow, my shoes crunching the popcorn that fell to the ground when my whole world was upended by the mother of all surprises.

Shannon helps Warren sit, and I sink down beside him. She frowns at me for taking the place she was going to sit in but recovers before Warren can notice, hovering over him instead. "Are you okay? Do you need to rest?"

She reminds me of a curly-winged gnat. No matter how many times you shoo it away, it won't leave you the fuck alone.

"Shannon?" Warren asks, looking at her. His expression is appreciative, but it also says she's worn out her welcome for the time being. "Can I get some time alone with Addison?"

"Of course," she murmurs.

Over his head she gives me a hostile look, acid covered in sugar, before turning on her heel and disappearing behind a row of tents.

"She means well," Warren comments, looking after her. "She's suffocating though." He grabs for his throat with both hands, miming his words.

When I don't crack a smile, he waves a hand at the sky. "The weather is nice."

I'm not interested in small talk, though it seems Warren is. I know this is hard for him, probably more than I realize.

But guess what? This is an out-of-body experience for me too. Chatting about the weather isn't going to cut it right now.

"Warren, how are you here?" I angle my body toward him, my knee propped on the bench and my arms draped along the back. I can't believe it's his face I'm seeing right now. He dominated my thoughts for so long.

He turns to me, and his skinny face swells before my eyes. Love, desire, longing, they fill the hollows in his skin formed by months of inactivity. "I woke up," he says simply, as if there is no more explanation than that.

"Right," I say slowly, nodding, understanding his answer but still not absorbing it. "But, how? And when?"

His head travels slowly back and forth, as if the answers elude even him. "I don't know how I woke up. I just did. I opened my eyes, and I was in this room I'd never seen before. It was white with—"

"Watercolor paintings of flowers," I say, remembering all the hours I spent sitting in a chair beside a sleeping Warren.

"Yes," he breathes, reaching for my free hand. He intertwines his fingers through mine, and I stare down in amazement. This is Warren's hand. *Warren's.*

"I woke up alone," he continues. "I was frightened. And confused. I'd had so many dreams, and I wasn't sure if I was still in one. Then a nurse walked in, and she didn't notice at first. She was nearly to my bed when she looked at my face."

His lips curl into a smile as he remembers. "She shrieked. She dropped whatever she was holding and ran from the room. Then there were so many people in the room I thought there was no way another person could fit. Only a couple were doing anything useful; the rest just wanted to see me. And I still didn't know what it was they were looking at. I wondered if I was disfigured."

My heart lurches, picturing the curious and astonished gazes. It must have been terrifying.

"The doctor explained to me that I'd been in a coma for about ten months and—"

My hand flies to my mouth. "I left only days before the ten-month mark." Shannon's phone call, when she'd asked for Warren's concert shirts... He'd been awake then.

Warren's fingers tighten around mine. "I'm not mad at you for giving up. I was told someone in my position should have been a lost cause." An empty chuckle rises from his chest. "They call me a miracle."

"I'd call it miraculous." I want to ask him what his family

told him, if he knows about the bakery, but now isn't the time. "Do you remember the stroke?"

He shakes his head.

I don't know what else to say. What does someone talk about with their ex-fiancé who was in a coma and now is not? Politics? The rate of global warming? The new giraffe born at the zoo?

A burning sensation starts behind my eyes. This is all too much.

Warren sees the tears starting. They haven't even tipped over onto my cheeks yet, but he is there, ready to cradle me, banish the tears the way he always did when I came home upset. To *our* home. The one I rented out. The one currently occupied by someone else.

My hands touch Warren's back as he holds me, and I feel the jutting shoulder bones, my fingers *bump, bump, bumping* over the backside of his ribs. His atrophied muscles will regain their strength, the fibers regrowing and binding into the sinew he stood in front of the bathroom mirror and flexed when I was nearby. I'd once told him that his back muscles were a turn-on, and it was all the encouragement he needed. He had no qualms using against me the ammunition I'd handed him.

"I'm here now, Addy love. We'll get through this together."

I stiffen at the nickname. Months ago, I'd wished he would wake up and call me that. Prayed for it.

I pull away, replacing my hands in my lap. "Warren, you should know that—"

Warren stops me with a shake of his head. "Whatever you did while I was out, it's okay. These last ten months are like a black hole. For me, and for you. For us."

He takes my left hand, raising it to his lips and kissing

the space where my engagement ring should be. He swallows hard and looks into my eyes, his gaze intense, deep and penetrating. I know Warren, and this is how I know he is about to deliver a speech he practiced the whole flight here. "I love you, Addison. I woke up as in love with you as I was the last night I went to sleep in our bed. I know you've been working to move on since you were told I was a hopeless case, but I'm right here, and I'm going to get us back to where we were. I'm going to put that ring back on your finger, maybe not today, but soon. When you're ready for it. You're going to fall in love with me again."

I stare, caught, his words slipping into me.

Tell him about Brady.

I should tell him how Brady makes my heart soar, how he breathed life into me when my oxygen supply was low. Tell him about what it feels like to be loved by Brady, like being in a misty rain, the vapor settling gently onto my skin. Soft and cool, all-encompassing and refreshing.

I should tell Warren it's not as simple as he thinks, that his return doesn't come with a broom, sweeping away the detritus of the life that went on while he slept. His well-meaning declarations can't polish us, make us shine once again.

I look into his eyes, knowing he deserves only the truth.

But then I see the small crescent-shaped scar on his hairline, the one he got when he lifted me on his shoulders at a concert and I got scared and gripped his head, my pinky nail digging into him.

And I lie.

"We've checked in at the hotel down the street." Shannon shades her eyes from the sun with one hand and points with the other.

She rejoined Warren and I not too long after I opened my mouth and said, "Okay."

Okay.

Okay, you can try to make me fall in love with you again.

Okay, you can put that ring back on my finger someday.

Okay, I'll give you hope, even when I'm in love with another man.

Shitty. I'm a shitty person.

"That's nice," I tell Shannon, unsure of what to say in response to the hotel.

I glance down at my watch, groan internally when I see the time. It's late, and I promised Brady we'd have dinner together. And now, alongside the pasta, I'll be serving a heaping portion of shock. "I'm sorry, I have to go home." I don't say more. It's another lie. One by omission, this time.

Shannon turns to Warren. "Would you mind going to the hotel and booking us a table for an hour from now? The man at check-in said they fill up early."

Warren gives her a look. "Try being a little more obvious, Shannon." Despite this, he listens to her. He kisses my cheek, his hand running the length of my forearm as he leans in.

I offer him a smile and watch as he goes. I wonder how long it will take him to gain back all his weight?

"So?" I tilt my head, waiting for Shannon to start with whatever it is she sent Warren away to say.

"Does Warren know you've moved on with someone else?"

I stare hard at her, my arms crossing in front of myself, as if I can block myself from the indignation I feel wafting off her. I don't know how she knows about Brady, but I'm not going to bother asking.

My chin lifts an inch. "I haven't told him yet."

Her mouth curls into a hateful smile. "Don't worry, the guy you moved on with already knows about Warren."

My hands, limp at my sides, flex into fists. "How would you know that? Did you tell him? How do you even know who he is?"

"I didn't tell him anything. He saw for himself."

It's not the answer I was expecting. "What do you mean?"

I hate the satisfaction on her face, the curve of her smile. "It was earlier, right after you saw Warren. A man was standing nearby with a guy and girl—"

Relief washes through me. I shake my head, certain. "Whoever you saw, it wasn't the guy I'm dating." Brady has two male friends in Lonesome, and so far that's it.

Shannon cocks an eyebrow. "She was" —her hand hovers a couple inches off her flat stomach— "maybe four months pregnant. Barely showing. And it was definitely your guy. I noticed him, because who wouldn't? Tall, dark hair, muscles and a face like that?" She laughs. "You clearly have a type. Anyway, I was watching him when he turned and saw you. You didn't see him because you were too busy getting reacquainted with my brother's lips."

"Nooo," I mutter, my voice low and guttural.

"Yesss," Shannon purrs. "If Warren's return presented a problem for you, then I think you managed to solve it all on your own."

"I have to go." I grab my purse and shopping bag from the bench and jog away, not waiting for Shannon's response. By the time I get to Grandma's Jeep, my hairline is sweaty.

The wind from the drive home dries the sweat. I park the Jeep, skipping the house and going straight to cabin seven.

I knock once. Twice. Three times.

No answer.

From my purse I find the list I used to shop yesterday, and I tear it in half. Grabbing a pen, I write a note to Brady.

It's not what you think. I love you.

I slip it in the crack between the door and the doorframe. Before I go, I lay a palm on the door and bow my head, saying a quick prayer.

On my way to the main house I check my phone, hoping for something, *anything*, even an angry voicemail, but there's nothing. I call him twice, but it rings and rings and then voicemail picks up.

I don't know what to do. I guess I'll start with dinner.

My grandma comes into the kitchen just as I'm taking the ingredients from the bag. I stop what I'm doing and fold myself into her.

"Addison?" she asks, patting my back.

"I think I may have ruined it." My voice is muffled by her shoulder.

"Ruined what, honey?"

"Things with Brady."

"Addy, disagreements are normal. Now you get to make up." She pulls back and winks at me. "That's the fun part."

I shake my head, tears brimming. "This is much more than a disagreement. Warren is here, Grandma. He woke up."

Her fingers touch her lips in surprise, blocking her gasp. "Oh shit."

She leads me to the island and pulls out two stools. "Sit," she instructs. "Tell me everything."

I fill her in on every detail, and she stays quiet, nodding the whole time. When I'm done, she says, "I don't envy you."

I laugh, an empty, dry sound.

"Do you still love Warren?"

This is what I've been wrestling with. Before Warren, I didn't have any consequential exes. I never had to run into them and remember the good times, the little things that made them special in the first place. Are glasses always tinted rose when you look back on a relationship that ended because of circumstances?

The truth is, I do love Warren.

But I don't love him the right way, not anymore.

I don't answer my grandma, and she doesn't press me. "Are you making dinner?" she inclines her head at the uncooked pasta on the counter.

I stand. "I was supposed to cook for Brady. I was going to start teaching him."

"Brady's a good man, Addy. He's not going to run away. He'll confront you. You'll tell him your side. It will all work out."

I think back to the first few days Brady was here at Sweet Escape, how broken he was over Lennon. Over the girl who didn't choose him.

I want every one of your kisses and sighs and irritated looks. I want to love you loudly. I want to love you messy. Brady's words from two nights ago.

I can only hope he meant it when he said messy, because this is the very definition. He couldn't possibly even know it was Warren who was kissing me. At this point, Brady thinks I was cheating on him, right after he told me he loves me.

I set to work making the sauce, but the smells of garlic and oil make me nauseous instead of hungry. Grandma leaves the kitchen, but she's back a minute later, keys jingling in her outstretched hand.

"What's that?" I ask, her wide eyes scaring me. I can't take any more right now.

"The keys to cabin seven."

My lower lip quivers. She uncurls her fingers and I slip the keyring from around her pointer finger.

I don't run to his cabin, because I'm terrified of what I might find.

Nothing.

No sweatshirt hung over a chair.

No toiletries on the counter in his bathroom.

No clothes in his dresser, shoes lined up in the small closet, or his suitcase stashed away.

I arrive at cabin seven and let myself in, and the only thing I find is that I was right.

He's gone.

My steps are slow and heavy. I'm almost out the door when I see a folded piece of paper on the ground. Hope flurries through my heart, a dash of excitement. A note from Brady! *He knew I'd get the key, that I'd come here looking for him.* I bend, snatching it from the floor, and open it.

My hope crashes to my feet. It's the note I left when I came here the first time, without a key to let me in. I tuck it into my back pocket and lock the cabin behind me.

When I get back to the main house, Grandma is stirring the sauce I'd left behind on the stove. Hope is evident on her face, too.

Hope. Such a dangerous thing. I know that by now.

I shake my head, and her face falls.

"He's gone." My voice is jagged. I blink back my tears, taking over for my grandma at the stove. I stare into the sauce, my wooden spoon cutting a path through the thickening cream. I'm saving my tears for later, for when I'm in the shower and I can scream silently.

Grandma leaves the kitchen, sensing my desire to be alone. When there's a knock at the front door, nobody but me is around to get it. I dump my noodles into the boiling water, droplets sailing over the side and sizzling on the cook top. I rush out of the kitchen, smoothing my hair and wiping beneath my eyes.

"I'm coming," I yell, before Brady can lose his nerve and leave.

Here it is again. *Hope.*

I pull open the door, my lips poised to proclaim *It's not what you think.*

"Hi," I say awkwardly, rearranging the shape of my mouth.

Warren smiles nervously, and I see it on his face too. *Hope.*

26

BRADY

My phone lights up. Addison's name flashes across the screen.

"Are you ever going to answer it, Brady?" Lennon gives me a look that tells me just what she thinks I should do.

The pad of my thumb swipes over my lower lip as I study her name, then the screen goes dark. "At some point, yes. Just not yet." I need to hear Addison out, but the truth is that I'm afraid of what she'll have to say.

Lennon turns back to her book, and I know she's swallowing her opinion.

I tossed and turned all night, thinking about what I saw in the market yesterday, and I think I've figured it out.

I've gotten myself into another situation where nothing is fair. It wasn't fair to Lennon that both her best friends were in love with her, and it's not fair to Addison that her comatose ex-fiancé woke up and came for her right after she fell in love with me.

It stuns me how unfair life can be. How it trucks along, wreaking havoc, unapologetic about its wrath. I thought Addison and I had a good thing, two broken hearts coming together and mending one another, but no. It appears there's just more heartache for me. Life is starting to feel like a pie-eating contest, where the only prize is more pie.

I blow out an irritated breath and stand. "I'm going to the lobby to grab a newspaper."

Lennon looks up at me. Her legs are curled beneath her on the couch. "Grab me one of those cookies they keep near the coffee?"

I nod, a small smile turning my lips upward. Lennon's never been shy about her appetite, but she has been eating like a linebacker since they arrived.

I slip out the door and take the elevator down. I was lucky yesterday when the hotel where Finn and Lennon are staying had a room available on their floor.

The lobby has three newspapers, and I choose one and sit down. Finn went out to get lunch for the three of us, and Lennon's reading her book. I might as well sit down here and page through this newspaper.

Plus, I'm sulking.

I take my paper to the far corner of the lobby, to a place where there are three chairs and zero people. I start with the sports section, move on to world news, and then the front page stories. People have been coming and going through the lobby, but as far as I can tell nobody pays me any mind. It takes a full half hour for anybody to sit down in one of the nearby chairs.

I finish my article, glancing up as I turn the page. My gaze stills, locked on the guy reading a different paper. He glances over; he must've felt me staring.

He dips his chin, his gaze returning to his paper. It's an acknowledgment and also a polite instruction not to talk to him. Normally I'm all for leaving strangers alone, especially ones who are reading.

But this guy happens to be the guy I saw kissing my girlfriend yesterday.

Tossing the paper aside, I lean forward and extend a hand. A false show of civility. When he reluctantly places his hand in mine, it's all I can do to keep from tightening my grip.

"Warren?" I say his name like it's a question, even though my instincts told me who he was yesterday, and they're screaming the same today.

He eyes me warily. "Yes. Do I know you?"

I take my hand back, straightening my shoulders. "Brady Sterling. I'm Addison's boyfriend." It's a liberty I feel like taking. We hadn't gotten around to discussing titles, but saying I love you catapults us past the conversation where we determine the relationship.

Warren laughs, shaking his head disbelievingly. "Okay, buddy."

I feel bad for the guy, I do. But not that bad. "Addison and I are dating. And I get that you've come back here for her. I'm guessing you're a medical miracle, right?" I rush forward, not letting him answer. "And I'm happy for you. I'm sure you're a celebrity in the field of science."

"I woke up thinking I had a fiancée," he hisses, stabbing a finger at the ground.

"It's a shitty situation. And we're all in it, not just you. You could've called Addison, but you didn't. You came here because you knew what it would do to her to see you. You hoped that would work in your favor. You preyed on her kind nature."

His chest puffs up, but his shirt hangs off him and it doesn't have the intended effect. It's not his fault. What happened to this guy was awful.

"She's my fiancée. Mine." He smacks his chest to emphasize the word. "And I'm not above using any advantages I may have."

I stand, tossing my paper onto the seat. "Have you asked Addison what she wants? Or did you just use her guilt to coerce her?"

If Warren responds, I don't hear it. I don't get more than a few feet away when I see Finn standing nearby, bags of takeout dangling from his hands.

"The ex?" he asks, giving Warren a hard stare over my shoulder. That's what best friends do. They're on your side when they don't even know who they're opposing.

I nod, reaching the place where Finn stood watching. We head to the elevator.

"I feel for him. His situation is shit." Reaching out, I press the button for our floor. The doors open, and we step on. When nobody else gets on and the doors close, I look at Finn. "But I wish he hadn't woken up. That's awful, isn't it? What a terrible thought." I glance up at the ceiling of the elevator, decorated in metallic swirls.

"It doesn't make you a bad person, Brady. It makes you human."

"Since when have I wished ill on someone? Is this what love does? Makes you capable of things you're otherwise unable to fathom?"

"Yes," Finn answers, and the hard way he says it makes me stare at him, but he doesn't look at me. "Do you want to mix a sleeping pill into his drink and put him on a train to Chicago?"

I chuckle. "Something like that."

The elevator stops on our floor, the doors open and Finn steps off first, pausing to look back at me. "It's okay to love someone so much you'd do anything for them."

The doors begin to close but Finn's foot shoots out, halting them. They slide open again and I step off.

"I'm glad she has you." I clap him on the back.

I mean it. Lennon has someone who loves her so much he'd do anything for her.

And so does Addison.

In fact, it sounds like she may have *two*.

27

ADDISON

I KNEW LETTING WARREN STAY FOR DINNER LAST NIGHT WAS A bad idea. But what was I supposed to do? He stood there on my doorstep, his expression as optimistic as a dog when its owner reaches for its leash. And he brought flowers. My favorite, of course, because he woke up in love with me, still remembering my preference for roses even if they are cliché. He'd told his sister to eat alone, and come out to Sweet Escape.

I spent the day alternating between calling Brady and busying myself. Call Brady, go for a run. Call Brady, check the amphitheater because *what if he's there?* Call Brady, make lunch. Call Brady, take a nap as restless as my sleep the night before it. He hasn't answered yet. Soon I'll have to resort to text messages to get my side heard. I'd rather be face to face, but beggars can't be choosers. He needs to let me explain what he thinks he saw.

Warren called late-afternoon, asking me to come to his hotel so we could talk. I agreed quickly, ready to tell him about Brady. Hurting Warren's feelings is inevitable, and the longer I allow him to hope, the worse off he will be.

I arrive at the hotel, breathless from running in the rain. The sky opened up as soon as I parked. Thankfully I saw the angry gray sky before I left Sweet Escape and pulled the top up on the Jeep.

I push the hood of my raincoat off my head and shrug it down over my shoulders, hanging it on the coat rack just inside the doors. Repositioning my purse, I look around for Warren. I don't see him, but Shannon catches my eye. She's leaning against a pillar, watching me.

I grumble to myself as I make my way over to her. Why wouldn't she just call out to me when she saw me looking around?

"Warren's this way," she says as I approach, glancing around the lobby. She pivots and beckons me with a hand.

My eyes narrow. What's with the cloak and dagger behavior?

She leads me into one of the hotel's restaurants. It's an upscale place, white linen napkins folded smartly and real china. My jean shorts and damp t-shirt are hardly appropriate attire. Ahead of Shannon, I spot Warren's figure, seated at a table by the glass wall, in full view of half the lobby. It's an odd choice of table. Especially when so many others are available.

Not that it matters. We don't need privacy. Or maybe we do. I'm not sure how this conversation is going to go.

"I see him, Shannon. Thanks." *Beat it, you mean person.*

"Addison, hi." Warren stands as I approach. He brushes a kiss onto my cheek. "You look lovely."

"Warren, I thought you wanted to talk?" I take in his slacks, his collared shirt and dress shoes.

"I do." He gestures at the table. "Can we eat dinner and talk at the same time?"

I sit without answering, letting the action do the

speaking for me. And then I see the table. Pictures of us, printed to look like Polaroids, in various spots around the table, and all pointed in my direction.

I lift up the one of us at the beach on Lake Michigan, studying it. Warren had wrapped his arms around my middle, lifting me. My head is thrown back in laughter. One of his friends snapped the photo.

Around the table, there we are, little pieces of evidence to prove Warren's case. He's fighting so damn hard.

A short candle sits in the center of the table, its flame flickering over the plains of Warren's face. The restaurant lights are turned down low, juxtaposed with the brighter lights of the lobby on the other side of the wall. I feel like an animal on display.

"Do you remember that day?" Warren lightly touches the top of the photo I'm holding.

"Of course." I haven't forgotten any of our days.

A server comes to take our drink order. Warren orders a bottle of wine, one he knows I like. Another piece of evidence. *See how I remember what you like to drink?*

He watches me, silent, as I piece through the other pictures, like taking a shovel to our past. Only right now, I don't have to dig; everything sits on the surface, ready and waiting to be reclaimed.

The server comes back, brandishing the bottle and presenting it to Warren. He waves his hand, expediting the presentation. The server pours my glass, then Warren's.

I take a big drink, an attempt to calm my nerves. I came here to tell Warren about Brady.

Warren reaches across the table, his fingers curling over the top of the palm I've flattened against the starched tablecloth.

"Addison, I—"

I shake my head. "Warren, please. I need to tell you something." The heat of his fingers burns into my skin as he brushes them back and forth across my palm. Taking a deep breath, I say, "I know you said that these past ten months are a black hole for our relationship, that all is forgiven and forgotten. But I have to tell you about someone."

"I met Brady today."

My head flies back as if slapped. "Where?"

Warren glances out to a cluster of chairs off to the side of the lobby, then back to me. "Here. He was reading a paper. I sat down nearby, not knowing who he was. Somehow, he knew who I was. He introduced himself to me."

I squeeze my eyes tight, trying to wrap my brain around what Warren's saying. Questions scurry through my mind, but they aren't the kind I can ask him. *How was Brady? Did he look okay?*

"What else?" I ask, forcing myself to look across the table.

"He told me he understood the predicament we're in, and that he doesn't want to get in the way of two people who belong together. He said he'd bow out."

"Oh," I whisper, my hand coming up to touch my throat, sliding down over my collarbone. I don't know why I'm touching myself, other than to check that this is really happening. I'm really here, learning that Brady gallantly gave me up because he thought he was doing what was best for me.

My lower lip quivers and I bite the skin on the inside, trying to still the quaking. I need something to do with my hands, so I take another big drink.

"Addy love?"

I turn away from Warren, needing to get my bearings before giving him my full attention. I look out into the lobby, toward the people standing at the front desk, and at Brady.

Brady!

He's staring at us. His cheeks grow taut and his eyes look pained as he takes in the scene before him. We lock eyes, and I reach out, my hand bumping into the glass wall. Brady rips his gaze from me and stuffs his hands in his jacket, heading for the front door.

"Brady, no," I yell, pushing away from the table. Dimly I'm aware of the teetering wine glasses.

I hear my name behind me as I hurry from the restaurant, stopping at the spot where Brady stood and looking for him. I glance right and see Warren, still seated at our table. The pain in his eyes is so similar to Brady's. No matter what I do, someone is hurting.

I can't deal with Warren right now, I have to find Brady. He might be willing to bow out, but I'm not willing to let him.

Grabbing my jacket from the coat hook, I thread my arms through, pull my hood over my head, and hurry out into the driving rain.

"A man just came through here," I yell to the valet who stands beneath an awning. "Which way did he go?"

He points right, and I head that way, instinctively ducking my head to keep the rain from pelting my face, but I give up quickly when I realize I can't see.

Come on, Brady, where are you?

I look into shops as I pass them, but come up empty. Finally I see him, only a short distance away, seeking refuge under the purple awning of a coffee shop.

"Brady," I yell, waving my arm. He looks at me, and I see the yearning, the love, the hurt. Is that the face of a man who has decided to bow out?

He waits for me, his eyes on me until I'm standing beside him.

He's quiet, expectant, and now that I'm here, I don't know what to say. Getting to the point is probably best.

"What you saw in the market wasn't what it seemed."

Brady's mouth forms a thin line. "And that romantic dinner for two back there?" He points behind me. "Was that also not what it seemed?"

"No!"

He shakes his head and looks away. "I don't like being lied to, Addison."

"You're not being lied to. Warren asked me to come to the hotel and talk. I was going to tell him about you. He said he doesn't care what I was doing while he was out, but he doesn't know that you're not just some guy keeping my sheets warm. He doesn't know I'm in love with you."

"Do you still love him?"

I hate that I have to think about the answer, but I'm not about to lie to Brady. I open up my mouth to tell him everything I'm feeling, everything I'm confused about, but the despair on Brady's face stops me. To him, my delayed response has answered his question.

His shoulders hunch forward, his hands tuck into his pockets. "I'm not interested in another love triangle, Addison. Been there, done that. Good luck at the baking competition tomorrow." He replaces his hood on his head and runs out into the rain.

"I choose you, Brady. I choose you!" But he's too far away to hear me, the rain acting like a soundproof wall.

I walk back through the rain, and this time my chin falls all the way to my chest.

When I reach the hotel, I don't go inside. I hand my

ticket to the valet, and he runs to retrieve my car. I climb in, my soggy shorts and jacket squishing on the seat. I pause before I shift into drive, tipping my head back against the seat and taking a deep breath.

My eyes shoot open in alarm at the sound of my door opening. I watch, shocked, as a girl climbs into my passenger seat.

"I'm not a driver, I'm sorry. I think you got into the wrong car." I have very little patience or apology for the confused woman.

She looks at me, and although her brown hair is damp from the rain, I know that I've seen her somewhere.

"Are you Addison?" she asks, her eyebrows raised.

I nod, trying to figure out what's going on.

"Then I'm in the right car." She sticks her hand into the space between us. "I'm Lennon."

"Oh shit," is all I can think to say.

She laughs. "*Oh shit* is a pretty good response considering what's happening in your life right now."

A waving arm outside the car catches my eye. It's the valet and he's pointing at a car behind me. I put the Jeep in drive and pull away from the curb. A block away, I find an open space and park.

Turning to Lennon, I say, "You have to know that I love Brady. I didn't know my ex was going to show up here. He was in a coma. For ten months! I'd moved on. And then he shows up, telling me that he's going to fight for us, even if I am seeing somebody else." Lennon waits patiently for me to continue. "He just needs to understand that I'm in love with Brady, that I've moved on and I can't go back."

Lennon runs a hand over her tiny baby bump as she listens to me. I'm not sure she's even aware she's doing it.

"Does Brady know all this?"

"I just saw him." I look down at my soaked clothes. "It's why I look like I swam in a pool fully clothed. I chased him down in the rain. He asked me if I still love Warren and—"

Lennon holds up a hand. "Please tell me you said no."

"I couldn't lie to him. I *do* still love Warren. I love that he's a good person, and that he came here to find me, and I'm so fucking sorry for the situation we're in right now. But I'm not *in* love with Warren, not anymore. And Brady wouldn't let me say that. He ran into the rain and disappeared the moment I tried to explain."

Lennon moves her head slowly from side to side. "Brady is a little, uh" —her lips twist as she searches for the word— "*sensitive* to having competition for another person's love. At least he is right now." A blush warms her cheeks. "That would be my fault. I'm sorry you have to deal with the baggage I created."

I nod. "He said as much."

Lennon eyes me. "You love Brady?"

My chest rises and falls with my deep breath. Thoughts of Brady roll through me. "I love him like crazy, with this weird feeling in my chest where it feels like the contents are greater than the outside. Somehow, I love him more than I loved Warren, even though we haven't known each other very long. I guess when you know, you know."

Lennon's eyebrows raise. "Weren't you engaged to Warren?"

"Yes. And I was in love with him. But the person who was in love with Warren wasn't a person who watched her fiancé fall into a coma, who walked through grief and learned to rely on herself. I'm different now, and it's a different person who loves Brady. He thinks there's a competition and he's refusing to be a part of it, because he's scared he won't be chosen." The heel of my palm smacks the steering wheel in my frustration. "But there is no competition. And he won't listen long enough to let me tell him that."

"Brady needs to feel chosen. Warren's arrival really threw him."

I groan, running a hand over my eyes. "Speaking of competitions, I'm in one tomorrow. A legitimate competition. And the prize is a bakery."

Lennon raises her eyebrows. "Let me know if they want help judging."

Despite the somber air in the car, I chuckle. "Will do."

I back out of the space and turn around in the middle of the street. The rain has let up, but she's pregnant and I'm not going to make her walk. When I pull up to the front of the hotel, Lennon grins.

"I like you, Addison."

She reaches over, hugging me in this small space.

"I was a little jealous of you when Brady told me about everything," I admit. "He loved you first."

Lennon snorts. "Believe me, he loves you way more than he loved me. It's so flipping obvious."

Her words bring me peace in an otherwise war-torn day.

She gets out of the car, waving at me before disappearing into the hotel. The same one where Warren and his snake of a sister are staying. And Brady, too?

I feel just a tiny bit better on my drive back to Sweet Escape. Nothing has changed, not really, and yet everything has. Lennon being on my side means Brady could perhaps listen to me. I just might have a shot.

Grandma eyes my wet clothes when I walk in the door, but I shake my head and tell her not to ask. In the upstairs bathroom, I undress and step under the hot spray of the shower.

Tonight, I need good sleep. Yes, my life is in turmoil.

But I'm a damn good baker, and tomorrow is my chance to prove it.

28

BRADY

"Brady Sterling, you're a fool."

Lennon sits cross-legged on the couch in her and Finn's hotel room.

"Is this one of those super-emotional pregnancy outbursts?" The door swings shut behind me with a loud thud and I step cautiously into the room. "I already apologized for forgetting your Chinese food last night."

Lennon frowns. "That's not what this is about. And don't worry, because that place delivers." She scoots over and pats the space beside her. "Come on. It's time we had a heart to heart."

I look around. "Where's Finn?"

"He went downstairs to the gym."

I should've done the same. Instead, I responded to Lennon's message to come to their room, and Finn is suspiciously missing.

I sink down onto the couch, leaning forward and resting my elbows on my knees. Dust motes dance in an arc of sunlight shining through the window. Last night's rain has given way to today's clear skies.

"What's up?" I ask Lennon, the reluctance plain in my voice. "I hear I'm a fool?"

"I talked to Addison last night."

My head turns sharply to meet Lennon's gaze.

"How?"

"I was in the lobby, looking for *someone* who was late with my dinner, and saw Addison out front getting her car. There was an opportunity and I took it."

Great. Just great. "And?"

"This is how I know you're a fool." Lennon blinks, waiting, but I don't say anything. She continues. "Addison loves you, Brady."

I breathe out a short, angry stream of air from my nose. "Right. And she also loves Warren. Therein lies the problem."

Lennon rolls her eyes.

Was she always this willing to display her true emotions? I don't remember a lot of eye-rolling and being called a fool before. But that was back when she was managing my feelings. She no longer has to worry about that. This turned corner in our friendship is interesting, but not necessarily bad.

"You're being an ass, Brady." She crosses her arms.

I can't help my smirk. "So now I'm a fool and an ass?"

"Yes. You're a foolish ass. She's not in love with Warren. You didn't let her finish yesterday when she went after you in the rain."

My mouth drops open. "She told you everything?"

Lennon nods. "She needed someone to hear her out. Which is how I know that she loves him in a perfectly normal way. The way you love someone who loved you once upon a time." Lennon takes my hand. "She loves Warren the same way I love you now, Brady. I love what we almost were, because it's a part of our story and a part of my story as an individual. It's an experience I'll treasure, because of what it taught me. You're a part of me, but I'm not in love with you. Warren is a part of Addison, but she's not in love with him."

My stomach sinks to somewhere around my kneecaps. "Oh, shit."

Lennon grins. "That's what Addison said last night when I jumped in the passenger seat of her car and introduced myself."

I want to laugh, but I can't push the sound past the forlorn feeling in my chest. "When I talked to Warren, he told me in no uncertain terms that he was here to fight for Addison, and he was going to use all the tools in his arsenal, including the underhanded ones. He has no problem exploiting her guilt and using it to his advantage. What if it works? What if he tips the scale in his favor?"

"That will only happen if you keep being a foolish ass and don't let Addison tell you herself how she feels." Lennon tugs on my hand, forcing me to meet her gaze again. "You might not want a competition, but I'm afraid Warren has brought it to you anyway. You fought for me for years, Brady. Are you exhausted, or afraid of losing again?"

I rub the bridge of my nose with my finger. "A little of both, probably." I don't like admitting it.

"Great. Now, it's time to get out of your own way. And if you don't fight for her, then I will. And I'll fight dirty just like her ex, because nobody suspects a pregnant woman." She pats her belly and smiles triumphantly.

I wrap an arm around Lennon's shoulders and pull her into me. Her hair smells like the Lennon I remember, but it doesn't do things to my heart the way it used to. My heart wants only Addison.

"I love you, Lennon."

She hugs me back. "I love you too, Brady."

Finn walks into the room, sweaty, eyeing us with a bottle of water tipped up to his lips. "Should I be worried?" He asks the question in a voice that holds no concern.

I release Lennon and stand up, striding across the small room. Patting his back, I say, "Here, hold my trophy while I kiss your girlfriend."

Finn spits out his mouthful of water, some of it flying into the air and some of it dribbling down his chin. "I forgot about that shirt," he says, smiling and wiping the back of his hand across his chin.

"Ugh, I didn't." Lennon's lip curls.

Finn goes to Lennon, using one finger to lift her face for a kiss. "That shirt was awesome."

"Seventh grade Finn was awesome," she clarifies. "Seventh grade Finn's shirt was not awesome."

"Bye, guys," I say from the door. If I waited for their banter to cease, I'd be waiting for hours.

"Where are you going?" Lennon asks with a cautiously excited expression.

"To win my girl."

"Yes!" she whoops, tossing her hands in the air. She high-fives Finn. "It worked," she tells him, continuing her celebration dance.

I slip out the door and hustle back to my room. I need to hurry if I'm going to make it to the results of the baking competition.

Lonesome Day is in full swing. Main Street has been blocked off by local police, so I'm forced to park my truck a couple blocks from the bakery and hustle.

I turn the corner and see people crammed onto the front lawn at Lucy's, hovering on the sidewalk and spilling out into the street. A rectangular table sits on a platform, and five people are positioned behind it.

The table holds seven trays of baked goods. It must be the goods made by each entrant, which means one of them is Addison's. I search the trays for treats I recognize, and three from the left I spot butterscotch blondies piled beside rows of cupcakes and muffins.

I walk through the crowd, my eyes seeking out every blonde and quickly eliminating them all. Where is Addison? She has to be here somewhere.

A loud voice booms through the crowd. "People, we have a winner!"

My gaze swings up to the stage, where Lucy, the owner of the bakery, stands with her arms open. "This wasn't easy, but there was one tray of goodies that pulled ahead with a special treat we all have an affinity for." She beams. "Addison West, I hope your blueberry muffins are permanently on the menu at your new bakery!"

The crowd lets loose with a raucous cheer. Lucy's eyes scan everyone, looking for Addison just like I am. Her smile wavers every second that passes without Addison's presence.

"Uh, our winner seems to be missing in action," Lucy says, her tone confused and slightly annoyed.

I raise my hand, maneuvering my way through the crowd. "Lucy, hi, I'm Brady, Addison's boyfriend."

Relief makes Lucy's chest sag. "Everyone, Addison sent a proxy to accept her win." She points at me. "This is her boyfriend, Brady."

I turn and face the group. All the gazes are excited and expectant, until my stare lands on a frown of disapproval.

Warren.

I look away from his sour face, addressing the group. "Addison had something important to take care of. When she learns she won the competition, you will probably hear her celebration from wherever you are in town."

A collective chuckle rolls through. I don't look at Warren, because I don't give a shit how he's feeling right now.

"On behalf of Addison, thank you to everyone who came out today" —I sweep my arm behind me— "to the judges for being willing to make what was undoubtedly a tough choice, and to the fellow competitors who worked hard and gave my girl a run for her money." I step away from the front with a nod and a smile.

There is more applause and a few claps on my back as I make my way into the crowd. I offer polite smiles and thank you's, but my focus doesn't stay on any one person for long. I want to find Addison.

People move past me, surging forward, ready to sample the trays of treats now that the event is over. I'm tall enough to see over the heads of three quarters of the people here, and when I look up to the judges table, I see a certain someone surreptitiously swipe a blueberry muffin from the tray Addison baked.

Beatrice. Her thick eyebrows draw together as she takes an angry bite from the top of the muffin, not bothering to peel off the wrapper. Her features soften and her eyes close. The look of enjoyment lasts for only a second. Her eyes snap open and her gaze darts around, checking to make sure she hasn't been caught. She doesn't see me.

I can't wait to tell Addison about Beatrice. But, of course, first I have to find her.

I slip onto the sidewalk. I'm going to start my search at

Sweet Escape, and if Addison isn't there, I'm going to look every place I can think of.

"Brady," a deep voice behind me says my name.

I'm slow to turn around, mostly because I don't have time for this right now.

"Warren." I tip my chin down in greeting.

"You're an asshole, you know that?"

My eyes look fixedly over Warren, considering his position. Maybe I am an asshole. But I've been the nice guy my whole life, never making waves.

I want Addison, and if I have to be an asshole to get the girl I plan to love until I'm old and wrinkled, then so be it.

"Yep," I say to Warren. "I know that. And I also know what it feels like to be in love with someone and not be the guy they choose. But I got over it. And you will too. I wish you the best man, I really do. But this happily ever after belongs to me, not you."

I leave him open-mouthed and walk away, and when I get in my truck I point it toward Sweet Escape.

"I'M SORRY, BRADY, SHE'S NOT HERE. SHE HASN'T BEEN HOME since this morning when she left for the bake-off." Louisa's apology floats through the air in the open doorway.

With a pang, I realize it's not only Addison I've missed, but Louisa too.

I back up a step. "Would you mind if I explored the woods a little? There's a spot we went to once..."

"Have at it, Brady."

I thank her and head down the front porch steps, stopping only when Louisa calls out to me.

"Did she win?"

I turn back, beaming with pride. "She won."

"I knew it!" Louisa pumps her fist into the air.

I continue on around the side of the house, over the slope of the backyard, past my cabin, and onto the path. I keep going, winding my way deeper and deeper, until I reach my destination.

But my hopes of finding her at the amphitheater are dashed. I stand at the top of the steps and look around. Nothing is here but dirt and pine straw.

Disappointed, I walk back through the woods and out to my truck. Louisa stands on the front porch, and we lock eyes. Her raised eyebrows ask the question, and the shake of my head answers it.

I get back in my truck and pull onto the main road.

By late afternoon, I've checked every place I can think of. My heart sinks lower and lower with every failed stop.

Finally I head back to my room at the hotel.

It's my fault she's gone. My fear kept me from listening to her.

Tomorrow, I'll call my dad. I've never asked him to pull strings for me, but I'm not above it. Not when it comes to finding Addison. He must know someone who can search her transactions, find out where she last spent money.

I slip my key card in the slot. When the light flashes green, I push open the door, walking slowly inside with shoulders that feel so heavy I don't want to stand upright any longer.

"Hi."

A soft voice reaches into me, its sound a melody.

I RUSH FORWARD, THE WEIGHT SUDDENLY GONE FROM MY shoulders.

Addison hurries to me. "Brady, I—"

My lips swallow her words. I've been accused of not listening to her; one more time won't hurt. My fingers thread through the hair at the nape of her neck, my other hand grips her hip possessively. She moans into my mouth, and I swallow that too.

My tongue slips into the seam her lips create, and she parts them quickly. We're needy, desperate. Our kisses become apologies and our touches feel like promises.

Addison pushes me toward the bed, grabbing at my shirt as we go. We're a flurry of eager hands, our breathing turning to panting as we attempt to rid one another of clothes.

Addison lies back, her hair fanning out around her as I lean over her. I place a kiss on her heart.

"So sorry," I murmur against her.

"Me too," she says, her breath heavy.

Pushing myself up on my forearm, I drag a fingertip across her ribcage, over her hip, and down her thigh. Curling a hand around the back of her knee, I hitch it up and she wraps it around my back.

"I've missed you." My voice is thick with everything I'm feeling.

Addison's eyes are clear and bright. She stares up at me, her eyes roaming over my face. "So much," she agrees. Her arms encircle my neck, pulling my face down to hers.

She kisses me deeply, devouring, her lips meshing against mine.

Her chest rises with a sharp intake of breath when I push inside her. A hot rush of air slips through my teeth. Addison feels like a home I don't ever want to leave.

Burying my face in Addison's neck, I work to show her how much she means to me, how sorry I am for the past few days.

With my lips, I tell her I love her, with my body I show her how deeply I cherish her.

She is not just a good thing. She is the very best.

29

ADDISON

"Don't go," Brady groans, reaching for me from his spot under the covers.

I laugh, stepping back from the edge of the bed so he can't reach me. "I need to. I told him I'd be there by now."

Brady lifts his head from the pillow, grimacing. "I still think I should go with you. He might try to lie and tell you I'm bowing out again." His lips draw together in a hard line.

I shake my head. We went through this last night, after we came up for air. We'd ordered room service and Brady finally let me tell him everything, and that was when we discovered Warren's lie. I could be angry with him, but I'm not. I don't have it in me, not when he's been through so much, and traveled here to find me.

When I'd said I needed to see Warren and make sure he understood we were over, Brady tried to convince me to let him tag along.

He's a very good lawyer, and I have a feeling he was using some fancy lawyer tactics on me, but I didn't waver. What I'm going to tell Warren will be hard enough on him; he doesn't need an audience.

"What are you going to do while I'm gone?" I ask, slipping my feet into my shoes.

Brady sits up, looking around the room. "Pack, so I can go back to Sweet Escape. Assuming your grandma hasn't given away my cabin by now."

"Don't worry," I tell him, running his hairbrush through my hair. I look down at the clothes I wore yesterday. A little rumpled, but they'll do. "The cabin is still yours."

"How long will you be?" He frowns as he speaks.

"Not long. My day is pretty full, and I want to get started on it. I have to go by the bakery and hear how exactly I'm going to officially take over the space. I want to write down my ideas and figure out what's a priority." A smile splits my face as I talk. I can't believe I won. The space will be mine, and not anybody else's. Nobody can kick me out when they think I've misbehaved.

"And you have to leave room for your boyfriend," Brady adds, winking at me. He climbs from the bed, naked, beams of sunlight sweeping over him.

He sees me eyeing him in all his glory and smirks. "Don't you have somewhere to be?"

"Yes," I say through gritted teeth. "I'll come back here when I'm finished downstairs." With superhuman strength, I drag myself from the room and down to the lobby.

WARREN WATCHES ME AS I APPROACH. THE AIR AROUND HIM has changed.

He's no longer trying.

"Hi." I wave, taking a seat opposite him.

"You came from the elevator. Not the entrance." He says it matter-of-factly.

"Yes." It's a confirmation he doesn't need.

"You've made your choice, then?"

I stare at him, at the face I loved, the face that kissed me goodnight and made me smoothies in the morning. For me, this relationship was over a long time ago. For him, this wound is new.

I don't tell him what I told Brady last night. I don't tell him how there was never a competition, because Brady was my first and only choice.

I tell him I've chosen, and that my choice is Brady.

"I don't know what to say. I'm sorry." My eyes fill with tears. I hate what I'm doing to him, but I'd hate a life without Brady even more.

I used to think sacrifices were a selfless act, and perhaps some are. But I'm willing to break a person's heart in the quest for my happy ending, and that's about as selfish as it gets. It's not like I'm the only one; it happens everywhere, all day long.

Right now, this sacrifice is the only one I care about.

"Warren, I have to be honest with you." I take a deep breath, because he deserves the truth. "Before your accident, I was having doubts about us."

His head jerks back. "Were you going to break things off?"

"No, I wasn't. I would've married you."

He balls up a napkin, angrily tossing it on the table. "I guess you were happy when the coma took care of your problem for you."

I shake my head quickly, horrified at his words. "Not at all. Just because I wasn't certain about us doesn't mean I didn't love you. I grieved you, Warren. It took me months to feel well again."

"How nice."

I flinch at his biting sarcasm but forge on since I know I'm the one who caused it. "I appreciate that you came here." His hand rests on the table, and I place my hand on top. He starts to pull away, but I press down firmly, stopping him. "I want the best for you, Warren. I want you to find happiness with someone."

"Sure, sure," he says quickly, looking off to the side. "Listen, I better get going. I need to get back to Chicago. Plenty to do, starting with taking back our apartment."

I move my hand from his and he tucks it into his pocket. "I'll sign whatever documents are needed to take my name off it." He nods and stands, and so do I. I want to hug him, but I'm not sure he'd allow it.

"Good luck with everything, Warren. I mean it." I try for a smile, but it's half-hearted.

"Thanks, Addison. I hope he... Brady..." He says the name like it's not something he wants to do. "Makes you happy."

And then he hugs me. A fleeting, awkward side hug.

I watch him walk away and punch the button for the elevator.

A deep sigh fills my chest, and I close my eyes to release it.

"You're a piece of work."

The words are spoken quietly, squeezing through a clenched jaw. And they don't surprise me at all. I stand so I'm on her level.

"Hi, Shannon."

"Don't greet me like we're old friends," she seethes. "I told him not to come here, but he insisted on seeing you in person. I told him he was better off forgetting you. And I was right."

The triumph on her face makes me sick. I step closer,

right into her personal space, close enough to make her feel my breath on her cheek. "Get a life, Shannon. Your brother will move on, and you're going to need something to move on to also."

I back up and pivot, walking to the elevator Warren used just a few minutes ago. I step onto the next open elevator and take it up to Brady.

"Are you serious? Tell me more." I laugh, lifting my beer to my lips.

Under the table, goosebumps form as Brady runs his hand up and down my thigh.

We've been sitting at the restaurant for the past two hours with Finn and Lennon, and my cheeks are beginning to hurt from laughing.

"Brady—"

"My turn," Brady interrupts, shooting a look at Lennon. She sticks her tongue out at him.

He removes his hand from my thigh and uses it to gesture. "Lennon is conveniently forgetting to tell you anything embarrassing about herself."

Lennon tosses her hands into the air. "I knew you wouldn't be able to resist."

Finn kisses her cheek. "It's a good one, babe. You have to admit."

She turns her face to him to get one more kiss, this time on the mouth. "Fine, yes, it's a good one," she says in mock exaggeration.

"So," Brady turns to look at me while he tells the story. He's so close I want to pounce on him, but I force myself to listen. "Growing up, Lennon went to church every Sunday.

One Sunday, when she was...sixteen?"—he looks to Lennon for confirmation, and she nods— "she went to church with her skirt tucked up into her underwear. And somehow, all those nice men and boys chose not to tell her."

My eyes widen in horror. "When did you finally realize it?"

"I told her," Finn says, laughing.

"Wait." My eyebrows knit in confusion. "I thought you didn't go to church." An earlier story provided me with that insight.

"Hardly ever," Finn explains, "but this one Sunday I had something I wanted to, uh,"—he glances at Brady, a fleeting look of guilt riding over his face— "tell Lennon."

Brady snorts. "What he means is that he was after a secret make-out session with her."

Pink rises on Lennon's cheeks, but there's pride on Finn's. "Yeah, I was." He playfully hammers a fist down onto the wooden table. "And I got it, too," he winks at me.

My shoulders shake with my laughter. I look across the table at Lennon. She rolls her eyes upward, but there's a smile on her face.

"Uh, guys." Brady looks around, then back to us. "I hate to break it to you, but I think we've overstayed our welcome."

I peer around Brady. We're the last table in the place, and our server is sitting at a booth, scrolling on her phone.

We stand up and walk out, exchanging hugs and good-byes outside the door. When Lennon hugs me, I whisper, "Thanks for letting me into his room."

"I'm just happy I thought to swipe his extra key card," she responds, laughing quietly.

Brady wraps an arm around my waist and pulls me to

him. "Alright, ladies, enough secrets. Rectangles don't tell secrets."

"Huh?" Finn, Lennon, and I all stare at Brady.

"Rectangle," he repeats. "A shape with four sides. You know, because we used to be a triangle, but now Addison made us a rectangle."

Lennon groans. Finn shakes his head and says, "I'll be calling on you when I need some dorky dad jokes."

Brady playfully punches Finn's shoulder. "You sure you have to go home?" he asks.

Finn and Lennon are scheduled to leave tomorrow morning, but I wouldn't mind if they accidentally-on-purpose missed their flight.

"You can come home anytime, Brady," Finn responds.

Brady squeezes the arm he has wrapped around me. "I am home."

We have another round of hugs, then part ways.

Brady drives us back to Sweet Escape. He parks the truck and we walk down to cabin seven.

Once we're inside, he pulls me to him. "Thank you. You have no idea how happy it makes me that you get along with them."

"You mean, with Lennon?" I'm pretty sure if I'd met Lennon on my own, she'd become my best friend. Anyone who jumps into a car with someone they don't really know, just to help out a friend, is a person I want in my life.

Brady looks unsure of what to say next, so I help him out. "Don't worry, Brady. We both came to Lonesome with baggage." My baggage is probably back in Chicago by now.

Brady's fingers slip into my hair, gripping either side of my head. His gaze grows soft, and it warms my chest, like he's sending his love directly into my body.

"We're not each other's first loves, and that's okay." He

leans in, rubbing the tip of his nose against mine. When he speaks again, I hear it, but I also feel it, his words against my skin and in my heart and zinging through every cell in my body. "Because we're going to be each other's last loves."

And then he releases me, only to pick me up and carry me into his room.

30

EPILOGUE

Apparently I chose the right profession. This handyman business is better suited for someone who knows what he's doing.

When Louisa asked if I could install security lights on her house, I said yes. What I should've said was *no.* Along with cooking and laundry, I don't know what I'm doing when it comes to minor home improvements or repairs.

I am, however, a smart enough guy that I can figure it out the way I figured out how to bake that cake for Addison. *Internet tutorials.*

I watch the video a handful of times, and once I'm confident I've got it down, I climb up the ladder and get to work.

It's not nearly as difficult as I thought it would be, now that I know what I'm doing. If anything, the challenging part is staying focused on the task when I can see Addison through the front window. She and Louisa stand in the living room, folding baskets of towels and sheets.

When I'm done installing the two new motion-activated security lights, I turn the electricity to the house back on and go inside in search of my girl.

I find her in the kitchen, dividing up baked goods into the brown wicker baskets Louisa leaves in each cabin as a welcome to the new guests. Tomorrow is Sunday, and I've been around long enough now to understand that means it's a big day for guest check-out and check-in.

Tomorrow also happens to be a big day for me and Addison. We're flying to Phoenix, to attend the christening of Finn and Lennon's baby boy.

"Hey there," I say to Addison, winding my hands around her waist and burying my nose in her hair. "You smell like a dream I don't want to wake up from."

Addison laughs and turns around, her hands running over my chest. "I was watching you on the ladder, installing the lights. You looked pretty sexy working a screw driver."

"Oh yeah? How about I take you home and show you how I can work a—" I clear my throat and pull my grinding hips off Addison. "Hello, Louisa."

Louisa smirks at me on her way to the cabinet, where she grabs a glass and fills it with water. "You know, Brady, I was just thinking about that terrible real estate lady who came to my door that day. If it wasn't for you, who knows if this place would still be mine?"

That conversation turned out to be integral in more ways than one. It's what convinced Addison I was worth a shot. Or at least a ride to town, anyway. "It was nothing, Louisa. We were just fortunate I overheard."

Louisa nods, and as she passes us, she says, "Addison's bed is still available for use upstairs. One might've thought you two had calmed down by now." She laughs and leaves the kitchen.

"I prefer our bed at home," I murmur, grazing Addison's forehead with a kiss.

"My work here is done," Addison says, standing on tiptoe to plant a light kiss on my lips. "Why don't we go home?"

Our apartment is in one of the newly-constructed buildings in town. It's close enough to the bakery that Addison can walk there when the weather is nice.

"Are we going home to pack?" I ask, running the tip of my nose across her cheek.

"Among other things," she whispers.

***

I CAN'T HELP IT. MY EYES ARE DRAWN TO THE BEAUTIFUL blonde across the airport bar. She lifts her glass of wine to her pink lips, taking a delicate sip. She looks around, her gaze landing on me.

I'm not one to flirt, but a woman like this requires it. Because if I don't, someone else will.

I offer a shy smile, though shy I am not, and look away. It's a ruse, meant to make her think I don't do things like this often.

It works.

She leaves her seat, slinking over to me. She wears a white blouse tucked into a lavender skirt, long, shapely legs extending from beneath the short hem.

I lean back against my seat, motioning to the empty chair beside me. She slides in, and her perfume wafts over me. She looks at me, licks her lips, and the muscles in my stomach tighten.

"Brady," I tell her, offering my hand to shake.

"Addison," she responds, placing her soft palm in mine. She leans forward, her blouse falling open.

I unabashedly take the bait, glancing down into her shirt to see the swell of her breasts. I've never been envious of an article of clothing before, but here I am, wanting to switch places with her white lace bra.

I look back up at Addison and catch the quivering of her lips.

"You're breaking character," I softly admonish, rubbing my thumb against her chin.

Last night, as Addison looked at the packed bags I'd lined up next to the front door of our apartment, her eyes lit up with an idea.

"Let's re-do the first time we met." She grabbed my hand, eyes pleading. "Tomorrow, when we're waiting for our flight. Let's go to the bar and re-do it."

I actually like the way we met, it's a funny story. But Addison's idea sounded fun, and also like I might gain entry into the mile-high club. So I agreed.

Addison clears her throat, trying to get back into her role. "So, Brady who I've never met and am not hopelessly in love with, why are you visiting Arizona?"

I take a sip of my beer, trying to control the urge to drop the act and push her into the family restroom I spotted across from our gate. "My best friends just had a baby, and I'm going for the christening. I'm his godfather."

Addison feigns surprise. "So weird, I'm going to Arizona for a christening too."

I palm my stubble. I've promised Addison I'll be clean-shaven for the ceremony. "Would you like to meet me for a drink when we're there?"

Addison leans closer, wrapping her arms around my neck. She's done with the role-playing. "I'll meet you for a drink anywhere, Brady Sterling."

My stomach muscles clench again, but not for sexual reasons this time. Has she found what was in my duffle? I was so careful to hide it.

I force myself to relax. That day at the amphitheater when we spoke our truths, Addison didn't see me slip the small wooden stick into my pocket, and there's no way she found it last night. I wrapped it in an old t-shirt and placed it under the clothes I packed. I'm not worried about her finding the ring; that's safely stowed in my pocket, until we reach Arizona and I find the right time to tell her the truth about how I want to spend the rest of my life.

A bored voice booms over the loudspeaker, announcing the imminent boarding of our flight.

"That was fun," Addison grins, kissing me.

"We can have even more fun on the plane..." I grab my backpack from the ground under my seat.

"You need to study," she reminds me.

How can I forget? The bag of books I've just hefted over my shoulder is reminder enough. When Paul came to me a month ago with his idea, I turned him down. But then I spent the next few days thinking of what he'd said and remembered what practicing law felt like at its core. And I remembered how much I loved it. Going into practice with Paul wouldn't be anything like the intense firm I was a part of in Chicago. So I ordered some books and signed up to take the Oregon state bar exam.

For someone who wanted to run away from his problems, I didn't get very far. And, somehow, what I ended up with was everything I wanted. A slower pace, the chance to practice law my way, and a woman who made my life better simply by being in it.

And I'll never, ever let her go.

The End

ALSO BY JENNIFER MILLIKIN

Hayden Family Series

The Patriot

The Maverick

The Outlaw

The Calamity

Standalone

Here For The Cake

Better Than Most

The Least Amount Of Awful

Return To You

One Good Thing

Beyond The Pale

Good On Paper

The Day He Went Away

Full of Fire

The Time Series

Our Finest Hour

Magic Minutes

The Lifetime of A Second

Visit Jennifer at jennifermillikinwrites.com to join her mailing list and receive a free novella. She is @jenmillwrites on all social platforms and would love to connect.

ACKNOWLEDGMENTS

I can't believe Brady's happily ever after has arrived! First, a gigantic thank you to my family, for dealing with a zombie for the last few weeks as I read and re-read and then re-read *just one more time*!

Thank you, from the deepest depth of my heart, to my mom squad. Olivia, Jody, Erin, Kristin, Julliana, Sarika, and Lana I love you ladies!!! Olivia, thank you for using Beyond The Pale as your January book club pick. Your support of my work makes me want to cry!

Julia, Crystal, and Jody, my rockstar beta readers. I love you for making my stories better.

Kristan, my soul mate, my sister-from-another-mister. If I didn't have you to eat fried cauliflower with me and listen to my writing woes, I don't know what I would do. I love you long time.

ABOUT THE AUTHOR

Jennifer Millikin is a bestselling author of contemporary romance and women's fiction. She is the two-time recipient of the Readers Favorite Gold Star Award, and readers have called her work "emotionally riveting" and "unputdownable". Following a viral TikTok video with over fourteen million views, Jennifer's third novel, *Our Finest Hour,* has been optioned for TV/Film. She lives in the Arizona desert with her husband, children, and Liberty, her Labrador retriever. With fifteen novels published so far, she plans to continue her passion for storytelling.

facebook.com/JenniferMillikinwrites
instagram.com/jenmillwrites
bookbub.com/profile/jennifer-millikin